Praise for earlier Cramp mysteri

CW01336402

"A fun read with humour throughout…"
Crime Thriller Hound

"An excellent novel, full of twists and turns, plenty of action scenes, crackling dialogue - and a great sense of fun."
Fully Booked

"A good page-turning murder mystery, with a likeable protagonist and great setting."
The Bookworm Chronicles

"A highly enjoyable and well-crafted read, with a host of engaging characters."
Mrs Peabody Investigates

"An amiable romp through the shady back streets of 1960s Brighton."
Simon Brett, Crime Writers' Association Diamond Dagger winner

"A highly entertaining, involving mystery, narrated in a charming voice, with winning characters. Highly recommended."
In Search of the Classic Mystery Novel

"A romp of a read! Very funny and very British."
The Book Trail

"Superbly crafted and as breezy as a stroll along the pier, this Brighton-based murder mystery is a delight."
Peter Lovesey, Crime Writers' Association Diamond Dagger winner

"It read like a breath of fresh air and I can't wait for the next one."
Little Bookness Lane

"By the end of page one, I knew I liked Colin Crampton and author Peter Bartram's breezy writing style."
Over My Dead Body

"A little reminiscent of [Raymond] Chandler."
Bookwitch

"A rather fun and well-written cozy mystery set in 1960s Brighton."
Northern Crime

"The story is a real whodunit in the classic mould."
M J Trow

"A fast-paced mystery, superbly plotted, and kept me guessing right until the end."
Don't Tell Me the Moon Is Shining

"Very highly recommended."
Midwest Book Review

"One night I stayed up until nearly 2am thinking 'I'll just read one more chapter'. This is a huge recommendation from me."
Life of a Nerdish Mum

The Comedy Club Mystery
A Crampton of the Chronicle adventure

The Comedy Club Mystery

A Crampton of the Chronicle adventure

Peter Bartram

Deadline Murder Series Book 3

THE BARTRAM PARTNERSHIP

First published by The Bartram Partnership, 2019

ISBN: 9781096270980

For contact details see website:
https://www.colincrampton.com

Text and Cover Design: Barney Skinner

Chapter 1

Brighton, England. 8 November 1965

My news editor Frank Figgis took a drag on his Woodbine and blew a perfect smoke ring.

He said: "Did I ever tell you about the legal trouble we had when we ran that picture of a stud bull with no testicles?"

I said: "Now that does sound like a balls-up."

Figgis harrumphed.

He narrowed his eyes to show he didn't welcome the interruption.

I ignored the signal and said: "In any case, I don't see what that's got to do with me. My byline reads Colin Crampton, crime correspondent. Hector Smallhouse is the night lawyer. The paper's legal trouble is his line of country."

We were in Figgis' office at the Brighton *Evening Chronicle*. The room had green walls hung with mounted front pages of the paper's greatest scoops.

The ceiling was a kaleidoscope of yellow, red and brown nicotine stains. If Michelangelo had smoked Woodbines, the Sistine Chapel ceiling would have looked a bit like it.

Figgis sat behind a desk scarred with cigarette burns and overflowing with galley proofs. The place smelt like a campfire was smouldering in the corner.

Figgis' hard eyes peered out of a grizzled face. He had a scrawny neck. His thinning black hair was shiny with Brylcreem and parted down the middle. He looked like a bad-tempered gnome.

He took a last drag on his fag. He stubbed out the dog-end in the Watney's Red Barrel ashtray he'd "borrowed" from the Coach and Horses.

He said: "The trouble happened before your time here. But

1

talk of night lawyers misses the point. When you've got legal trouble on a newspaper, the last person you want on the scene is a lawyer. Best to sort it out yourself. Just as I did with the bull with no bollocks."

I lifted a questioning eyebrow. "You sewed back his cobblers personally?"

"In a manner of speaking. You see, what happened was that Len Bryant, one of our photographers, had been up at the Royal Sussex Agricultural Show taking some shots. There was this prize bull – best in show – that had won a ton of prizes. I seem to recall the animal was called Goliath. Ugly beast, if you ask me. But, apparently, in the previous six months it had serviced forty-three heifers. Earnt his owner a small fortune in stud fees. As Goliath's general and two colonels were still in full working order, the lucky farmer expected a rich harvest of fees in the next breeding season. And then our picture appeared over a report of the show – and the cowpat hit the fan."

"I don't see why. What about 'there's no such thing as bad publicity'?"

"Not in this case. Len had taken pictures of the animal from all angles. He'd planned to use a shot of the beast's head."

"And after forty-three heifers, no doubt with a smile like a giant banana on his face."

"Not exactly. He looked like a miserable brute. Not the kind you'd put into a pasture with Daisy the heifer and hope that a good time would be had by all."

"So he used a different shot?"

"One taken from the rear. The only trouble with that was Goliath's undeniably impressive meat and two veg were centre stage in the picture, if you see what I mean."

I could see what was coming.

"And so Len airbrushed them out," I said.

"He said readers like maiden ladies living in Hove would be embarrassed when they turned the page."

"And young brides up on the Whitehawk estate would be viewing their new husbands with a disappointed eye," I added. "That's as may be. The next thing we knew a libel writ had landed on my desk."

"I suppose the owner claimed the picture showed the animal he was hiring out at big fees wasn't match fit. And that, therefore, he was a fraudster."

"He wanted damages and an apology in the paper."

"Looks like he'd put the balls in your court," I said.

Figgis harrumphed again.

He said: "The last thing I wanted was the night lawyer crawling all over the case. So I told Len to reprint the picture from the unbrushed negative and we ran it on the round-up page the next day under the headline 'Now that's what we call a ballpark figure'. The owner was delighted – at least, he was by the time he'd downed the sixth double Scotch I'd bought him in the Coach and Horses. We heard no more about it."

I leaned back in my chair and glanced out of Figgis' grimy window. Rain was dripping off the trees in the Pavilion gardens. In was the kind of November day when dark clouds hang low in the sky like wet blankets.

I switched back to Figgis.

"A tale for our times," I said. "But what's brought it on?"

"This," Figgis said. He took a bundle of papers from his in-tray. His thick eyebrows beetled together as he studied the densely typed text. His forehead furrowed like a freshly ploughed field.

"It's a libel writ," he said.

"Not for me, I hope."

"Not this time. This one is for Sidney Pinker."

"Our theatre critic. What's he been up to?"

"It was that piece he wrote about the death of music hall in last Friday's paper."

"I never read obituaries," I said. "But it doesn't strike me like a topic that would have people screaming defamation."

Figgis put down the libel papers, rummaged among his galley proofs, and produced a press cutting.

"This is the piece from the paper," he said. "Read the first paragraph in the second column."

I took the cutting and read: "Music hall was in the sick room even before that great Brighton entertainer Max Miller died two years ago. But since then its condition has become critical. And no wonder when the patient is attended by witch doctors like theatrical agent Daniel Bernstein. Mr Bernstein was best known as Mr Miller's agent and manager. But since Miller's sad death, Mr Bernstein has played the variety theatre-going public for fools by supplying only second-rate acts. Singers who can't hit the right key. Dancers with two left feet. And comics whose jokes would take the bang out of a Christmas cracker."

It rambled on in the same vein for a couple more paragraphs.

I passed the cutting back to Figgis.

I said: "How did this get into the paper? You'd spot a libel like that within seconds of it hitting your desk."

Figgis avoided my eyes.

He picked up a paperclip and bent it out of shape. Tossed it into his wastebasket. He glanced towards the window, then at the ceiling. There was something he didn't want to tell me.

He dragged his gaze back to the writ on his desk.

"I was out of the office," he said.

"Business meeting?"

"No."

"Day off?"

"No."

"You were playing hooky."

Figgis' thin lips compressed. It was the closest he ever came to embarrassment. He looked like a naughty boy caught with his hand in the sweetie jar.

"If you want to put it like that." He wagged a finger at me. "I expect you to keep that confidential, of course."

"Of course. But for my private interest, what were you doing?"

"You don't need to know that. What you should know is that we must clear up the libel problem quietly."

"You mean without His Holiness hearing about it?"

Figgis nodded.

Gerald Pope, the paper's editor, was a patrician throwback to the age when the editor was a gentleman and everyone else on the paper was a prole. Pope had zero news sense. His idea of news was Alvar Lidell reading the Court Circular on the BBC's Home Service. Pope had landed in the editor's chair only because his father had known someone else's father. Figgis had kept trouble, like libel, out of Pope's way. So Pope trusted Figgis. As a result, Figgis was left to run the paper while Pope spent his time sending out memos about the correct use of the semicolon. Or whether there were too many black squares in the crossword puzzle. There was a thick file of the things on the bookshelf in the newsroom. Nobody ever read them.

But if something happened which made His Holiness' faith in Figgis waver, who knew what might happen? He might even decide to try running the paper himself. And then what?

Après Figgis, le déluge.

I said: "Does Pinker know a libel writ is heading his way?"

Figgis reached for his ciggies, shook one out of the packet, and lit up.

"He heard yesterday. He was in here like a quivering jelly. Talk about going to pieces. I thought he was going to end up as a stain on the carpet. I told him to say nothing. And I insisted he steered well clear of Bernstein."

"Will he?" I asked.

"He'd better, if he knows what's good for him. He should leave us to sort this mess out."

"Us?" I queried.

Figgis took a drag on his fag and relaxed a little.

"Why do you think I told you that story about the bull with no goolies? I sorted out that problem with Len Bryant. His Holiness was none the wiser. We – you and I - can do the same with Bernstein."

"I don't even know Bernstein," I said.

"Then he won't know what a crafty devil you are. You can sweet-talk him into withdrawing the writ."

"How?"

"Offer him a flattering feature in the weekend supplement. Meet Mr Show Business. That kind of thing. You'll have him drooling down his kipper tie."

"I might have him using it to throttle me."

"Then he'll be on a murder charge and the writ will be forgotten."

I pushed back my chair and stood up.

"And you'll be without a crime reporter."

Figgis shrugged. "It's a small price to pay," he said.

Fortunately, when a dead body turned up it wasn't mine.

Chapter 2

I headed back into the newsroom trying to think of a way to get out of the job Figgis had just landed on me.

Perhaps I could do what he'd just done. Hand it on to someone else. Trouble was, Figgis would only find out. Then he'd think up some fresh way to waste my time. Or he'd cavil about small items in my expenses. Or tell me to interview some duff old body with a dull mind and a monotone voice.

Best just to get the job done.

I hated having to sort out the mess created by someone else, but I didn't have much choice. Figgis was right about keeping trouble away from Pope. There was no telling what he might do if he actually tried to edit the paper. We'd end up running front-page splashes about his wife's charity tea parties.

What made Pinker's problem worse for me was the fact it involved theatricals. They flounced around and called each other "darling". And they never paid for their round in the pub.

I headed across the newsroom towards my desk. The place was gearing up for the first deadline of the day. Twenty journalists had their heads over typewriters and rattled out stories. The noise sounded like a machine-gun attack.

Cedric, the copy boy, drifted around the place. He had freckled cheeks and goofy teeth. He looked like a train-spotter but there were rumours he was ace at pulling the girls down at Sherry's dance hall on a Saturday night.

He walked up to me as I sat down.

"Any copy for the subs, Mr Crampton?"

"Not for the first edition, Cedric."

"We could do with one of your murders."

"I don't commit them – I just report them. And, anyway, there's not much chance of that."

Cedric ambled off across the room.

I picked up a sheaf of press releases that had arrived overnight and stuffed them into my bin.

I sat back and considered how I was going to tackle Bernstein. I thought Figgis' idea that Bernstein would drop his libel writ in return for a flattering profile was a long-odds bet. I'd rather put my money on a three-legged nag in the Grand National. People don't generally issue writs unless they intend to go through with them. Figgis had struck lucky with the farmer who owned the bull with no balls. Bernstein sounded like a tougher customer. As an agent, he'd be used to dealing with contracts. So he'd be in regular touch with lawyers. When it came to the law, he'd know which kind of case would fly and which would shrivel up and wither away.

More than that, he was used to negotiating with theatre owners so he'd be familiar with the cut and thrust of deals. He'd know how far he could push someone. If it came to brinkmanship, I'd be dealing with an experienced operator who'd been to the brink and back more times than I'd cursed Frank Figgis.

So before I set up a meeting with the man, I'd need some leverage. Something I could use to pressure him when the deal-making got tough. I was willing to bet that anybody who inhabited Bernstein's world would have some skeletons they'd prefer to keep locked in their green rooms. I had to find one of those skeletons and rattle it in his face.

But where?

Perhaps Sidney Pinker would be able to point me in the right direction. But that raised another question. Where was Pinker? I hadn't seen him around the paper this morning.

The telephone on my desk rang.

I lifted the receiver and said: "Colin Crampton."

A voice as taut as a violinist's bowstring said: "Oh, dear boy, thank heavens I've reached you."

Sidney Pinker, the errant theatre critic and part-time libeller, sounded more fraught than usual.

I said: "What's up, Sidney? As it happens, I wanted to talk to you."

"I can't speak for long," Pinker said.

"Why not?"

"I'm making my one phone call."

"We don't ration phone calls at the *Chronicle*."

"I'm not at the *Chronicle*."

"I know that. Where are you?"

"At the police station."

"That's my beat."

"Just listen, dear boy. Danny Bernstein is dead."

"The Danny Bernstein who's an agent?"

"Yes, the one who took exception to my piece in last Friday's paper. Although everything I said was true."

"How did he die?"

"The police say he was murdered."

That had my attention.

"So why are you at the police station?"

Sidney gulped back a sob. "Because, dear boy, the police say I killed him."

I felt the muscles in my shoulders tense, the way they always do when a big story breaks. It felt like a bolt of fire had shot down my spine. Tired old neurons in my brain lit up like they were the neon around Piccadilly Circus.

Pinker started to say something else, but a gruff voice interrupted him: "That's all. You've had your phone call."

The line went dead. I sat at my desk and stared at my phone.

I felt like I'd just missed the punchline of a bad joke.

Ten minutes later, I was in an interview room at Brighton Police Station arguing with Detective Chief Superintendent Alec Tomkins.

Tomkins was a big man with a fleshy face, piggy eyes, and thick dark hair which he combed straight back from his forehead. He was wearing a dark grey pin-striped suit and brown brogue shoes. Tomkins had become the top detective in Brighton less through his penetrating powers of deduction and more from knowing when to roll up his trouser leg. He had a habit of feeling the wrong collar – and I hoped he'd made the same mistake with Pinker.

I said: "I want to see Sidney."

Tomkins curled his lip in a sneer and said: "You're not his lawyer."

"I'm here as his colleague and the person he wants to provide him with advice."

"You should tell him to plead guilty."

"That's against my religion."

"Then you'll end up in Hell with Pinker."

I gave Tomkins a flinty look. "See you down there," I said.

Tomkins laughed.

I said: "Suppose you tell me what you know so far."

"I've got Ted Wilson heading a team at Bernstein's office taking statements and collecting evidence."

That was a lucky break. In the Sherlock Holmes Award for Brilliant Deductions, Ted would bring up the rear. But he'd still think he'd done a pretty good job. He was an honest cop. Most important of all, he was my only helpful contact on the force.

I said: "Any early results from Ted's investigation?"

Tomkins pulled an irritated face. "There's no doubt about the main facts," he said. "Bernstein was killed with a sword."

My eyebrows jumped at that.

"Where would anyone get a sword from?"

"It was mounted on the wall of Bernstein's office. A memento from one of his former clients, apparently. One Suleiman the Sword Swallower."

"Former client?" I queried.

"We understand he died on stage. Got a bad attack of hiccups in the middle of his act. Forgot to take his indigestion tablets before he went on. They had to bring down the curtain."

"So the show didn't go on?"

Tomkins ignored that and said: "It looked as though Bernstein had tried to defend himself. He'd seized an Indian club from the wall – memento from a juggler client. The club was on the floor by Bernstein's chair."

I said: "Pinker is no swordsman."

"That's not what we're hearing. Sally Ashworth, the receptionist, walked into the room to find Bernstein pinned to his chair like a butterfly mounted on a card. Pinker was laughing hysterically. And he had his hand on the sword's hilt. Forensics will confirm that when we test for fingerprints."

I couldn't believe it. Pinker couldn't fillet a sardine without going all squeamish.

Tomkins said: "We've nailed the method of murder and the opportunity. Now all we need is the motive. But I'll crack Pinker on that under questioning."

So Tomkins didn't yet know that Bernstein was suing Pinker for libel.

I said: "Before you interview Sidney, I must speak to him."

Tomkins laughed. "You and whose army?"

"You've just said you plan to crack Pinker. I'll take that as a clear intention to use violence when you interview him. I'll be leading on that in the story I write for the *Chronicle*. I shall put it on the wires for the national press as well."

Tomkins face flushed like a boiled beetroot. "I was using a figure of speech."

"Tell that to the officer investigating you for misconduct."

Tomkins stood up. He quivered with anger. He wanted to hit me but knew that would only prove my point. "Five minutes, not a second more."

He stamped out of the room and slammed the door.

Two minutes later I was sitting on a hard deel chair facing

Sidney Pinker.

We were in interview room one, usually reserved for hard cases like armed robbers. It had bars on the windows and the room's two upright chairs and deel table were bolted to the floor. Long ago, the walls had been painted with cream emulsion. Now they were covered with scratches and dark blotches. Down by the floor an unknown wag had scratched, "This way to the escape tunnel" into the paintwork.

Pinker sat slumped on his chair. He looked like a wraith from a ghost story by M R James. His face was white. It shone like melting wax. His pale blue eyes were clouded with panic. They seemed to have sunk deeper into his skull. He was shaking his head in misery.

He was wearing a tan brown jacket over a pale green shirt open at the neck, and a flowery cravat. It didn't look like the kind of gear you'd wear for a spot of swordplay. A breastplate or cuirass would have been more à la mode.

When I entered the room, Sidney looked at me like I was the executioner come to cut off his head. Then he recognised me and his lips twitched into a wan smile.

"Dear boy, it's you. Have you come to take me back to the office?"

I sat down on one of the bolted chairs.

"No, Sidney. I've come to find out what's happened. I've just been told an incredible story by Tomkins about Danny Bernstein being run through with a sword."

"It's true, but I didn't do it."

"Tomkins said you had your hand on the sword's hilt."

"When I saw that awful scene, I just collapsed, my dear. I just didn't know what I was doing. I think I must have been trying to pull the sword out."

I leaned my elbows on the table, rested my head in my hands, and took a long look at Pinker.

I said: "Let's start at the beginning. When Figgis learnt about the libel writ Bernstein had issued, he told you to stay well away from him. Why didn't you do that?"

Pinker shook his head from side to side. "It was last night. I just couldn't sleep. Wesley said I should have some hot chocolate, but I said, 'No, sweetie, you know it puts pounds on my pecs'. Wesley would never look at a man with flabby pecs. So I just lay there with it turning over in my mind."

"The threat of the writ?"

"Of course, dear boy. Not the worry about my pecs. Anyway, by the morning, I'd decided the only thing to do was to sort the matter out man-to-man. I asked Wesley about it at breakfast. While he was straining his carrot juice, I said, 'Do you think I could appeal to Danny Bernstein?'. And do you know what he said?"

"Tell me," I said wearily.

"Well, Wesley, the saucy scamp, said, 'In those boxers you could appeal to the massed bands of the Brigade of Guards.' And I said, 'In that case, I'm going to ignore grumpy old Figgis.' And do you know what I did next?"

I shook my head. "I wasn't with you, Sidney."

"More's the pity, dear boy. Anyway, I immediately picked up the telephone and I dialled Bernstein's office. But there was no-one there. Too early, I suppose. So I said to Wesley, 'I'm going round there straight away.' And Wesley said, 'Better put your trousers on first. At least before you arrive. You don't want that Danny Bernstein to get the wrong idea.' And I laughed."

Pinker's face flushed as he chuckled. But the chuckle choked in his throat and turned into a gulping sob.

I gave him a moment to compose himself. Then I asked: "What time did you arrive at Bernstein's office?"

Pinker glanced at his watch. Or rather he glanced at the hairs on his wrist. It turned out his watch had been taken from him – along with his belt and shoelaces – when he'd been arrested.

He said: "It was just after nine. I know that because I heard the Town Hall clock chiming the hour as I reached the place."

"Did you go in straight away?"

"Yes. That is to say, dear boy, no."

"Which was it, Sidney?"

"It was yes. I only hesitated to furl my umbrella. It'd been raining. Just a light shower but it stopped as I arrived."

"Did you go to Bernstein's office immediately?"

"Immediately. Or, rather, after a short delay."

"What kind of delay?"

"I asked Sally – she's the receptionist there, and a lovely girl as girls go – if Danny Bernstein was in. She said he'd arrived about ten minutes earlier and gone straight to his office. That is to say, he didn't go straight to his office, because, apparently, he hung up his raincoat in the coat cupboard under the stairs. It's at the back of the building. Sally asked me if I wanted to leave my umbrella there."

Sidney's hand flew to his mouth. "Oh, my golly golly gum drops. My umbrella is still there. And it's a present from Wesley. He'll be just furious if I've lost it."

I said: "At the moment, Sidney, a lost umbrella is the least of your troubles."

A lone tear trickled down Sidney's cheek. He pulled out a paisley handkerchief and brushed it away.

I said more gently: "Did Sally say whether anyone was with Bernstein when you arrived?"

"Not in so many words."

I huffed a bit and said: "Sidney, what did she say?"

"She said that a man had come in while she'd been talking to the postman and signing for a registered letter. That was about five minutes before Bernstein arrived. The man had gone straight to one of the two top floors – they've got a chartered surveyor and an insurance claims assessor up there. She didn't have time to ask for his name. But he'd left five minutes before I'd arrived."

"So there was no-one else in the building apart from Bernstein – and Sally?"

"Not as far as Sally knew. She didn't think any staff were in yet at the surveyors or the insurance place. That's probably why the man left. Both the other offices were closed. And Evelyn Stamford, Bernstein's personal assistant, wasn't in either."

"Did Sally show you into Bernstein's office?"

"No. I'd been there before – a few months earlier – and I knew where it was. The door of his office was ajar, so I knocked lightly and pushed it open..."

Pinker shivered. He belched loudly, put his hand to his mouth. Leaned forward and clutched his stomach as though he were in pain.

"Take it slowly, Sidney," I said. "Tell me what you saw."

"It was Bernstein. He was sitting in the chair behind his desk. The chair was swivelled sideways so I could only see the side of his head. I didn't see anything else at first. I suppose I wasn't expecting to. My mind was in a turmoil about what I was going to say to him. And then I realised something was wrong."

Pinker rubbed his hands nervously together. His tongue flicked over his dry lips.

"Then the telephone on his desk rang. I jumped in shock. I don't know why. It was only a telephone. But I felt like my body had been invaded by an evil spirit. I knew that something terrible was going to happen to me. The bell was the warning. A ghostly voice sounded in my mind. It said, 'For whom the bell tolls... it tolls for thee.'"

Pinker swallowed hard. "I stood there shaking with fear as the telephone rang and rang."

Chapter 3

Sidney Pinker shivered and clasped his trembling hands together.

I said: "Pull yourself together, Sidney. So the telephone rang. What happened next?"

Pinker said: "It stopped ringing."

"Is that all?"

Pinker entwined his fingers like he was praying. Perhaps he was.

"I wish it had been," he said. "How I wish it had been. When the phone stopped, I looked back at Bernstein and that's when I saw the sword for the first time. It was terrible. I thought I was going to throw up. I was worried about gobbing all over my new suede shoes. There was already blood all over the floor. It must have shot out like a geyser when the sword went in. My mind was all over the place, dear boy. I wanted to rush to the bathroom, but then I realised I didn't know where it was."

I leaned forward and patted Pinker's arm. I said: "Slow down, Sidney. Take it easy. You're babbling – quite understandable. But you need to stay calm."

"But I wasn't calm. My mind was racing. I thought that if I pulled the sword out everything would be all right. So I moved around the desk. I felt like my body was possessed. Of course, that's nonsense, I know. What a silly sausage you must think I am."

"Forget the sausages, Sidney. Just tell me what happened."

Pinker swallowed hard. "I walked up to Bernstein and grabbed the sword. I don't know why I did it. I was just acting on impulse. I tugged on the sword but it wouldn't move. The blood had soaked the front of Bernstein's shirt and jacket. It had pooled in his lap. I felt so faint. The world seemed to be revolving around my head. I stood there clasping the hilt of the sword. I knew if I let go, I would swoon."

"Swoon?"

"Fall, dear boy, on the floor. Like that dying swan in the ballet. But without doing a pirouette first. I felt like my brains were seeping out of my ears. I could feel warm tears trickling down my cheeks. And then I heard the scream."

"Where from?"

"Behind me. I turned around and Sally, the receptionist, was in the room. She was holding her head in her hands and she screamed and screamed. And so I started to scream as well. I couldn't help myself. It was a weird kind of ecstasy. We were both hysterical. I don't know how long it went on, but I suppose we must have stopped. Because then Sally pointed her finger at me and shouted 'You've killed him.' But I hadn't – at least, I didn't think I had."

I held up my hand. "Wait a moment. What do you mean, you didn't think you had? You've already told me you saw Bernstein with the sword buried in his chest."

Pinker took out his handkerchief and wiped his forehead.

"By this point, dear boy, I didn't know what I was doing."

I said: "I understand you were in a panic and that scrambles the mind. But in a couple of minutes, Detective Chief Superintendent Alec Tomkins is going to walk in here and ask you some tough questions. You need to gather your wits and think straight. You certainly don't want to tell him you think you might have stuck a sword in Danny Bernstein. I mean, who the hell did you think you were in there? The Count of Monte Cristo?"

Pinker took a deep breath. He wiped his forehead again and stuffed the handkerchief back in his pocket. He nodded slowly – like someone who's just unravelled one of the deeper puzzles of the universe. Like how you know a black hole is there when you can't see it.

"I understand," he said.

I wasn't convinced he did.

So I said: "I'm going to arrange for a lawyer from the paper to come. Don't answer any questions until he arrives."

"What if Tomkins insists on an answer?"

"Tell him statements given under duress are not admissible in court. So he should put his thumbscrews away."

Pinker forced a thin smile. "I'll do that."

I said: "What puzzles me is why you wrote the article that riled Bernstein."

Pinker's eyes flared. "Because I hate the man," he said. "All theatrical agents are leeches, but Bernstein was one of the worst. He exploited young entertainers, booked them into lousy venues, and then took an unfair percentage of their fees. No wonder live variety theatre is dying in this country."

I said: "You're entitled to your views Sidney, but I'd keep them to yourself while Tomkins is around."

Pinker shrugged. "I suppose so."

The door opened and Tomkins walked in. He had a smirk on his face like he'd just eaten a pot of raspberry jam. He was followed by a uniformed sergeant I didn't recognise.

Tomkins leered at me and said: "Time's up."

"It is - for your career, if you put a foot wrong while you're interviewing Sidney," I said.

I stood up and walked towards the door, turned towards Sidney.

I said: "Don't let Tomkins rile you. After all, you're the innocent one around here."

I glanced at Tomkins. For a moment at least, I'd wiped the jammy smirk off his face.

I called Frank Figgis from the telephone box opposite the police station.

He groaned when I described my meeting with Pinker but agreed to arrange for a lawyer to head to the cop shop pronto.

He said: "We'll have to carry a story on Bernstein's killing but we'll hold off mentioning the cops have arrested a suspect. It looks bad if one of the paper's journalists is on a murder charge."

I said: "We can't do that. Tomkins will already have told Jim Houghton on the *Evening Argus* that he's arrested Pinker. You can bet a Woodbine to a Havana cigar that the *Argus* will splash the story in their midday edition. If we tell only half the tale, it'll look like we're hiding something. Then people won't believe any of what we write. We need to be open about this from the start."

"It's still going to look like the *Chronicle* has a theatre critic who's a potential killer."

"Not if we make it clear from the start that the cops have arrested the wrong man. I'll dictate a piece to the copytakers which suggests the police have blundered and the real killer has scarpered. That should put the *Argus* and Tomkins on the back foot. Then I'll head round to Bernstein's office and see what I can pick up from the crime scene."

Figgis grunted something I didn't hear. There were a couple of clicks and a copytaker came on the line.

"Take folio one," he said.

I began: "The police hunt for the killer of theatrical agent Daniel Bernstein got off to a bad start today when the cops arrested the innocent man who found the body…"

A dozen rubberneckers were clustered around the crime scene tape outside Bernstein's office.

His agency – Bernstein Performers – occupied the ground floor of a three-storey building in a side street near the Old Steine.

I ducked under the tape and strode up to the front door. A grumpy old constable I'd seen before had landed the sentry duty role. He had a walrus moustache and flat feet. I nodded pleasantly to him.

He said: "We didn't think it would be long before the vultures descended."

I said: "Look on me as a carrier pigeon. I've come bearing interesting information from your boss."

"The Big Tommo?"

"The very same."

"What's the gen from Tomkins?"

"Sidney Pinker has confessed. He got the sword for his birthday and he wanted to see if it worked."

The cop's moustache wobbled from side to side while he laughed.

I said: "Any other journos beaten me to it?"

"Not while I've been here. There was a short bloke with legs as thick as telegraph poles and a nose like a ripe tomato. Claimed he had business in the building. He sounded like an American so I sent him on his way."

"Very wise," I said. "I take it Detective Inspector Wilson is inside."

Without waiting for an answer, I brushed past him.

I stepped into a corridor which ran from the front to the back of the building. To the right were stairs which led to the upper floors. To the left, an open plan area held a few chairs for visitors and a desk. A worn Indian rug added a downbeat homely touch.

A young woman with cropped auburn hair was sitting behind the desk. She was dabbing her eyes with a paper tissue.

I could hear voices at the far end of the corridor. Before anyone appeared and I was asked what I was doing there, I crossed to the desk.

The young woman looked up as I approached. She stuffed the tissue into a drawer, sat up, and straightened her hair. Tried to pretend nothing had happened. The perfect receptionist.

I said: "You must be Sally."

She said: "Sally Ashworth. But how do you know?"

"Sidney told me how brave you were this morning."

Actually, Sidney had told me he'd joined her in screaming like a banshee. But it does no harm to build up people who've had a traumatic experience.

Sally gave an involuntary shiver. "Is that the man who killed Mr Bernstein?"

"Sidney didn't kill Danny Bernstein," I said. "Sidney's a theatre critic. He ends bad actor's careers with his waspish words, but words can never kill in real life."

Sally's brown eyes moved from side to side as she thought about that.

"I suppose you might be right," she said. "But he had his hand on the sword."

"Sidney had gone to pieces," I said. "He doesn't have your courage. He didn't know what he was doing."

Sally nodded. "I suppose that's right. He was curled up on the floor crying when the police arrived. I had to give him three of my tissues."

"I'll buy you a new box. But you might be able to help me with one point. Sidney told me that a mystery man you didn't recognise had arrived while you were with the postman."

"That's right. He came in a minute after the postman arrived just after half past eight and went straight upstairs. The postman had a registered letter for Evelyn Stamford, Mr Bernstein's assistant. I had to sign for the letter."

"And by the time you'd signed, the mystery man was upstairs?"

Sally nodded. "Yes. And a few minutes later, Mr Bernstein arrived. It was only quarter to nine and I was a bit surprised."

"Why was that?"

"Because he normally comes in much later – sometimes not until ten o'clock. I handed him his post and he went straight to his office."

"Straight to his office?"

"Well, I think he hung up his coat in the cupboard under the backstairs first."

"So the mystery man didn't come to see Mr Bernstein?"

"I don't think so. He'd gone upstairs and Mr Bernstein's office is at the back downstairs."

"Do you know who the mystery man was?"

Sally shook her head. "I don't know. I'd never seen him before."

"What did he look like?"

"I didn't get a good look at him. He was sort of medium height and slim. He had a trilby hat on."

"Anything else?" I said. "This November weather is a bit chilly to go around in the buff with only a hat."

Sally grinned. "He was wearing a grey suit."

"Could he have been a client of the firms upstairs?"

"It's possible. But they don't open their offices until half past nine. There was no-one up there at the time."

I said: "Why should a visitor go upstairs when there was no-one up there to visit?"

"There's a small landing on each floor with a couple of chairs for visitors to wait. I suppose he could've been waiting for someone to arrive and left when they didn't turn up."

"And he left no message?"

"No."

"How long was he up there?"

"I'm not sure, but I think it must've been about ten minutes. Not more."

"And then he left?"

"Yes, a few minutes before Mr Pinker arrived just after nine o'clock. The man hurried down the stairs and just flashed through the door. I didn't even have time to ask who he was."

"So the man in the grey suit left as mysteriously as he'd arrived?"

"Yes." Sally's eyes flashed with indecision. "But I've now realised, something was strange. When he left, he wasn't wearing the grey suit."

"He'd taken it off?"

"No. What I meant to say was he had the suit on but he was wearing a raincoat over it."

"But he wasn't wearing the raincoat when he arrived?"

"I don't think so." Sally put a finger to her lips while she thought about that. "I'm certain he wasn't."

"Could he have been carrying the raincoat over his arm when he arrived?"

"It's possible. I only caught a glimpse of him. But I don't remember seeing it."

"Could he have taken a raincoat from a hanger upstairs?"

"None of them leave their coats overnight. And, anyway, the upstairs offices are locked when there's no-one there."

I thought about that for a moment. He must've been carrying the coat, I decided. Rain had been forecast and a shower even fell earlier in the morning.

Sally said: "Shortly after the man had left, a call came through for Mr Bernstein. I put it through to his office but the phone wasn't answered. There's an extension in Miss Stamford's room but she wasn't in yet. So I went to Mr Bernstein's office to see whether he was there. And it was then…"

I said: "Don't distress yourself. I know the rest."

I heard the sound of boots clumping down the corridor.

I said: "Thanks for your help. I won't forget about the tissues."

I turned away from the desk just as Ted Wilson stepped around the corner. His forehead had wrinkled into a frown. His eyelids drooped with tiredness. His lips were compressed with tension. He was wearing a tweed jacket and flannel trousers. There was splash of blood on his right shoe. He didn't look like a man who'd just come from a carnival.

He said: "A messy murder and no breakfast. And, then, just

23

when I think it couldn't get any worse you turn up."

I said: "I can't do anything about the killing, but I can solve the breakfast problem. Full English suit you?"

Chapter 4

Ted Wilson leered at the food a waiter had just put in front of him.

The plate held three rashers of back bacon, two sausages, a grilled tomato, a mini mountain of mushrooms, a heap of bubble-and-squeak, a slice of fried bread, and two poached eggs.

Ted said: "Now that's what I call a breakfast."

"You haven't got the black pudding," I said.

Ted belched loudly. "I've seen enough blood for one day."

He hoisted his knife and fork and tucked in.

I reached for my croissant and took a bite. I sneaked a quick peak at Ted's bulging belly to remind myself why I hadn't joined him in the full English.

We were in Marcello's. The early morning rush had ended. We'd taken a quiet table towards the back. It was about ten minutes since I'd met Ted in the corridor at Bernstein's office.

Bernstein's former office, I should have said.

Right now, ever the agent, he was probably standing at the Pearly Gates waiting to make an entrance. He'd be trying to gull St Peter into believing he could top the bill at the London Palladium.

I dunked the croissant into my coffee and said: "Even as you stuff that forkful of bubble-and-squeak into your mouth, Tomkins is trying to fit up Sidney Pinker for a murder he didn't commit."

Soggy flakes of the croissant fell off before I could take a bite.

Ted said: "I wouldn't be so sure. It's the quiet ones who surprise you. The gentle ones that commit the most brutal killings. But I'll admit I can't figure what Pinker's motive would've been."

I kept silent about the writ Bernstein had issued. A dead man can't sue, so perhaps the writ would wither away and everyone would be none the wiser. Or perhaps it wouldn't.

In any event, I didn't think Pinker would kill over a libel writ. We were all threatened with them from time to time. We knew that most of them never came to court.

I watched Ted attack his fried bread and said: "I can't understand why Tomkins has got it in for Sidney. It's me he's supposed to hate."

Ted picked up his coffee cup and washed down a mouthful of sausage with a couple of gulps. "That's because you don't know what I do," he said.

"And I suppose it's going to cost me another coffee to prise the secret out of you." I signalled to Marcello to bring another.

Ted stuffed some egg into his mouth and wiped a dribble of yolk from his chin. "Tomkins' wife Hilda is a fanatic for amateur dramatics. She's in some kind of am-dram group that runs shows in a church hall up at Patcham."

"Don't tell me Sidney gave her a poor notice in the *Chronicle*."

"Last year," Ted said. "The thespians were putting on *Blithe Spirit*."

"The Noel Coward comedy about the man who's visited by the ghost of his first wife."

Ted nodded. "Hilda was cast as Madame Arcati, the medium who calls up the spirits of the nether world. Hilda tops the scales at twenty-two stone. Apparently, you could hear the boards in the stage creak when she made an entrance. Anyway, in his review, Pinker wrote: 'If Hilda Tomkins is a medium, I'd hate to encounter a large.' Tomkins told me Hilda was so upset by the comment, she was off her food for fully five minutes."

"And now Tomkins is getting his own back."

"Tomkins may be the superintendent around the station, but I hear he's the rookie at home. Hilda gives the orders, especially in the bedroom. His tough line with Pinker will get him off night duty with Hilda for a couple of days, I shouldn't wonder."

"That's why he left you to run the crime scene."

"There was no way he was going to give up the chance to grill Pinker personally."

"Let's hope for Pinker's sake that Tomkins has left his red-hot pliers with Hilda."

Ted used a piece of bread to wipe the last egg yolk from his plate. He sat back and launched a burp that would have won him a round of applause in Turkey.

I said: "I didn't have time to have a good look round the building this morning. But the place seemed modest to me."

"Yes. Bernstein's operation wasn't exactly the Rank Organisation. But he did well enough. Drove a Jag, had an expensive watch on his wrist, lived in a big house out at Withdean. Hard to say how he keeps that up from a small agency with a string of second-rate performers."

"The fruits of his years with Max Miller, perhaps," I said.

"Maybe. Miller died in May 1963, but a quick glance at Bernstein's bank statements shows he's had plenty of cash coming in since then."

"Is there any chance of me getting a quick look at the murder scene?" I asked.

Ted shook his head. "No chance. But I can tell you, Bernstein had a large office at the back of the ground floor. It looks over a small yard through a window."

"A window big enough to climb in?"

"Not unless you were a midget and had brought a pair of stilts. The window is high up on the wall."

"What's beyond the yard?"

"There's an alleyway which runs behind the buildings. There's a gate from the alley into the yard. It's usually bolted on the inside. But it wasn't this morning. I checked. There's a back door on the ground floor out into the yard, but that was locked. Overnight the key is kept in reception. It was in its place this morning."

"So someone could have got into the yard, but not through

the back door?"

Ted nodded. "That seems reasonable. There's a kitchenette also at the back. A set of backstairs come down into that area from the upper storeys. There's a door at the bottom of the stairs which is kept bolted on the inside so no casual visitors on the ground floor can use the backstairs to reach the upper storeys."

"You sound like an estate agent showing me around the place," I said. "Why all this detail about what it looks like?"

"Because you need to understand what I'm about to tell you now."

Ted had that smug smile on his face when he thought he had one up on me. This time, it looked like he had.

I said: "If this is good, I'll pay for your lunch as well."

Ted said: "Won't have time for lunch today, but I'm going to tell you anyway. However…" He tapped the side of his nose. "…you didn't hear this from me."

"Get on with it," I said.

"Whoever killed Bernstein had an accomplice."

"How do you know?"

"Because we believe the murder was committed in pursuit of a theft. We found a cigar box on the floor of the yard outside the window. We believe the killer threw it to an accomplice in the yard."

My eyebrows lifted at that. "You're not seriously telling me that Bernstein was croaked because someone wanted to get their hands on his fine Havanas?"

"H Upmann's as it happens. But, no, the box never had any cigars in it. He kept it locked in his desk drawer. We found the key still in the lock. Bernstein had a second key on a ring in his pocket. It was what was kept in the box the thief wanted."

"And what was that?" I asked a touch impatiently.

Ted grinned. "Max Miller's Blue Book," he said. "The notorious Blue Book."

I sat back and absorbed that information. It changed

everything.

A year ago, someone had told me about Max Miller and his Blue Book.

That someone was Sidney Pinker.

Twelve months earlier, I was sitting in Prinny's Pleasure enjoying a large gin and tonic.

In fact, that's not quite right. Prinny's Pleasure wasn't the kind of place where you "enjoyed" drinks. It was a back-street boozer where you downed your noggin from a grubby glass and hoped you didn't go down with cholera.

The Prinny in the place's name was the Prince Regent, later King George the Fourth. He'd spent time in Brighton because he could do things in a louche seaside resort he couldn't in full view of the stuffy court in London or Windsor. The Pleasure was Prinny's top squeeze, Mrs Maria Fitzherbert. She lived in a smart townhouse in Old Steine, not far from the pub.

Jeff Purkiss, the pub's mine host, was convinced the pair had used the place for secret assignations. In those days, it used to be called the Old Goat. Jeff had changed the name because he thought its link with royalty would drum up trade and he'd become rich. As a business decision it ranked alongside that bloke who turned down the opportunity to buy the patents to the telephone from Alexander Graham Bell.

As a result, I was frequently the only customer. Which suited me just fine. A crime reporter needs a quiet spot to meet contacts with dirty secrets to tell.

Anyway, I was sitting in the corner wondering whether to risk another drink when the door opened and Sidney Pinker walked in.

He was wearing a blue and white striped rowing jacket, pale cream shirt, and polka-dot bowtie. He wore a pair of pink slacks and had Italian loafers on his feet. The loafers looked like they'd have cost a few million lire on the Via Veneto.

I couldn't have thought of anyone less likely to drink at Prinny's Pleasure. Sidney's usual watering hole was a bar called Fancy Nancy in Kemp Town.

Sidney stood framed in the doorway and looked around the place. He sniffed, and his nose wrinkled, like he'd just walked through a farmyard. He stepped over a sticky bit on the carpet and headed towards me.

I said: "What brings you here, Sidney? Is Nancy's place being raided by the cops again?"

Pinker frowned and brushed an imaginary piece of fluff off his jacket.

"You can mock, dear boy. But Fancy Nancy attracts a quality clientele."

"So does Prinny's Pleasure."

Sidney glanced around the room. "I can't see anyone."

"I was referring to myself. Can I buy you a drink?"

Pinker peered at my glass. "If that's the standard of cleanliness in this place, I think I'll wait until I go on somewhere."

"Actually, this is one of the better glasses. But if I can't buy you a drink, what can I do for you?"

Pinker sat down and pulled his chair closer towards mine. He leaned towards me and rubbed his hands together. For a moment, I thought he was going to give me a playful chuck under the chin. I would have returned the compliment with a friendly punch on the snout. But Pinker thought better of it.

He looked around like there was a nest of conspirators earwigging us and said: "I think I'm onto a big story."

I said: "That must make a nice change from writing theatre crits."

"I prefer the term notices, dear boy. But never mind. The point is I'd be the first to admit I'm a little rusty on breaking hard news. I wondered whether I could confide in you."

"Confide away."

Pinker drew his chair even closer. "You'll have heard of Max

Miller, the famous music hall comedian."

"Of course, he was born in the east Brighton slums back at the turn of the century. Became the most highly paid entertainer in Britain. He made millions. A true rags-to-riches story. Didn't he die a couple of years ago?"

Pinker nodded. "And left a mystery behind him."

"That sounds more like my kind of story."

"Max was known as the Cheeky Chappie – and for good reason. Some of his jokes were risqué. In the variety theatre, this was just what the punters wanted. They lapped it up. But Max was banned by the BBC once for telling a filthy joke on the radio."

Sidney gave me a wary glance.

We fell silent.

I let the tension between us build, then said: "Well, what was it?"

Sidney beckoned me closer and lowered his voice. "Max was going through his usual patter and said, 'So I was walking along this cliff top path. It was so narrow you couldn't pass anyone coming the other way. I came around a bend and there was a naked woman coming towards me. Didn't have a stitch of clothing on. Good looking girl, too. I didn't know whether to toss myself off or block her passage.'"

"Hilarious," I said in a deadpan voice. "No doubt it was the way he told them."

"He was never at his best on radio. He needed a live audience," Pinker said defensively.

"Better than a dead one."

Sidney frowned. "The fact is, audiences loved him. He'd come out on stage and say, 'Now would you like a joke from my White Book or my Blue Book?' The clean jokes were white and the dirty jokes blue. Of course, the audience always wanted the Blue Book jokes. Max would whip out the book and start telling them."

"Where's this leading, Sidney?"

"Well, Max always used to keep his Blue Book very private. Nobody got to see it apart from him. There were all sorts of rumours about it. Like it contained scores of jokes Max hadn't yet told. No wonder that other comedians would have liked to get their hands on it. But, then, Max died – and the book vanished."

"So that's your big story is it? Joke book goes missing."

Pinker pulled his chair nearer to me.

I said: "If you come any closer, Sidney, you'll be sitting on my lap."

"Chance would be a fine thing, dear boy. But, no, my story's not about a missing joke book. It's about the fact that the Blue Book has been found."

"When did this happen?"

"In the last few days. And it's a weird story. It seems that after Max died, his widow found a box of H Upmann cigars in his room. She knew Max wouldn't be able to smoke them, so she gave them to Danny Bernstein, the agent who'd handled so many of Max's bookings. Danny put them to one side meaning to smoke them, but forgot about them. A few days ago, he'd run out of cigars and remembered he had them and opened the box. And do you know what he found under the cigars?"

"The Blue Book."

Pinker looked at me with wounded eyes. I'd stolen his punchline.

"You knew," he said.

"It was obvious," I said. "How did you hear about this?"

"Through a source."

"Which, quite rightly, you won't reveal."

"But I would like your advice."

"What about?"

"I haven't seen the book, but the journalist who breaks this story will have the show business scoop of the year."

"So tell Bernstein you know he's got the book and you'll give him favourable coverage if he lets you see it."

"That's the trouble. Bernstein and I have never got along. He's a lush who drinks heavily at lunchtimes and then sleeps in his office in the afternoon."

"How does he run his agency like that?"

"He's got an assistant – Evelyn Stamford – she knows more about the business than Bernstein does," Sidney said. "But Bernstein is a mean-spirited old cuss and he swindles his clients. I'm sure he even took Max for a tidy sum. He'll know the Blue Book would be worth a prince's ransom to another comedian. I don't think he'll see me."

"Then that's your way to trap Bernstein into letting you see the book," I said. "Write the story based on what you know so far – the cigar box tale is a neat twist. But give the story a downbeat angle – you know, Miller's been dead for a year, television is killing off variety theatres, blue jokes aren't suitable for the telly. You'll be able to think of other reasons. Then let Bernstein see your copy, but make it clear you're happy to spike it if you can write a better story. He'll want to show you the book. He won't want the paper printing a piece that talks down the Blue Book's value."

Pinker's mouth had dropped open as I spoke. He hugged himself with excitement.

He said: "I don't know whether I've got the bare-faced cheek to do that."

"Of course, you have. Be strong and you'll act strong."

Pinker sat up straighter. "Yes, I will," he said. "I can be strong. When that horrid Rupert Ponsonby-Jones said my new cravat looked like a distress signal at half-mast, I didn't shed a tear. I just looked him in the eye and said 'And your fly buttons are undone, but it looks like no-one's at home.' If his face had turned any redder, it would have caught fire."

"So you can do it," I said.

But I wasn't sure that he could.

Even so, Pinker clapped his hands like a delighted child.

"I'd kill to be the reporter who breaks the Blue Book story," he said.

In Marcello's, Ted Wilson said: "You haven't been listening to a word I've said."

I summoned up my steely gaze and focused it on Ted. "Sorry, I was thinking about something."

He said: "You looked as though you were light years away."

"No, only one year. But don't let it worry you."

Ted had a slurp of his second coffee. "I was telling you it looks as though Bernstein was murdered by a thief and his accomplice made off with Max Miller's Blue Book."

This wasn't the time to reveal what Pinker had told me a year earlier. That he'd be willing to kill to get his hands on the Blue Book. Besides, people use that 'I'd kill' expression all the time. It doesn't mean they will.

But I realised this new information meant I'd have to think again about Pinker's innocence – or guilt.

Ted said: "I can't sit here all day watching you moon about."

I said: "Thanks for the tip-off about the Blue Book. Usual non-attributable terms of course."

"Of course," said Ted.

I said: "One other point. Where was Bernstein's assistant Evelyn Stamford when all this happened?"

"She arrived about half past nine, a good half hour after the receptionist Sally found Pinker with the body."

"I'd like to talk to her."

"We've had to keep her out of her office this morning. She has a separate room from Bernstein at the front. But we've said she can come back in this afternoon. Mind you, if it were me, I'd never set foot in the place again."

Chapter 5

I used Marcello's telephone to call in an update on the story to a copytaker at the *Chronicle*.

Then I ordered another coffee – strong and black – and sat thinking about Pinker.

A year earlier, Pinker had taken my advice about the Blue Book. He'd written a negative story playing down the book's value. He'd shown it to Bernstein. He'd hinted that if Bernstein let him see the book, he'd write an upbeat piece about it.

But when you're playing that kind of scam to get a story, you need to radiate confidence. Your target needs to believe you really mean what you say. And Pinker would've had doubt written all over him. In big black letters.

He'd told me all about it afterwards.

Pinker had handed Bernstein the negative story typed out on copy paper. Bernstein had read it. His eyebrows had knitted together like he couldn't believe what he was reading. His gaze lifted from the paper and he gave Pinker a death stare. He ripped the paper in half and tossed it in his waste bin. Then he threatened to throw Pinker into the street if he wasn't out of his office in ten seconds.

Pinker arrived back in the newsroom quivering like a shell shock survivor from the First World War trenches.

Afterwards, I'd tried to persuade Pinker to use the carbon of his story he'd kept at the office in his regular showbiz column. But his heart was no longer in it. A few days later, the *Evening Argus* ran a flattering piece about the Blue Book. They'd had no more information than Pinker.

And then the story seemed to die.

Pinker had never had much respect for Bernstein. But now he hated him with a passion. Despite that, I firmly believed Pinker would never make a murderer. I didn't think he had it in him.

Now I wasn't so sure.

Suppose the killer did have an accomplice, as Ted Wilson had suggested. If Pinker had a sidekick, could he have put enough fire in Pinker's belly to turn him into a killer?

I didn't have an answer to the question.

I picked up my coffee mug. The dregs of my coffee were cold. But I drank them anyway.

It was mid-afternoon by the time I made it back to the building where Bernstein had his office.

A uniformed plod was playing the sentry role outside the front door. But he'd been briefed by Ted to let me in.

The cops were still busy collecting forensics in Bernstein's chamber of horrors. But Evelyn Stamford's room at the front of the building hadn't been affected by the drama.

The door to Evelyn's office was closed. I knocked lightly, opened it and looked inside.

There was no-one at home.

There was a desk in the centre of the room piled with files. I thought of having a quick shufti but that would be too big a risk even for me.

But I pushed the door so it opened wider.

And then a voice behind me said: "Where do you think you're going?"

I spun around. A woman had appeared at the far end of the corridor. She had a slim figure like an athlete's. She was wearing a dark blue skirt and a checked jacket over a cream blouse. She had a fancy bow arrangement around her neck. She had brown hair trimmed to the nape of her neck. Her hair was held back from her face by two tortoise-shell combs. She had a firm chin, a broad nose, and thin lips. She reminded me of the kind of librarian who gives you a nasty look if you start talking in the reference section. The first crow's feet had begun to appear around her hazel eyes. I put her age at about fifty.

She gave me a look she wouldn't use on a bloke who'd come to tell her she'd won a thousand quid on the Premium Bonds.

I switched on a hundred-watt grin and said: "You must be Evelyn Stamford. I knocked politely on your door but answer came there none."

"Most people would have assumed the room was empty and left the door closed."

"I thought I'd better check to make sure there wasn't another dead body on the floor."

"I can assure you I'm very much alive and have every intention of staying that way. And your remark is in poor taste."

"Sorry. I blame my rough upbringing."

She strode towards me. I stuck out my hand for a friendly shake. She ignored it and walked into her office.

She moved over to her desk. I followed her into the room.

I had a quick look around while she fumbled with buttons on her jacket. She took it off and hung it on a coat hanger in the corner of the room.

The place wasn't exactly a home from home. Three metal filing cabinets were lined up along one wall. A large pinboard filled with notes hung from another. A bookcase next to the door held copies of *Spotlight*, the tome that lists theatricals looking for work, plus some street directories, and a couple of old railway timetables. There were few of the softer touches you'd often see in a woman's office. No stylish curtains – just a dusty Venetian blind at the window. No vase with cut flowers. No dish of pot-pourri. No photo of hubby with the kids.

The one artistic touch was a set of three large playbills hanging behind Evelyn's desk. One was for Vesta Tilley, an Edwardian music hall performer. She'd dressed in trousers, top hat and tailcoat as an upper-class toff called Burlington Bertie. She sang a popular song about a day in the life of the character.

A second playbill featured Hetty King who dressed in a seaman's uniform to sing All the Nice Girls Love a Sailor.

And the third featured Valentine Redcar who didn't seem to have made it into the hit parade. But she'd appeared as Dick Whittington in a pantomime back in 1936.

Evelyn settled herself behind her desk and said: "If you're here about a job, you're too late."

"Yes, I know Danny Bernstein has taken his final curtain call. That's what I wanted to talk to you about."

"I've already been interviewed by the police."

"I'm Colin Crampton from the *Evening Chronicle*."

"Then you can turn around and exit stage right, out of that door."

"Before I do, would you like to hear why it wouldn't be in your interests for me to do that?"

Evelyn shot me a sly sideways glance. "I'm listening, but make it brief."

"I have to write an obituary on Mr Bernstein for the *Chronicle*," I lied. "I can do this by talking to the friends and colleagues who knew him best. And my obit will reflect the warm words they had to say about him. I'm guessing that none knew him better than you. But if you don't want to talk, I'll have to speak to other people whose opinion of him might not be so high. Which group do you think Mr Bernstein would have preferred?"

Evelyn frowned and fidgeted in her chair. She picked up a handful of files and put them on top of some others.

She said: "All right. Sit down. I'll give you ten minutes."

I grabbed a spare chair and pulled it up to the desk.

I took out my notebook and said: "How long had Mr Bernstein been running his agency here?"

"Since before the Second World War. He had the luck to sign Max Miller as an early client. Of course, Max was just beginning to make his name in the nineteen-thirties. Mr Bernstein booked him into variety theatres all over the country. Soon Max was playing the biggest theatres like the London Palladium and the Holborn Empire. With Max on the books, it wasn't difficult to recruit other clients."

"When did you join the firm?"

"Immediately after the war. I'd toured in variety in the nineteen-thirties and been in ENSA during the conflict."

"That would be the Entertainments National Service Association. The body that organised shows for the troops."

Evelyn sniffed. "ENSA signed me up as a singer. I performed in the Middle East, and in Europe after D-day."

I made a note in my book. I didn't mention that ENSA was known by its audiences as Every Night Something Awful.

Crampton, master of tact.

I asked: "Did you continue in show business after the war?"

"I didn't think I'd make it any further as a performer. There were too many wartime stars like Vera Lynn filling the theatres."

"And that's when you joined the agency here?"

"Yes, I'd met Mr Bernstein on one of my tours and he asked me to become his assistant."

"Apart from Max Miller, did Mr Bernstein have other big-name clients?"

"He had many clients including a lot of speciality acts – jugglers, escapologists, magicians, acrobats, unicyclists – even a performing dog act, Professor Pettigrew and his Pixilated Poodles. It was enough to keep us busy for many years."

I didn't mention Suleiman the Sword Swallower whose blade had done for Bernstein.

Tact. It was becoming a bad habit. I'd have to do something about it.

I said: "I'd heard that traditional variety theatre is dying now that everyone watches television."

Evelyn shook her head. "We're not as busy as we were in those years immediately after the war. But we still manage some good acts."

"But Max Miller's death two years ago must've been a blow," I said.

Evelyn nodded. "Yes. The agency has missed him. And not just for financial reasons. When he was in Brighton, Max often used to pop into the office. He'd sit in the back room with Danny and a bottle of whisky. They'd jaw about the triumphs they'd had in the theatre."

"So Bernstein was a friend as well as an agent to Max?"

"Yes."

"One to whom Max would like to leave his Blue Book?"

Evelyn gave me a wary glance. "You already know that it arrived in the cigar box. But, yes, I believe that Max would have welcomed the knowledge that it was owned by an old friend."

"Why did Mr Bernstein never share its contents with other Max Miller fans?" I asked.

"I think he felt that as Max had kept the contents private during this life, that wish should be honoured in his death."

"Do you know what Mr Bernstein intended to do with the Blue Book on his death?"

"He never confided that in me. But whatever his intentions, they've been thwarted by the thief who took it and killed him."

"His death must've come as a big shock to you."

Evelyn nodded gravely. "When I arrived at the office at half past nine to find the police swarming over the building, I felt sick to the pit of my stomach."

Evelyn glanced at her watch. "And now, if you'll excuse me, I have work to do. Someone has to serve our clients."

"The show must go on," I said.

"Yes," she said in a deadpan voice. "The show has to go on."

For the first time, Evelyn looked as though the emotion was getting to her.

I said: "Just one more question. Do you think Sidney Pinker killed Mr Bernstein?"

"Mr Pinker reacted badly when Danny refused to show him the Blue Book. There were angry phone calls. I could hear Danny shouting down the phone in his office. And then Pinker wrote that disgraceful article in your newspaper. It's no wonder that Danny had had enough and decided to sue. I suppose it pushed Pinker over the edge. I understand Sally found him with the murder weapon and splashed with blood. That's what I call being caught red-handed."

Half an hour later, I was in the *Chronicle's* morgue, the place where thousands of press cuttings were filed.

There hadn't seemed much more to say after Evelyn Stamford had delivered her damning verdict on Pinker. Her mind was closed to any other explanations. And I was struggling to think of one anyway.

I'd persuaded Henrietta Houndstooth, who ran the morgue, to pull the cuttings we held on Max Miller and Daniel Bernstein. As I'd suspected, the Miller file was three inches thick. The Bernstein file was its skinny relative.

I'd expected Bernstein's murder to be the talk of the morgue. But Mabel, Elsie and Freda, Henrietta's assistants, who clipped and filed the cuttings, were taking a stroll down memory lane. The three, known around the paper as the Clipping Cousins, turned out to be fans of Max Miller.

"He was outrageous," Mabel said. "I remember seeing him about fifteen years ago at the Hippodrome. He came on stage wearing that floral jacket and plus-four trousers. He looked more camp than a row of tents. I was sitting in the fourth row of the stalls. I was laughing as soon as he came on. He pointed at me and said, 'If you're wondering, ducks, I'm not. But I help 'em out when they're busy.' I just shrieked. So did the rest of the audience."

Elsie said: "I saw him at the Finsbury Park Empire on a trip to London. I thought a lot of his jokes were corny, but his personality was so warm, you wanted to be his friend."

Freda said: "The best bit was when he sung his closing song."

"Mary from the Dairy," Elsie said.

"That's right," Mabel said.

"I loved that song," Freda said.

"Whenever I'd seen Max Miller I used to hum it all the way home," said Mabel.

They looked at one another… and burst into song. "I fell in love with Mary from the Dairy…"

I turned to Henrietta and said: "As it seems to be cabaret time, I'll take these cuttings back to the newsroom."

Henrietta smiled and shook her head in mock despair.

But the way my mission to save Pinker was going, I should've been the one in despair.

At my desk in the newsroom, I started to study the press cuttings.

Max Miller had been a big personality in Brighton. So Henrietta had been thorough in compiling cuttings about him. She'd included items from the theatrical newspaper *The Stage*, and the legal eagle's journal *The Law Society Gazette*, which I hadn't seen before.

The tips of my fingers became inky as I flipped through the flaking clippings.

Miller, it seemed, had lived his life in a spotlight, but he'd created a world of shadows after his death. The first mystery was where all his money had gone. He'd earned millions as a star of stage and screen. But he'd left just £27,000, a fraction of the wealth that had passed through his hands.

He'd left £7,000 to his former secretary, Ann Graham. His wife Kathleen had been well provided for in the will, the *Law Society Gazette* informed me, but had remained tight-lipped about Ann's bequest.

Then there was the mystery of the Blue Book. I already knew that it had been hidden in the cigar box. But if it had the value Bernstein had told Pinker, why hadn't Kathleen tried to get it back? The *Law Society Gazette* hinted at some reasons. Perhaps Kathleen was miffed at the money Ann had received and didn't want to draw any more attention to Max's financial affairs. Perhaps she was doubtful whether she could legally reclaim what she'd given as a gift. And if she could get it back, Bernstein would already know its content – which was where its real value lay.

But a further cutting deepened the mystery. There was another claim to the Blue Book. That came from Ernie Winkle, a comedian who'd regularly appeared as a supporting act on the same bill as Miller.

I leaned back in my captain's chair as I read a cutting from *The Stage*. "Comedian Ernie Winkle is taking legal advice about suing for the Blue Book," *The Stage* reported. The cutting noted that Winkle owned a comedy club in Brighton, the Last Laugh. I'd seen the place in one of the side streets that ran off Marine Parade. But I'd never been inside.

The Stage cutting went on: "Mr Winkle said, 'I worked with Max Miller for years, and appeared with him all over the country. A load of the gags in that book will be ones I told Max. He promised me I'd have the book when he passed on. And now I want that promise honoured. I will do anything to get the Blue Book.'"

Did "anything" include murder? I wondered. It was time to pay Winkle a visit.

Perhaps I would have the last laugh at the Last Laugh.

Chapter 6

My Australian girlfriend Shirley Goldsmith flashed me a smile and said: "I like a laugh but the one thing I can't stand is mother-in-law jokes."

I said: "You mean like the one about the two men in a pub."

"Don't say it," Shirley warned.

But I like to live dangerously, so I continued: "The first man said, 'My mother-in-law is an angel.' His friend knocked back his beer and said, 'You're lucky mate. Mine is still alive.'"

Shirl gave me a not-so-playful punch on the arm.

We were walking along Marine Parade towards the Last Laugh comedy club. It was one of those November evenings when you think stories about English weather can't all be true. There was a cloudless sky and a full moon. The moonbeams cast long fingers of light across the sea. The waves broke on the shingle with a soothing rhythmic splash. A breeze as gentle as an angel's sigh wafted in from the south-west.

Shirley said: "It's not fair that mothers-in-law are always the butt of weak comedians. They should even up the score. Why are there no father-in-law jokes?"

I said: "There are."

"Prove it."

"A woman is talking to her best friend. She says, 'Every time my father-in-law comes to dinner, he criticises my cooking. But, actually, I've got a soft spot for him. It's that patch of earth by the trees in the cemetery.'"

Shirley said: "If you ever give up journalism, don't apply for work in comedy."

"No danger of that. Frank Figgis is the only stand-up comic around the *Chronicle*. And even he doesn't know why people laugh at him."

"Yeah, your Figgis sounds like a joke. But I don't get it.

When you said you were taking me to a club, I thought we'd be dancing. That's why I'm wearing this funky gear."

Shirley had dressed in a silver print mini-dress with crazy flared sleeves. She was wearing knee-length black disco boots. She had a silver band in her blonde hair. She looked every inch the fashion model she'd become in the past year. I was tempted to scrub the Last Laugh and take her to Sherry's.

But there'd be time to play after I'd landed my story. I only hoped Shirley would see it that way. I hadn't yet told her that we wouldn't only be watching the show. I had work to do.

We crossed the road and headed up the street towards the Last Laugh.

Shirley said: "If I were opening a comedy club, I wouldn't call it the Last Laugh. That makes it sound like someone is getting one over on a sucker. I hope it's not us."

"I hadn't looked at it like that. But if I were a comedian, I'd be more worried about getting the first laugh."

We found the Last Laugh half way up the street. The club was housed in a run-down old cinema. But the ghosts of John Wayne and Katharine Hepburn would have left long ago. The place looked like it had been put up when cinemas used to be called bioscopes and Rudolph Valentino made audiences swoon. The women, that is. And, as we were in Kemp Town, some of the men, too.

There was a pair of swing doors underneath an awning to keep the rain off queues of eager filmgoers. Above the awning, we could see the rust marks where the cinema's name had once been spelt out in lights: CORONATION.

"I wonder whose coronation that was," Shirley said.

"George the Fifth's I shouldn't wonder," I said.

There were glass display cases on each side of the doors. The cases would once have displayed playbills announcing next week's attraction. Perhaps Boris Karloff in *Frankenstein*. Perhaps Vivien Leigh in *Gone with the Wind*. Perhaps Errol Flynn in *Robin*

Hood. More ghosts from the past.

The display case on the left held a poster which had faded with age. It showed a picture of a man with a lined face, a scrawny neck, and hunched shoulders. He was looking straight at the camera with a leery grin. His black hair had been plastered with so much hair cream it looked like his head had been coated with tarmac.

The foot of the poster delivered the punchline:

ERNIE *"Mind your manners"* WINKLE

Merry moments with Brighton's main mischief maker

Shows nightly

So this was the owner and star attraction of the Last Laugh.

Perhaps the place wasn't so badly named after all.

Shirley pointed at a poster in the display case on the right. "Hey, look there's going to be a Laugh-a-thon."

"A what?"

I switched my attention from the mischief maker.

"A Laugh-a-thon. It's a joke telling competition. According to this, five comics battle it out to raise laughs. The winner gets a spot on *Sunday Night at the London Palladium*."

"That's a top TV show. Millions tune in every week to watch," I said.

I took a closer look at the poster. It showed thumbnail photos of the five finalists – Billy Dean, Teddy Hooper, Jessie O'Mara, Peter Kitchen and the mischief-maker himself, Ernie Winkle.

"I've never heard of any of these," I said. "I wonder whether Sidney Pinker knows anything about them."

"You can find out in three days," Shirley said. "That's when the Laugh-a-thon takes place – and it's here."

"I wonder whether this is in the *Chronicle's* news diary."

This was the kind of story Sidney Pinker would usually file. But Sidney had other things on his mind at present.

We pushed open the swing doors and stepped into the foyer. The place had one of those ceilings with lots of swirls and curls in the plaster work. The walls had been covered with red flock wallpaper, probably before the projector had shown its first "talkie". Half a dozen portraits of Hollywood stars lined one wall. I spotted Veronica Lake, Humphrey Bogart and Bette Davis among them.

Between Humphrey and Bette there was a dog. I suppose that must have been Lassie.

To the right of the foyer, there was a ticket kiosk. It was one of those old-fashioned ones with a glass front and a small hole in the glass to talk through. The hole is usually too low so you have to bend down to buy your ticket. It makes you look like Uriah Heep begging for a favour.

Meanwhile the ticket seller inside is sitting on a comfy seat. No doubt the bending and crawling makes them feel superior.

The young woman in the ticket booth had curly fair hair, brown eyes, and a bored expression. Her name badge read Cilla Mullen.

I leant over and said: "Are you fully booked?"

Cilla's eyes lit up, like a battery had been turned on in her head. She he-hawed like a horse with a sense of humour.

She said: "Fully booked? That's the funniest thing I'll hear tonight. You, too."

I glanced at Shirley. She rolled her eyes.

I said to Cilla: "The show's that bad?"

Cilla said: "Let me put it this way. I've had more laughs having a tooth pulled."

Shirl nudged me in the ribs. "Let's beat it. We can grab a drink somewhere and then go bopping."

I shook my head. "I need to see this."

"Like you need to watch a puddle drying."

I said to Cilla: "Two tickets, please."

Shirley said: "Hold hard, buster. Before you book me into this fun palace, what's the score?"

"What do you mean?"

"Why are we here?"

"To see the show."

"There's more to it than that. It's time to level with me, bozo."

I shrugged. "I wasn't going to mention it in case we couldn't get in, but I need to find a way to interview Ernie Winkle."

"What would you want with the merry moments mischief maker?"

"It's to do with Sidney Pinker."

"Your guy who's on a murder rap?"

"He's not my guy. And Tomkins is fitting him up for a killing he never committed. I'm trying to get to the bottom of it."

Shirley's eyes flared. "Well, you can get to the bottom by yourself. And stay there, as far as I'm concerned. You said we were going to a club and I'm dressed to dance. And that's what I'm gonna do. Perhaps I'll find a guy who knows how to have fun without tying work on the end of it. See ya!"

She flounced through the swing doors and out into the night.

I stood with my jaw hanging loose while the swing doors squeaked to rest.

Cilla tapped on the kiosk window.

"Will it be just the one ticket now?" she asked.

I pushed through the door into the auditorium clutching my single ticket.

I didn't feel much like any kind of laugh, let alone a last one.

I was annoyed with myself more than Shirley. I should have levelled with her from the start that this wasn't going to be a fun night out. But the fact was, there'd been too many cases lately when our date had ended as a work fixture. I knew Shirl was fed up when we finished an evening with a dash to the *Chronicle* to file copy. Or to the cop shop to get a quote from Tomkins or Ted Wilson. Or, worst of all, to a back-street house or a lonely spot in the woods where some unlucky passer-by had just found a dead body.

Shirl was a trooper, but she wasn't a traipser. And I could understand why she was less than enchanted with the prospect of traipsing around after my stories.

The auditorium had the same faded red flock walls as the foyer. There were those wall lamps which look like half a fruit bowl stuck to the wall. They gave out a reluctant yellow glow. At the front of the place, there was a small proscenium arch with a heavy curtain hanging behind it. The auditorium seats were arranged in rows. There was a little table between each seat. There were half a dozen glum looking punters dotted around the place. I noticed most were nursing drinks, which made me brighten up a bit.

If there were drinks, there must be a bar. I peered through the gloom – and, sure enough, there it was at the back of the room. I made my way up the aisle towards it.

Behind the bar, Cilla from the ticket kiosk was sitting on a stool and staring into space. She had the kind of eyes I imagine you get when your body has been taken over by aliens.

I walked up and clicked my fingers in a friendly way. As though I were Sigmund Freud bringing a patient out of hypnosis to tell him he was cured and no longer wanted to make love to his mother.

Cilla snapped back into the real world with a lop-sided grin.

I said: "You looked like you were out of it."

She said: "I wish I were. I hate working in this dump."

"It doesn't tickle your funny bone anymore?"

I asked for a gin and tonic - one ice cube, two slices of lemon.

Cilla served my drink and said: "Ernie Winkle has never got a laugh out of me. I tell a lie. I did laugh at him once."

"When was that?"

"It was the seventeenth of June 1963. He was playing the last house more drunk that usual. He fell off the stage and broke his arm. I laughed so hard the tears ran down my legs."

"I heard he was big in his day."

"Only in his own imagination. And then only when he'd made a dead man of his bottle of whisky. He'd have spent a lifetime playing second string working men's clubs in places like Rotherham if Max Miller hadn't taken him under his arm."

I took a sip of the G and T and asked: "Why was that?"

"It was long before my day, but the way I heard it, Max felt sorry for him. I only met Max once – he came here shortly after Winkle opened the joint. He was a kind man. But you'd expect that of a bloke who'd seen cruelty at its worst. He served in the trenches in the First World War, you know. He was nearly blinded in one attack. He couldn't see at all for three days. I guess if you go through something like that, you count your blessings and extend the hand of kindness now and then."

A bell rang behind the bar. Cilla glanced at it and shrugged.

"The ticket kiosk. Winkle's such a cheapskate I have to manage the kiosk and the bar. Anyway, looks like there's another sucker for the show. Got to go."

She pushed past the curtain back to the kiosk.

But it turned out there were two suckers. They came through the door from the foyer a minute later.

The first was a big guy with a square face and crooked jaw which looked like he'd walked into a brick wall. He had a couple of inches to spare over six feet, broad shoulders, and hands big enough to lift a hippo. He had a tanned face which wouldn't have come from spending November in Brighton. He was wearing a grey jacket with sleeves that were too short and scrunched under the armpits.

His companion was the kind of short man who struts around like a bantam cock. His thick black hair was combed back from his forehead. He had thick lips and a bulbous nose with a cleft. He had a barrel chest and a pair of legs which could have supported a grand piano. He was wearing a three-piece suit which must have been made to measure. Tailors simply don't sell ready-made stuff for people that shape. He swaggered into the room ahead of the bigger guy and surveyed the joint through insolent eyes.

His gaze reached me and there was a change in his eyes – from relaxed to sharper focus - as though he'd recognised me from somewhere. He realised I'd seen the change. He nodded to me like he was a new guy in town just getting friendly with the locals.

Cilla reappeared from behind the curtain.

The short guy ambled over to the bar like he was an old customer. Like he expected the barkeeper to serve up his usual. He chose a stool at the opposite end to me and hoisted himself onto it. The bigger guy moseyed alongside and leant on the bar. The shorter guy crooked a finger at Cilla and she moved up the bar to serve their drinks.

I took a long pull of my G and T and tried to think what to make of it. They didn't look like the kind of guys who'd hang out in a downbeat comedy club for fun. They didn't look like they laughed a lot. They looked like the kind of guys who'd get their entertainment from an evening strangling kittens.

I mulled this over while I finished my gin and tonic.

I was going to order another when the lights began to dim. The show was about to start. I moved into the main body of the auditorium and took a seat half way back.

I glanced behind me. My new friends had taken seats two rows back immediately behind. There weren't more than twenty people in an auditorium that must hold two hundred. So it wasn't chance they wanted to sit behind me. They didn't want me slipping out of their view when the auditorium became dark.

A spotlight shone on the stage. A pair of loudspeakers started up a tinny version of I Do Like to be Beside the Seaside. The curtain rose on an empty stage. The music ended. An uncomfortable silence descended on the place.

And then a man staggered onto the stage from the wings. One person clapped. It may have been a mistake.

The man walked uncertainly down to a microphone centre stage. He grabbed the mic's stand and swayed a bit. He leered at the audience. If his grin had been any cheesier it would have come with cracker biscuits and a pickled onion. He was a small round man, like a huge beach ball with legs and arms. He had a chubby red face with flabby cheeks and piggy eyes. He had a luxuriant head of hair. But not his own. His wig looked like the kind of cheap novelty you'd pick up in a joke shop. It had slipped slightly to the left so there was a bald patch above his right ear. He was dressed in a long flapping coat made out of material with stripes in bright primary colours. He wore a pair of plus fours tucked into the top of yellow socks.

He launched in on his act.

"Thank you, thank you for that warm welcome. After that I feel like I just rubbed up against an Eskimo. I got the cold shoulder. Seriously, I can tell you're going to be a great audience. You'll be right behind me. But I'm not worried. I'll shake you off when I reach the railway station. Anyway, for future reference, the name's Winkle. I'm the only winkle with its own mussels. Muscles, geddit? But I don't like to be shellfish."

Somewhere in the darkened auditorium a woman tittered.

"No, lady, none of that. Mind your manners, missus. Keep it clean. What did you think I was going to say? Mind your manners. We all need to mind our manners, don't we? I mean it was like the time I proposed to my wife. You know what she said. 'I like the simple things in life – but I don't want one for a husband.' I mean I could only say one thing. Mind your manners. That's what I said. Mind your manners."

Winkle ploughed on with his witless patter for another half hour. Now and then there was a snigger. Now and then a yawn. Towards the end I found my head nodding forward.

And then a reprise of I Do Like to be Beside the Seaside blasted over the loudspeakers

Winkle was waving at the audience. *"That's it for now. Thank you for your warmth and your laughter. Stay on for the late show in an hour's time.*"

And with that, he staggered towards the wings and the curtain fell.

I glanced behind to see what my two watchers had made of it all.

Their seats were empty. As the house lights came up, I looked around the auditorium.

They had vanished.

Chapter 7

At first, I felt relief – and then doubts crept in.

The pair had looked like trouble from the moment they'd swaggered into the club. Trouble for me. The short guy knew who I was and had given himself away when he'd looked at me. They'd made a point of sitting behind me.

And then they'd vanished.

Did that mean their job was over?

Or did it mean it would start up again another time?

And what the hell was their job? I had no idea.

But, I reminded myself, I had a job of my own. I had some pointed questions for Ernie Winkle.

The few punters had drifted to the bar at the back of the auditorium. Cilla was busy dispensing the drinks. I decided to slip backstage while everyone was otherwise engaged.

There was a door to the right of the stage. A sign on it read: Private Strictly No Admittance.

To a journalist, that's a bit like saying, "Come in, but wipe your feet."

I stepped smartly up to the door and opened it. I took a quick peak to make sure no-one was looking. Then I slipped inside.

I closed the door behind me and looked around. I was in a small room with black walls. A thin weasely little man was sitting behind a control panel twiddling the knobs. He was bald apart from a single strand of hair which he'd wrapped around the edge of his pate.

He looked up as I stepped into the room and said: "If you're looking for the lavs, it's the door on the other side of the auditorium. Use at your own risk – the porcelain's cracked, the taps don't work, and the cleaner hasn't been in there for three weeks."

I said: "I'm looking for a different dirty joke."

The bloke nodded. "He's back there. Dressing room number one. You can't miss it. There's only one dressing room anyway."

I left him turning his knobs and headed behind the stage.

I found dressing room number one – yes, it had a star on the door – next to a pile of old usherette ice-cream trays. They had a little light to illuminate the ices and a strap which the girls looped round their necks. Years ago, when the place was a cinema, the girls would have held the trays as they walked backwards down the aisles. Now they were covered in a thick film of dust – I mean the trays, not the usherettes. I wondered why Winkle hadn't thrown them out. No, not the usherettes, the trays.

I knocked on the dressing room door.

A voice within shouted: "Bugger off, unless you've brought my whisky."

I opened the door. Winkle was sitting on a stool in front of his dressing mirror. He turned as I entered the room. He screwed up his eyes and scowled at me.

I said: "How much do you want for the ice-cream trays?"

Winkle looked at me as though I'd just asked him to shoot his grandmother. His mind had jumbled with different thoughts. Who was I? Why did I want the trays? And was I a sucker he could make some easy money from? For the moment, he'd forgotten about the whisky.

He said: "Thirty quid. Or, if it's a cash deal, twenty-five. They're worth double that."

I said: "I'll think about it. While I'm doing so, could we talk about something else?"

"What?"

"Max Miller's Blue Book."

"I haven't got that. And if I had, it wouldn't be for sale. Not for a pony. Not even for a monkey."

"I hear there was once a time when you thought you'd inherit the Blue Book."

Winkle shrugged. Out of the stage lights, his face was like a grotesque mask. His cheeks were whitened with cream and he had thick black liner under his eyes. His lips had been painted carmine. His wig was still crooked.

"Yeah. There was a time when Max said he'd pass the book on to me, but that never happened. And, anyway, who the hell are you to ask me these questions?"

"Didn't I say?" I pulled out a card and handed it to Winkle. "Colin Crampton, *Evening Chronicle*."

"A reporter."

"Didn't think I'd fool a sharp cookie like you."

"So why did you ask me about those frigging trays?"

"Got you talking and stopped you throwing me out. By now, we're almost old friends."

Winkle grinned. "Clever bugger, aren't you?"

"If I ever need a testimonial, I'll ask you to put that in writing."

Winkle's dressing table was littered with jars of cream and tubes of make-up. Over the other side of the room, a rail held jackets and trousers. The place had a sweet cloying aroma but with a sharpness behind it. As though someone had dropped a whisky bottle in a perfume factory.

Winkle glanced in the mirror. He was thinking about what to do next.

He turned back to me. "Anyway, you may be clever, but you've wasted your time. I'm not talking about Max Miller or the Blue Book."

I pulled up a spare chair and sat down.

"Is that because you feel cheated out of it?" I asked.

"Max would have wanted me to have it," Winkle said. "He just never made that clear in his will."

"And then Daniel Bernstein got the book almost by accident."

"Yeah! It just fell into his lap. Like those girls who used to beg him to get them jobs as dancers."

That was something nobody had mentioned about Bernstein.

He had a casting couch. But didn't most theatrical agents?

I said: "How well did you know Danny Bernstein?"

"He was my agent from before the Flood."

"You look older than that. Or is it the make-up?"

"I'm supposed to be the funny man around here. But, you're right, it was back in the 'thirties when Max Miller's career started to take off. I'd got to know Max and he asked Danny to take me on. Said he'd like me to appear in his shows."

"And Bernstein agreed?"

"He'd do anything for Miller. Max was the only headliner he had on his books. But Danny was jealous of me, right from the start. I toured with Max week after week. We got to know each other like a pair of brothers. The kind of digs we'd stay in. The breakfast we'd eat. The drinks we'd have before a show. The girls we'd take out afterwards. Danny didn't like that. He knew I didn't like him. And I knew he didn't like me. But we both relied on Max for our success. All the while we lapped up that success, we kept the lid on our mutual dislike. But we knew that if Max's career went into a slide, that hatred would boil over."

"Did it?"

Winkle looked at me through weary eyes. He'd spent a lifetime trying to be funny. Perhaps it had only just dawned on him that he wasn't.

"You know it did," he said. "That's why you're here. You think I killed Bernstein. But I didn't. I couldn't – I don't have the guts for it."

"But when Bernstein refused to give you the Blue Book, you said you'd do anything to get it."

"I was angry. I didn't mean murder." He looked in the mirror again.

"Do you have any idea who did?"

"If I did, I'd have sent them a bouquet."

"Did you ever see Max's Blue Book?" I asked.

"Of course. He brought it out on stage most nights."

"But did you ever get to read its contents?"

Winkle shot a quick glance at the mirror. He turned back to me. I'd touched a raw nerve.

"Max guarded the contents, like it was the secret of eternal life. For his career, it pretty much was."

"And Bernstein never offered to show it to you when he got the book?"

Winkle looked into the mirror again. But this time longer.

"Bernstein wouldn't show me the way to my own grave," he said.

He glanced at his watch. "And now I need to prepare for the next show. And I haven't even drunk the first double yet."

I stood up, moved towards the door, and opened it. I glanced back.

Winkle had reached into a cupboard underneath the dressing table. He brought out a bottle of scotch.

"Yeah, I know what you're thinking," he said. "But if I drink enough before I go on, at least I can believe I'm funny."

I nodded at him, stepped outside, and closed the door behind me.

Back in the auditorium, most of the punters had bailed out.

They hadn't been tempted to stay on for Winkle's second show of the night.

Behind the bar, Cilla perched on a stool and flipped the pages of *Tit-Bits*.

I walked up, nodded at the magazine, and said: "Anything interesting?"

"Nah! Not unless you're a fan of Alma Cogan."

"That's the singer they call the 'girl with a giggle in her voice.'"

"Did you dig her take on Tennessee Waltz?"

"Not really. Sounds like she's singing in the bath. With a sponge in her mouth."

Cilla gave me a sharp look. "Are you going to order a drink or just run down popular singers?"

"Actually, I wondered whether you'd noticed what happened to those two blokes who came in after me?"

"The Yanks?"

"They were Americans?" I couldn't keep the surprise out of my voice.

"They spoke with Yankee accents. The small one called me 'honey'. Of course, they could've come from Haywards Heath and be putting it on. Nothing would surprise me here. But they left half way through Winkle's show. I suppose that's why Americans get on in this world. They don't sit around listening to crap."

"Did you catch their names?" I asked.

Cilla thought about that for a moment. "The small one called the big one Willis. I think the small one said his name was Gino. I think he hoped he'd pick me up. Like I'd be seen with a ball of grease."

So Gino and Willis had left. But why?

That was the question that was pounding in my mind. I was certain that they'd come into the club because they'd been following me. How long for I didn't know. But wait a minute. When I'd questioned the copper on the door at Bernstein's office, he'd said there'd been the usual rubberneckers. But a short guy with an American accent had claimed he had business in the place. The cop's description sounded like Gino. The cop had sent him on his way.

Could he have hung around and seen me go into the building later? But why should he be following me? If he'd had a cor blimey accent, I'd have him down as a reporter on one of the tabloids. He'd be using me as the pilot fish to guide him to the story. It had happened before. But never with an American. And I couldn't see the Yankee papers being interested in a murder in Brighton. At least, not being hot enough for the story to have me followed.

Anyway, the pair had cleared off. So, presumably, they'd finished their surveillance for the day. No point in worrying about that now. I'd pick it up in the morning. And I'd keep a close watch for anyone on my tail.

Cilla looked like she wanted to go back to her paper.

I said: "I think I'll skip Winkle's second show."

Cilla said: "With judgement like that, you'll go far."

"Tell that to Frank Figgis."

Cilla looked puzzled. So I headed for the door, passed through the foyer, and stepped into the street.

A white van had parked on the edge of the narrow footpath. The front of the van faced away from me, so I couldn't see whether there was anyone in the driver's seat. But the oaf who drove the thing had left less than a couple of feet between the van and the club's iron railings. These fenced off a flight of steps that led down to the club's basement. A gate opened onto the steps.

As I squeezed between the van and the railings the van's front door swung open blocking my way. I glanced around. The van's back door had been opened so it closed off my retreat.

Gino climbed out of the front seat. He was carrying a baseball bat.

Willis emerged around the back door. He wasn't wearing a pitcher's mitt. But with hands that size, he didn't need one. They probably didn't make them that big.

I said to Gino: "You have me at a disadvantage. I left my cricket bat at home."

Gino said in a New York drawl: "You won't need it. In this ball game, we're using your head for practice."

He stepped forward and swung the baseball bat at me. I jumped back. And felt Willis behind me grab my shoulders. I lifted my right leg and stamped down on his foot. Nothing too serious. Just enough to make his toes rattle around in his socks like bones in a butcher's bag.

Willis yelped like a hound dog in a trap. He let go my arms and staggered to one side. I turned and tried to push past him. But his floundering body and the van's back door blocked my escape.

Behind me, I sensed Gino advance with the baseball bat. I turned to face him. I needed a plan to get out of this. The only one I could think of was to duck.

Gino swung the bat at my head.

I ducked.

I made a good job of it. But the bat ruffled my hair as it missed the crown of my head by all of a millimetre.

At least that plan worked.

But now I was out of options. Because Willis' toes weren't rattling as much as I'd hoped. He grabbed my arms again. I hadn't stamped hard enough. That's my trouble. Too much compassion.

I struggled but Willis had a grip like a gorilla. And Gino had recovered from a lazy swing that would've ruled him out of major league baseball for life. He was moving in closer. Didn't intend to miss this time.

He raised the bat. Lined it up on my head like he was Willie Mays hoping for a home run. He grinned in a feral way – like a guy who gets a lot of pleasure from his work. He had yellow teeth. I guessed his bad breath could be just as deadly as the bat.

He swung the bat back, taking aim. And taking his time. Why rush something you'll look back on in years to come as one of the happiest moments of your life? He was savouring it.

The light changed in his eyes and I knew he was going to swing the bat. I struggled more but Willis' grip tightened. I tried the stamping trick again but he was too cute to fall for that plot now. He shifted his foot and kicked me in the back of the leg.

I yelled in pain.

I closed my eyes and waited for worse pain from the bat

to start. Perhaps there wouldn't be pain. Perhaps everything would just go black. For ever.

And then a scream rent the air. Long, loud and high-pitched. Full of anger and outrage. Like a snotty kid in the stands at a baseball game had just dropped his popcorn.

My brain closed down. And then I realised it wasn't me screaming. The scream came from the steps leading to the club's basement. The steps with the railings and the gate.

I opened my eyes. A figure hustled from the basement like the place was on fire.

The figure was Shirley.

She screamed like she was riding a bucking bronco. But she pounded up the steps. And she was carrying something big and red.

Gino's arm with the bat dropped to his side as he turned to see what the hell was happening.

Shirley stood at the top of the basement steps with a face like an avenging fury.

She raised the red thing – it was a fire extinguisher.

She pulled out a pin and yanked on the lever.

The first blast of the foam hit Gino right in the face. He hadn't been expecting it. The white stuff surged over his cheeks and ran down his shoulders. He looked like a bloke who'd just trekked through Siberia in a blizzard.

Shirley moved in like a commando with a machine gun.

Gino was helpless. The foam was all over him. It was in his eyes, in his ears, up his nose.

Willis' grip on my arms loosened. I struggled free. I turned around and kicked his left leg just enough to make him walk around like Hopalong Cassidy for the rest of his life.

He staggered sideways and Shirley charged in with the fire extinguisher.

Through the commotion, I heard Gino yell: "Let's beat it."

He hustled up to the van and jumped into the driver's seat.

Willis scrambled into the back.

Shirley sprayed the van with foam as Gino fired the engine and screamed away from the kerb.

She dropped the fire extinguisher on the pavement. She grinned and let out a long sigh.

"Now that's what I call a good joke," she said.

I brushed the stray foam off my jacket.

I said: "Does that trick with the extinguisher mean you still think I light your fire?"

Shirley said: "What I can't figure is why those drongos wanted to croak you."

"First things first," I said. "What were you doing down the club's basement steps?"

It was half an hour after the ruckus outside the club. After Gino and Willis had driven away, we decided we'd better skedaddle before any cops appeared on the scene. We were in Sherry's disco dancing to Sonny and Cher's I Got You Babe. There's nothing like a smoochy number to take your mind off a close encounter with death.

Shirley said: "After I'd stormed out of the Last Laugh, those two bozos were stepping out of their van. The short one gave me a dirty look – couldn't stop himself. And the big one said, 'Hey, boss, that's the broad who's with the mark.' The boss man gave him a filthy look and hissed, 'Button it.' But it was too late, I'd heard. I guessed something was up. I just knew I was gonna have to pull your nuts out of the cracker again. So I snuck down the basement steps and kept look out."

"And charged in like Boadicea when the attack went down. All you needed was a chariot with knives on the wheels."

"All I could find was that fire extinguisher."

"Couldn't have worked better had it been a Sherman tank."

Sonny and Cher finished their number and the DJ played The Byrd's Mr Tambourine Man. Shirley and I started bopping with the crowd.

I shouted above the music. "I've no idea why Gino and Willis wanted to kill me. I don't even know who they are. But I'm going to find out."

"You'd better watch your back then."

"I can't think of a way to thank you enough."

Shirl moved in close. She put her arms around my neck and kissed me.

"I can think of a way," she said.

It was nearly two in the morning by the time I reached my lodgings in Regency Square.

After Sherry's, I'd taken Shirley back to her flat. She'd let me thank her. Twice as it happened, but that's a personal matter I won't go into here.

I'd rented rooms on the fifth floor of a lodging house since I'd moved to Brighton. The place was run by a dragon landlady called Beatrice Gribble. She'd started letting out rooms after her husband Hector had died. I'd seen a picture of the old boy on the mantlepiece in her parlour. It showed a bald-headed bloke with the beaten expression of someone who knows he's destined always to be last in life's race.

The Widow – as tenants called Mrs Gribble, but never in her hearing – had her parlour on the ground floor. All the better to watch the comings and goings of tenants. But in the wee small hours she'd be in her bed and snoring like a chainsaw.

So I opened the front door with a devil-may-care shove and clumped into the hall.

The Widow shot out of her parlour before I could reach the first tread on the stairs. She was wearing a pink flannelette dressing gown and fluffy slippers with pom-poms. Her hair was tied up in a net arrangement like she was worried it might get away during the night.

The Widow moved across the hallway and cornered me by

the hat-stand.

She said: "I've had my evening's entertainment interrupted three times by telephone calls for you. The first when I was watching *Double Your Money*. The second when that delightful gentleman Richard Baker was reading the news on the BBC. And the third while I was meditating over the *Epilogue*. A very thoughtful talk on the meaning of life by a vicar from Chipping Sodbury."

I briefly wondered whether there was any life in Chipping Sodbury.

But I asked: "Who were the calls from?"

"They didn't say."

"Then how do you know they were for me."

"Because they just breathed heavily down the line."

I rolled my eyes.

"It's no good you taking that attitude with me," the Widow snapped. "Any more of these calls, and I shall ask you to pack your bags."

She stormed back into her parlour and slammed the door.

I trudged up the stairs wondering who had called and why they'd not left their name. It was another question I couldn't answer.

Chapter 8

The following morning, I arrived at the police press conference feeling like I'd slept in a hedge.

A thorn hedge.

I had a prickly feeling behind my eyes. My skin itched like it had been rubbed down with sandpaper.

So I was in a scratchy mood when Jim Houghton, my opposite number on the *Evening Argus*, lumbered up to me. Jim had a wrinkled face that looked like a squashed sponge. He had a shock of grey hair. He wore a moth-eaten tweed suit, a shirt with a crumpled collar, and a tie with a couple of gravy stains. He had a shaving nick on his chin and a bit of old meat stuck between the gap in his front teeth. It was the morning, so it would be bacon. (After lunch, it was Spam from his sandwich. In the evening, steak or kidney – sometimes both – from his pie.)

He gave the impression of a shambling old geezer who couldn't be trusted to take the right bus home. It was his secret weapon. In reality, he had a brain like a butcher's chopper. He'd scooped me on some big stories over the years. So as I saw him shuffling across the room towards me, I sharpened my wits.

Or what was left of them.

Jim ambled up and switched on his grin. He said: "Looks like your theatre critic will be reviewing the prisoners' benefit performances from Pentonville in future."

"What happened to innocent until found guilty, Jim?" I said.

"I look at the evidence. I hear Pinker was holding the murder weapon when he was discovered."

"Trying to pull it out so he could save a life, I understand. Not so much killer as saviour."

A cloud of doubt passed across Jim's face. "But Bernstein still died."

"Sharp as ever, Jim. Not many would spot that a murder case

involved a dead body."

Jim mumbled: "Cocky bastard. You'll get your comeuppance one day – just like Pinker."

He ambled off across the room and sat down in a seat on the end of the front row.

I took a seat at the back and surveyed the place. It was filling up with reporters from the national newspapers. A juicy murder case with a showbiz cast would keep the Sunday tabloids in headlines for weeks. They hoped.

There was the usual hubbub of conversation as journos swapped theories about the case with one another. Normally I'd be doing it myself. The trick is to advance a theory that's so outrageous you know it's untrue. You hope the bloke you're talking to will rubbish it and let drop a fact or two you hadn't heard.

It's the game you play when you're coming from behind on a story and you don't want to be scooped. But I wasn't playing this time. For starters, I knew more about the case than anyone in the room – probably including the cops. And, in any event, I still hadn't figured how I was going to get Sidney Pinker off a murder rap.

I was puzzling over this when Alec Tomkins swaggered into the room and sat down at the top table.

He had a thick sheaf of papers under his arm. He put them on the table and patted them into a neat pile.

He said: "I am going to read a statement and then I will take questions."

He put on his glasses, picked up the top sheet of paper from his pile, and started to read.

I'd flipped open my notebook but didn't write anything down. Tomkins' statement was a dull recital of everything we already knew.

He finished reading and put the paper back on his pile.

He surveyed the room with a self-satisfied smirk and said:

"Any questions?"

A reporter from the *Daily Sketch* asked: "Apart from the man you've arrested, are you looking for anybody else?"

Tomkins said: "No."

My hand shot into the air. Tomkins ignored it, but I asked anyway: "Does that mean you're ignoring other evidence – such as the mystery man that was in Danny Bernstein's office building shortly before he was discovered dead?"

Tomkins harrumphed. "We're pursuing several avenues of enquiry," he said pompously.

"Does that include seeking the identity of the mystery man?"

"It might do," Tomkins growled.

"So when you said 'no' just now, you should have said 'yes'."

"No. I mean yes. I think."

More hands shot into the air.

Tomkins stood up. "No more questions. I've got a murderer to catch."

"I thought you were claiming you'd already caught him," I said.

And on that confusing note, the press briefing broke up.

But I felt pleased. After my cross-examination of Tomkins, none of the other journos would be able to write that Pinker was definitely the killer. It was a result. But not the big prize. I needed to work more for that.

So I hurried up to Tomkins while he was picking up his pile of papers.

I said: "I want to see Sidney Pinker in the capacity of prisoner's friend."

Tomkins growled: "Yeah. With friends like you, Pinker would do better with enemies."

I frowned. "There's a rumour going around that you're giving Sidney a hard time because he once gave your wife a poor review in one of her amateur dramatic outings. Story hasn't hit the press yet, but it can be only a matter of time."

Tomkins leaned in closer to me. I could smell the heavy stink of his breath. "You lay off any mention of Hilda or you'll know what for," he said.

"You, too, if what I hear about Hilda is only half right."

Tomkins scrunched his papers angrily in his hand. He knew I'd backed him into a corner.

"A ten-minute visit to Pinker. Not a second more," he snapped.

He turned and stamped out of the room.

Sidney was brought up to an interview room from the cells a few minutes later.

He looked a lot less suave than the last time I saw him. There were grey bags under his eyes. His hair had matted. He hadn't shaved all the way under his chin.

The collar of his shirt was stained with sweat. His trousers had crumpled around the knee.

He sat down behind the table screwed to the floor on a chair screwed to the floor. I sat down on the opposite side of the table on another chair screwed to the floor.

From where I sat, everything around here seemed to be screwed – including Sidney. Unless I could find a way to prove he was innocent.

Sidney shrugged sadly and said: "They've taken away my cravat, dear boy. They said I might use it to do myself a mischief. Whatever they mean by that."

I said: "I think they're worried you might use it to hang yourself in your cell, Sidney."

"With a silk cravat from Hermes? Have they no taste, these vulgar plods?"

"As a general rule, no. But you can work with that if you know how to get around it. Besides, they used to hang peers of the realm with a silken rope."

"How decadent. But, really, these rough boys-in-blue aren't to my taste."

"In that case, we need to get you out of here."

"But how?"

"I need some information about some stand-up comics – Jessie O'Mara, Teddy Hooper, Billy Dean, Peter Kitchen and Ernie Winkle."

"This is no time for jokes, dearest heart."

"I'm well aware of that," I said testily. "But the five I've just mentioned could all have a motive for killing Bernstein."

Sidney's eyebrows jumped at that. "How come?"

I told him about the competition to win a spot on *Sunday Night at the London Palladium*.

"I could think of a whole laugh-line of comedians who'd kill to win a place on that show," Sidney said. "It could make their career. Which of them do you think did it, dear boy?"

"I don't know for sure that any of them did. But I need you to tell me as much as you know about each of them. I'm looking for something in their background that might suggest they'd be willing to kill Bernstein. Let's start with Jessie O'Mara."

Sidney looked at the ceiling and scratched his chin. "You know most of my work is in the legitimate theatre. Music hall is rather down there with the common clay. Now if you were asking me about Larry or Johnny Gielgud, I could keep you enthralled for hours."

I let out an exasperated sigh that sounded like the Flying Scot pulling into Kings Cross. "Sidney, don't think I'm sitting here because I enjoy it. I'm here on Figgis' orders to pull your arse out of the fire. Now concentrate."

"Sorry. I do get rather carried away some times."

"I wish you were."

Sidney frowned. "Jessie O'Mara. The 'Laughing Lass from Liverpool' it says on her bill matter. That's a laugh in itself. She comes from Birkenhead."

"That's only the other side of the Mersey."

"Tarnishes the tale, though. She comes on stage to the song

When Irish Eyes are Smiling. But she's got about as much Irish blood in her veins as my Aunt Freda. And she comes from Sidcup."

"So she's created a stage persona for herself. What's wrong in that?"

"Nothing if you can carry it off. For years she was a great favourite with pantomime producers at Christmas time. The kiddies who came to the shows loved her. She'd always be cast as the fairy queen. Played some big shows too – never quite made it to the Palladium, but was at the Opera House in Manchester and the Hippodrome here in Brighton. But that all stopped a couple of years ago."

Sidney paused for one of his knowing winks.

"Get to the point, Sidney," I said.

"It turns out the white-as-snow fairy queen got pregnant. Of course, a girl who's as tough as a blacksmith's apron soon solved that problem."

"She had an abortion?"

"Not yet legal either, although there's now talk of changing the law. Wouldn't have been a problem, except the news leaked out. Jessie escaped prosecution, but the bad publicity sent producers hunting for more virginal fairy queens. I hear that Jessie hasn't found bookings quite so regular as they had been since it all came out."

"But what's this got to do with Bernstein?"

"He was her agent. What a simple little soul you are. You don't think he hustled to get those great bookings for Jessie just because he liked the colour of her eyes, dear boy?"

I sat back in my chair. It didn't move and dug into my back. I'd forgotten the damned thing was screwed to the floor.

"I'm guessing that Jessie wasn't a Bernstein client after that," I said.

Sidney nodded. "She was always too good for him. Like Max Miller. Max was saucy but never smutty. It must stick in her craw that a grasping old lecher like Bernstein ended up with his Blue Book."

"Enough to want to kill him?" I asked.

"Who can say? Perhaps others have prior claim to that honour, dear boy."

"Such as?"

"Billy Dean, for instance. He's always been a basement comic."

"Basement comic?"

"The one whose name is always bottom of the bill. And that hardly ever. He's never had the kind of material that attracts the better class of variety theatre. I don't know much about him, but what I've heard makes my flesh creep."

"That must take some doing, Sidney."

Pinker licked his forefinger and used it to smooth his eyebrows. "Well, really, you know I've always been the epitome of fastidiousness. But Dean is not our type, dear boy."

"None of them are our type. They're all comics."

"I'd tip my Christian Dior Eau de Cologne down the toilet if Billy Dean stepped on to the London Palladium's stage as anything other than the cleaner," Sidney said.

"That bad?"

"He made what name he has as a comic who fills in between the strippers in Soho clubs."

"Like the Windmill Theatre?"

"Nothing so elevated for our Billy. He trades in grubby jokes with foul language. Apparently, for the punters in these places, the fouler the better. I think I'd faint if I ever heard it."

"Get a grip, Sidney. You're supposed to be a ruthless killer who plunged a sword into a man's body."

Sidney's face flushed. "Did you really have to bring that up again?"

"It's why we're here."

Sidney tossed his head. "Anyway, if Billy Dean is to win this competition, he'd need completely new material. But where's he going to get it? He writes his own jokes, probably while sitting on the lavatory. Now if he had the Blue Book, he'd have comic gold."

"And he'd kill for it?"

"Better than dying on stage," Sidney said. "For a comic, anything is better than the silence of a bored audience."

I said: "What can you tell me about Teddy Hooper?"

"He's a ventriloquist. He does this act with a dummy he calls the Honourable Percival Plonker. The joke, if you can call it that, is that Plonker is an upper-class twit who'd been to Eton."

"At least Hooper performs on the stage," I said. "I always thought it was stupid that Peter Brough with his dummy Archie Andrews did his act on radio. What's the point of a vent act if you can't see whether he's moving his lips?"

Sidney smirked. "If that's your test of a vent, you'd better advise Hooper to do his act at St Dunstan's."

"The home for the blind?"

"Yes. From what I've heard, Hooper is usually so drunk when he goes on stage, he doesn't know whether he's moving his lips – or any other part of his body."

"How does he still get bookings?"

"Some of the managements in older variety theatres don't even see the acts they book. They look at the takings for the week. If they're up, they'll book you again. Hooper has always had the good fortune to be on bills with at least one big-name draw."

"Still, word gets around."

"It does, and from what I hear Hooper has become pretty strange over the years. I've seen it before with vents. They start to treat their dummy like it's a real person. They're so used to speaking its words, they don't know when they're talking for the dummy or themselves. Leaves some of these guys with mixed-up heads. Like kind of two personalities rattling around in their mind fighting to come out on top."

"Could Hooper be mixed up enough to have killed Bernstein?"

"If Plonker told him to," Sidney said.

"Get real, Sidney."

"I'm serious. Hooper's personality is split between himself and Plonker. He doesn't just take Plonker on stage. He takes him everywhere. If you have a conversation with him, you find Plonker joining in."

"That's crazy."

"It was for Bernstein, so I hear. It was a few months ago. Apparently, Hooper with Plonker on his lap was having a row with Bernstein about his fees. Hooper had Plonker doing most of the talking. The dummy was calling Bernstein a 'smelly twister' and a 'mean old git' and some even less fragrant phrases. Eventually Bernstein got so exasperated by this, he grabbed Plonker off Hooper's lap and slung it across the room."

"And smashed the dummy?"

"Put it this way, if it had been a human it would have ended up in hospital encased in plaster and suspended from the ceiling by those ropes you see in intensive care wards. As it was, Hooper managed to get the creature repaired."

"And Hooper now hates Bernstein enough to kill him?" I asked.

"That's the spooky part about it. Whenever Hooper has the dummy with him, it's Plonker who spouts stuff about breaking every bone in Bernstein's body. It's as though it wants to see Bernstein dead."

"But Percival Plonker didn't stick a sword into Bernstein."

"No," said Sidney. "But Peter Kitchen has a violent temper."

"He's the satirist. I'd heard he was the new wave of comedy."

"If you can call poking fun at public figures comedy. But since that BBC TV programme *That Was The Week That Was*, there's been more of them around."

"I don't recall ever seeing Kitchen on the show or any of the others that started up after it."

"That's because he never got chosen – and he blames Bernstein. And Kitchen doesn't only have a vicious tongue. One night he was doing his act in a London pub. One of the audience got a bit mouthy. Heckled him. Comics should be able to handle that. The best have a stock of put-downs. You know – 'If you don't like my act, there's a bus leaving outside in five minutes. Be under it.' It turned out Kitchen's put-down was to step off the stage and thump the heckler. It ended the show and Kitchen was never booked at the pub again."

"And that ended his career?"

"It would take worse than that in showbiz to finish a man. But it was enough for Bernstein to turn him down as a client. I hear other agents followed Bernstein's lead. So Kitchen works alone – taking his own bookings when he can get them. Without an agent, he blames Bernstein for the fact he's never made it big on TV."

I thought about that for a moment. "When did Bernstein turn Kitchen down as a client?"

"I think it was after the first season of *That Was The Week That Was* finished. Kitchen hoped to get booked for the second season."

"That was two years ago. If Kitchen wanted to teach Bernstein a lesson, surely he'd have done so then? When he was most angry."

"Who knows how the mind of a satirist works?" Sidney said. "But you haven't asked me about the comic with the strongest motive."

"Ernie Winkle," I said.

"He never got over missing out on Max Miller's Blue Book."

"I know. I've seen his act – and interviewed him."

"More than I ever did, dear boy. You must have a strong stomach."

"I need to speak to the others. Where will I find them?"

"You can try Gloria's Rehearsal Rooms. You'll find it in Trafalgar Street."

"And ask for Gloria, I presume?"

"Yes, the place is run by Gloria Randle. She's known as Gloria the Crab. But I wouldn't mention that."

I raised an eyebrow.

Sidney filled in the detail. "Gloria used to be a magician's assistant – the Great Gilberto. But Gilberto wasn't so great when he came to the old trick of sawing a woman in half. Well, Gloria picked up the crab soubriquet afterwards."

Chapter 9

I decided I needed a strengthening cup of coffee before coming face-to-face with Gloria the Crab.

Besides, I needed time to think about what Sidney had told me.

Marcello's was quiet after the early morning breakfast rush. A fug of cigarette smoke and bacon fumes hung in the air. A couple of bus drivers from the depot munched on toast and marmalade at a table in the corner.

Marcello was behind the counter polishing up his smart new espresso coffee machine. It had long handles and knobs and a steam pipe. It had sleek lines and a fancy chrome finish. Add some wheels and it could probably have hauled a train.

I walked up to the counter and said: "If you can get a cup of strong white coffee out of that, I'll have one."

Marcello grinned. "This machine do everything but drink it."

"If you can fix that I won't even need to come in here."

Marcello pulled a sour face and turned to the machine. He heaved on some handles, twiddled some knobs, and passed me a glass cup and saucer with a pale brown liquid.

I took my coffee to a table well away from the drivers. The last thing I needed right now was an earnest discussion about bus timetables.

I sat at the table and took a sip of the coffee. I glanced up and saw Marcello watching me intently. The coffee was a bit weak and there was too much milk. But I gave him a thumbs-up and he beamed back a smile like a sunburst.

It warmed me more than the coffee. There hadn't been many smiles around since Sidney had walked in on Danny Bernstein's dead eyes looking down the business end of a sword.

And from what Sidney had told me, there wasn't going to be an excess of hilarity when I met the comedians. If Bernstein had been killed in order to steal the Blue Book, two of the comics would be prime suspects. Ernie Winkle thought Max Miller had promised him the book and was angry that Bernstein had gained it by chance. Billy Dean desperately needed some new jokes without four-letter words if he were to stand a chance of winning the Laugh-a-thon.

So did that mean I should concentrate on them and ignore the other three comedians? I took another sip of the coffee while I thought about that. The empty cigar box which had held the Blue Book had been found outside Bernstein's office window. So the book had been stolen at the time of the murder.

But that didn't mean it had been the motive for the murder. Jessie O'Mara, Teddy Hooper or Peter Kitchen had different motives for wanting Bernstein dead. If one of them had killed Bernstein, stealing the Blue Book would be a great way to misdirect the cops. It would distract attention from the killer's true motive. It wouldn't take much to have Tomkins chasing after the wrong clues.

So I had to consider all of them as possible murderers.

And, I reminded myself, Sidney Pinker also had a motive.

I drained the last of my coffee, stood up, and said *"ciao"* to Marcello.

Outside, the sun peeped out from behind November clouds. But the air seemed colder. Or perhaps it was just my mood.

Gloria's Rehearsal Rooms were halfway between two of Trafalgar Street's pubs – the Lord Nelson and the Prince Albert.

The place was an old Victorian building with soot-blackened bricks and small windows. There was a metal plaque with the name of the place beside the front door. The plaque could have done with some vigorous work with a tin of Brasso.

I opened the door and stepped into a surprisingly spacious entrance hall. The hall led into a corridor which ran towards the back of the building. There was a small desk with a bell and a notice which read "If I'm not here, ring the bell and wait, you impatient bugger."

I rang and lounged against the desk. I showed the kind of insouciance that would get me tagged as an infinitely patient bugger.

Somewhere down the corridor a door opened and closed. I listened for footsteps but there weren't any. But there was a kind of shuffling sound like a stiff brush being dragged over a rough carpet.

The sound became louder as the figure came closer.

And then Gloria the Crab edged around the corner. Her left shoulder came first, then her head. Her right shoulder followed. Gloria shuffled sideways rather like a climber edges along a cliff ledge. She shuffled one leg sideways, planted it firmly, then dragged the other alongside. It should have looked unnatural. But strangely it didn't. It just looked as though she were practising some dance steps. Not so much quick, quick, slow as shuffle, shuffle, stop.

Yet if Gloria moved sideways like a crab, that was where the resemblance stopped. I'd say she was in her early forties, but it was easy to see how with make-up under stage lights she'd have looked ten years younger. At least, as long as you weren't sitting in the front row of the stalls.

She'd have made a perfect magician's assistant with her full lips stretched in a broad smile and a what-happens-now look lighting up her eyes. Except right now she was glowering at me with a who-the-hell-are-you stare.

She said: "Have you been waiting long?"

"No."

"Pity."

Gloria shuffled over to her desk and sat down. She was wearing a yellow polo-neck sweater and some stripy stretch pants. She had carpet slippers on her feet.

I said: "Do I have the pleasure of speaking to Gloria Randle?"

"Who said it was ever going to be a pleasure?"

"Actually, my colleague Sidney Pinker, theatre critic of the *Evening Chronicle*. He's a big fan."

"Yeah, I know Sidney. Can't say I reciprocate. I thought Sidney was in the cooler on a murder rap."

"He's innocent."

"Aren't they all? Anyway, what brings you to my palace for practising performers?"

"I understand some of the comics in the Laugh-a-thon are rehearsing here."

"Yeah. Jessie O'Mara, Teddy Hooper and Peter Kitchen are all here. Ernie Winkle rehearses at his own club. Don't ask me where Billy Dean goes to try out his act. The nearest gutter probably."

"It must be fun having comedians in the place. A laugh a minute?"

Gloria nodded thoughtfully. "You don't know much about show business, do you?"

"Crime reporting is my beat."

"Yeah. Well, let me tell you of all the actors and variety performers you can have in your place, comedians are the worst. If you want to see neuroses walking around on legs, just go see comedians off-stage. If you want to feel a bruised ego surge into a room even before its owner's stepped over the threshold, look for a comedian. It's bad enough when they've just got a regular performance. But with this competition coming off, it's like having a convention of *prima donnas* in the joint."

"Tell them to go rehearse somewhere else."

Gloria gave a mirthless laugh. "You know I was a magician's assistant. Not a magician but I could make people disappear in a stage act. The trouble is in real life you see people you'd like to get rid of. The people you don't want around. But it's not so easy. You click your fingers and say abracadabra – but they're still there."

"For a quick 'hey presto', I'd disappear and go to speak with your *prima donnas*."

Gloria pointed to the corridor. "Jessie's in room one at the end of the passage. You'll find Peter Kitchen upstairs, first door on the right, room four. Teddy Hooper hasn't turned up yet. Perhaps Percival had a late breakfast."

I smiled a thank-you and turned for the corridor.

Gloria called after me. "By the way, thanks for not mentioning that thing."

"What thing is that?"

"You know… that crustacean thing."

"Never entered my mind," I said and hurried down the corridor.

I reached rehearsal room one and raised my fist to knock – but then I heard a woman talking inside.

Gloria hadn't mentioned that Jessie had someone with her.

Silently, I put my ear to the door and listened.

Eavesdropping – more value to journalists than shorthand.

A woman's voice said: "*You know, girls, men are a bit like those new Kenwood Chef food mixers that have just come into the shops. You need one, but you're not sure why.*"

Ah-ha! Jessie didn't have anyone with her. She was rehearsing her act.

I settled my ear comfortably against the door to earwig the show.

"*Say, girls, do you have as much trouble with your husbands as I have with mine. I said to him the other day, 'Why don't you help with the housework?' He said, 'I lift up my legs when you want to vacuum under them.' Typical! A girlfriend asked me 'what's the difference between a man and a bottle of Chateau Lafite?' 'That's easy,' I said, 'the wine matures.' My friend was asking me what she should give her husband for his birthday. 'What do you give a man who has everything?' she said. 'Penicillin,' I said. Anyway, I*" *mustn't complain. I'd like to thank my husband for a wonderful year of marriage. I'll let you know when it happens. So that's it, girls. Here's a final piece of advice. There's one certain place where you can always find a committed man. A mental institution. See ya!"*

The room went silent. Then two hands clapped. Jessie was giving herself a round of applause.

I opened the door and walked in.

Jessie was standing in front of a full-length mirror giving herself a quizzical look. She was wondering whether her act would raise many laughs in an audience of men and women.

I said: "If I were in the audience I'd be laughing and applauding. And my girlfriend Shirley would probably let out a whoop or two."

Jessie spun round to face me. She was a tall girl with the kind of full figure that gets many women looking anxiously at the bathroom scales. She had a full face with high cheek bones and big eyes that had a permanent surprised look. Her shoulder-length brown hair was frizzed and tied back with a red ribbon. She was wearing a Sloppy Joe sweater with the words "Proud Scouser" printed on the front and jeans.

She said: "Were you geggin' in on my act?"

I said: "Couldn't help catching the last minute of it. It was great."

"Yeah! I just can't get enough fans to listen at keyholes. Who are you?"

I pulled out a card and handed it to her. She looked at it and handed it back.

"Journalist. At least you're not some gobshite of an agent trying to steal my act."

I said: "That act is a one-off."

For the first time, Jessie grinned. "Yeah! I get to do it once and then I'm off."

"I'd like to talk to you about the murder of Danny Bernstein. I believe he is your agent."

Jessie's eyes darkened. "Was. Now there is a gobshite."

It looked as though Sidney might be right. Jessie looked like she could be as tough as a blacksmith's apron.

"You had an affair with him?" I said.

"Yeah. Why ask the question if you already know the answer? But you're wrong. It wasn't an affair. It was a matter of business. You know how many girls want to get on in show business? More than you'll ever pass the time of day with."

"You're answering your own questions now."

"Got a problem with that? Because I haven't. I've been asking and answering those questions since that gobshite made me pregnant."

"But you lost the baby?"

"That's one way of putting it. It wasn't the only thing I lost. I didn't want Bernstein near me. But he made life difficult. He put the word around and so now I've got no agent – and precious few bookings. This competition is my one big chance to get back as a headline act."

"You must hate Bernstein," I said.

Jessie slapped her thighs. It was a derisive gesture. "You're quick," she said.

"Where were you on Monday morning when Bernstein was killed?"

"Think I killed the bastard, do you?"

"I'm just trying to build background for an article on the killing."

"Yeah! Okay! I understand. I was out walking. I walk when I'm building an act. Movement helps me to think."

"Where were you walking?"

"Here and there. Along the seafront mostly."

"With anyone?"

"Like Greta Garbo I wanted to be alone."

"Did you see anyone you know?"

"Yeah! All my muckers from Liverpool were down for a day

by the sea."

So Jessie didn't have an alibi for the time of the killing.

I said: "I need to build a picture of Bernstein. I know you hate the man, but is there anything you can tell me about him?"

A cloud of indecision passed over her face. Her eyes flicked from side to side. She was wondering whether to tell me something.

"There is one thing…" she began.

But before she could continue, the door opened and a man wearing a stained dinner jacket, grubby white shirt and black bowtie lurched into the room. He was carrying what looked like a small man dressed in country tweeds. The small man had a waxen face, stiff lips and eyes that swivelled mechanically from side to side. There was a monocle over the left eye.

Ventriloquist Teddy Hooper and dummy the Honourable Percival Plonker had made an unwanted entrance, stage right.

Hooper staggered a couple of steps and steadied himself. His left arm swung free. His right arm had disappeared up the nether regions of Plonker.

Jessie flicked him a disgusted glance and said: "This isn't your room, Teddy. And you're drunk."

Plonker's eyes twizzled towards Hooper, then back to Jessie. They seemed to open wider.

"A drop hasn't touched my lips. I poured it straight down my throat."

Hooper voiced Plonker like an upper-class English aristocrat. As if to emphasise the point, he went into his routine.

"Where did you get that accent, old boy?" he asked Plonker.

"Eton, old sausage."

"Then you'd better stop eating old sausage."

"I have since I bought that sausage last week."

"What was wrong?"

"On the packet it said 'Prick with fork'. But there wasn't a fork."

"That's very rude, Percival. There's a lady present."

"I've never had a lady for a present. But I'm willing to try one."

"Not with your luck."

"Yesterday I backed a horse at ten to one. It came in at quarter past four."

"You should take it easy."

"I sleep like a log. I wake up in the fireplace."

"But you're in good health."

"I went to the doctor's last week and asked him if he could give me anything for wind. He handed over a kite."

Jessie moved towards them. She was on fire.

She said: "If that's the best you can do, you'll stand no chance in the competition. That's if you ever stagger on to the stage, you're so pie-eyed."

"Dear me," crowed Plonker's haughty voice. "The young virgin is having one of her turns."

Jessie's arm moved like a blur. She slapped Plonker's face his head slipped sideways and rested on his shoulder.

"You've killed Percy," Hooper whined.

His arm foraged inside the dummy to regain control and the head snapped back into position.

Jessie looked like she was lining herself up for another attack.

I moved between her and Hooper.

"No gentleman speaks to a lady like that," I said to Plonker. Realised I was talking to a lump of wood and turned to Hooper. "You owe Jessie an apology," I said to him.

Hooper slurred something that sounded like "Solly." Then he turned and staggered out of the room.

"Is he always like that?" I asked Jessie. Her eyes were still blazing.

"You've caught him on a good day," she said. "The man's poison – but not half as toxic as the words he puts into the mouth of that gargoyle he carries around with him."

"Not a fan, then," I said.

A single tear trickled down her cheek. "Now there's someone

I'd really like to see dead."

I never thought to ask whether she meant Hooper or Plonker.

Chapter 10

I left Jessie planning to rehearse her act again and went in search of Hooper and his poison pal.

I found them in a small room on the top floor. The place had grubby lino and whitewashed walls. It was lit by a single bulb hanging by a flex. I'd seen more comfortable prison cells. But I guessed if the rehearsal rooms hired by the hour this would be one of the cheapest.

And Hooper didn't strike me as the kind of man for whom paying rent would be a high priority.

Right now, he was sitting on the room's single chair. He had Plonker on his right arm and a half-bottle of Johnnie Walker in his left hand. He glugged from the bottle as I walked into the room.

Plonker's head swivelled around as I stepped through the door. His eyes widened, then he turned back to Hooper.

"Aren't the servants supposed to knock before they enter?" Plonker asked in his put-on posh voice.

Hooper nodded and took another pull from the bottle.

"Aren't gentlemen supposed to be chivalrous to a lady?" I said.

Plonker took a sly glance at Hooper. "Miss O'Mara is no lady," he said. "The word trollop comes to mind."

"The word murder comes to mind," I said.

This time Hooper gave Plonker a hard look. Hooper swigged some whisky.

Plonker said: "Stap my vitals! I do believe the fellow's making accusations against a member of the aristocracy."

"You're no aristocrat. The nearest you ever came to the landed gentry was being part of a tree on one of their estates."

I stood there astonished at myself. I suddenly realised what I'd just said. I was having an argument with a wooden doll. I needed to get a grip.

I moved closer to Hooper and said: "I'd like to ask you rather than your *alter ego* here some questions."

"Who are you?" They were the first words Hooper had said in his own voice since I'd come into the room.

"Colin Crampton, *Evening Chronicle*. I'm writing an article about the killing of Danny Bernstein and I want to talk to artistes who'd been on his books."

"Were on his books," Hooper said.

"We had to move on," Plonker added. "'At last he rose and twitched his mantle blue, Tomorrow to fresh woods, and pastures new.' I'd wager a king's ransom you don't know who wrote that, peasant."

"John Milton," I said.

"A little education makes the lower classes uppity," Plonker complained.

I turned to Hooper. "When Bernstein smashed your dummy…"

"Language!" Plonker interjected. "Who're you calling a dummy?"

I gave him a dirty look – I don't know why, I couldn't help myself – and continued: "Smashed your dummy, you must have wanted to kill Bernstein."

Plonker gave a derisive laugh. He turned to Hooper. "Murder is for folks with cash in the bank, isn't it my old retainer?"

Hooper shrugged. Not easy with a dummy on one arm and a bottle of whisky in the other hand. But he managed it.

"Couldn't afford to kill Bernstein," he said. "I needed money to repair Percy."

"I said he should've taken out private medical cover," Plonker said. "Instead you borrowed money from Bernstein to make me well. But then instead of paying it back, you spent your earnings on the demon drink."

"I need a glass after a day dealing with you," Hooper told

Plonker.

"So it's my fault that Bernstein sacked you when you couldn't repay him? And now we're living in reduced circumstances. And rehearsing in shitholes like this. Pardon my French."

I said: "Where were you on the morning Bernstein died?"

"In my box enjoying a dream – rather naughty actually – about Pinocchio. Oh, what one could do with that nose."

"Not you," I said. "Mr Hooper, where were you on Monday morning?"

Hooper took a long pull from his bottle. "I believe I was in the land of nod. I'd had a busy evening previously. Rehearsing hard, you understand."

"Of course. Was anyone with you?"

"Naturally. I always sleep with the Honourable Percival Plonker – although I want to stress there is nothing unnatural in our relationship."

"Taken as read." When dealing with a madman, humour him. "So there is no-one who could provide an alibi for you in court?"

"I would speak from the witness box on my friend's behalf," Plonker said.

I was about to explain that wooden dummies weren't allowed to give evidence in court, when the door opened and a man stormed in.

He was more than six feet tall. He had a shock of red hair, parted to the left in a casual way which had left a quiff over his forehead. He had piercing blue eyes. He had a tight little mouth that could look cruel when he was angry. And he was angry now.

He was wearing a checked jacket and grey trousers. He had a show handkerchief in his breast pocket.

He strode up to Hooper. I thought he was going to thump the man. Or possibly he was going to strangle Plonker.

He said: "You've upset Jessie, you fork-tongued old sot."

Hooper gazed at the man through bleary eyes.

Peter Bartram

Plonker swivelled his head. "Well, by Jove, if it isn't Peter Kitchen, the scourge of the mean and the mighty everywhere. And he's here in the role of knight errant."

"You shut up, or I'll rip your head off," Kitchen said.

"Ouch! Peter's in a temper," Plonker said. "Is it because you still can't get on that television satire show? Which one is it now? *That Was The Week That Was.* No, you missed out on that one. But then, you've missed out on all of them."

I stepped forward. "I'd heard you had a bit of a temper," I said.

Kitchen turned on me. "And who the hell are you?"

"Colin Crampton, from the *Evening Chronicle*, not from Hell. Although it sometimes seems like it."

"And what are you doing here?"

"I've been trying to interview Teddy Hooper about Danny Bernstein's murder. But now that you've turned up, I'd like to ask you a question."

"I've got nothing to say about Bernstein," Kitchen said.

"That's because he turned you down as a client," Plonker chipped in.

"Is that true?"

"I prefer to manage my own career."

"You don't have a choice," said Plonker. "And with no agent, you'll never get on TV."

"Shut that dummy's mouth or I'll shut yours," Kitchen roared at Hooper. "By the time you go on stage people won't be able to tell whether you move your lips 'coz you won't have any."

Hooper took a swig of his whisky.

I said: "Shall we have a civilised discussion?"

"Not possible with a peasant," Plonker said.

"I've got nothing to say to you," Kitchen said.

"Have the police asked you where you were on Monday morning when Bernstein was killed?" I asked.

"Yes. I've told them I was having my morning run up on

Devil's Dyke."

"Alone, I suppose."

"He's always alone," Plonker said. "He'd be alone even if he was smoking a cigarette in those vulgar television advertisements."

"If you're talking about the TV ads with that slogan 'You're never alone with a Strand', they've stopped making them," I said.

"The adverts?" Kitchen asked.

"No, the cigarettes."

"I don't smoke anyway."

"We're getting off the point," I said. "Did you have any witnesses to your run on Monday?"

"There were a few sightseers up there. Don't know who they were. Some may have recognised me."

"Ha, bloody, ha," Plonker said.

There was a gurgling sound as Hooper guzzled the last of his whisky. He slipped off his chair and slumped on the floor. His arm stayed inside Plonker.

Hooper looked like he was out of it for the next few hours. But Plonker's head turned towards me. And his eyes slowly closed.

Kitchen and I exchanged puzzled glances.

"I've got nothing more to say to you," Kitchen said.

He stormed out of the room, just like he'd entered it.

I glanced back. Hooper was asleep on the floor, snoring like a steam engine. Plonker was silent.

I wasn't going to get any more out of either of them. A welcome respite in the case of Plonker.

I stepped outside and went in search of room four where Billy Dean was supposed to rehearse. But when I opened the door, there was nobody there.

I headed back down stairs.

Jessie O'Mara was at the foot of the stairs looking up.

She said: "I heard shouting followed by a crash."

I said: "Peter Kitchen was defending your honour to Teddy Hooper. Teddy fell off his chair and is now snoring on the floor."

Jessie shook her head. "There are times when comedy is a funny business."

"I'm not sure which way to take that."

We fell silent. Jessie looked like she was thinking. Like she had a decision to make.

I said: "When we were talking earlier you were going to tell me something."

"Was I?"

"Yes. It was something about Danny Bernstein."

"It's probably not important."

"I sensed it was important. You weren't sure whether you should mention it. You still aren't."

Jessie gave a resigned nod. "You're right."

"Do you want to tell me now?"

Jessie nodded again. "Okay. But not here."

We left the rehearsal rooms and walked up Trafalgar Street to the railway station.

We sat at a corner table in the station's buffet. I ordered coffee and cheese sandwiches. The sandwiches had gone curly at the edges.

We sipped our coffee. Ignored the sandwiches. Jessie looked like all the troubles of the world were heaped on her shoulders. She didn't look like the Laughing Lass from Liverpool. More like a Miserable Miss from the Mersey.

She put down her cup and said: "If I tell you this, you don't let on that it came from me."

"You have my word." I reached over the table and gave her hand a reassuring squeeze.

"I have to be certain. What I'm going to tell you involves some bad people. Seriously nasty."

I said: "Jessie, informants have told me about seriously nasty people before. I've written about those people and what I've written has helped to put them in jail – away from people they'd otherwise harm. The most sacred pledge in the journalists' code is that we don't reveal our sources."

Jessie picked up a spoon and gave her coffee an unnecessary stir. Something to do while she thought about what I'd said.

I sat silently trying not to let my tension show. But it's always like this when you think someone is about to tell you something that will set you on the trail of a big story.

Jessie said: "All this happened when I was having... well, you know, that thing I had with Bernstein. I wish I hadn't..."

She broke off. Took out a handkerchief. Wiped a tear from her eye.

I said: "Don't let regrets ruin your life. Be strong – like Edith Piaf."

Jessie managed a thin smile. "*Je ne regrette rien*," she said. "But she died young. I don't want that to happen to me."

"It won't," I said.

Jessie nodded. "Then I'd better let it all out."

I relaxed a bit. Decided not to take out my notebook yet. The thought her words were being taken down might make Jessie nervous about what she said. Instead, I had a sip of my British Rail coffee. It tasted much the same as their tea.

Jessie said: "I wasn't the only girl Bernstein had in his office. And when I say 'had' I think you know what I mean."

I nodded.

Jessie said: "There were girls who used to come to the office looking for work. Most of them were daft little dolls with their heads stuffed full of dreams about showbiz. They wanted to be dancers, singers, chorus girls. Most of them couldn't dance or sing or kick their legs up in the air like the Tiller Girls. But if Bernstein liked the look of one, he'd promise her work, after she'd had a special audition."

"A special audition on the casting couch?" I asked.

Jessie nodded.

"And then shown the door?" I asked.

"No, that's where Bernstein was clever. He knew that if he had his wicked way with girls, then turned them out on the street with nothing, one of them would eventually blab."

"You're right. For newspapers, there's nothing more appealing than a 'wronged woman' story."

"So Bernstein would promise them nightclub work. They'd start entertaining guests at nightclubs and work their way up to a featured spot in the club's cabaret. And, he'd tell them, who knows what that would lead to? The silly little madams thought they were going to be Judy Garland in *A Star is Born*."

"But they ended up as nightclub hostesses," I said.

"Yeah. As tarts. They made commission from drinks they persuaded punters to buy. It was never enough to live on. So too often they had to provide the randy goats with a quickie in a back alley for a fiver. Or a split lip. Not many of them lasted long. So Bernstein had a ready market for new talent."

I drank some more of the tea-tasting coffee. Then I asked: "Did Bernstein's legit clients know about this?"

"No, and I wouldn't if I hadn't been so close to him. I was waiting for him late one night at his office. He'd been at some gobshite event like a Masonic dinner. He said he wanted to see me after it. There'd only be one reason, but in those days I thought I needed him. He did get me some great bookings. Anyway, this girl came to the office. She said her name was Julie. She had a black eye. She showed me bruises on her arms – horrible blue marks where a man's powerful hands had gripped her. She told me her whole story. About what Bernstein had done to her and the promises he'd made. She'd been working a nightclub as a hostess but she'd got a bit lippy about the way she was treated. The owners threw her out. After they'd given her a beating. She wanted Bernstein to know. I told her he wouldn't care. But I would. I wasn't there when he came back from his

Masonic dinner. And, afterwards, we went our separate ways."

"What happened to Julie?"

"I gave her a couple of quid to help her get out of town. Never heard from her again."

I raised my coffee cup for a sip. "Who beat her?" I asked.

"The Hardmann brothers."

I clunked my cup down so hard it cracked the saucer.

"You mean Tommy and Terry Hardmann?" I said.

Jessie's lips were compressed hard together in a moue of disgust.

"Yeah! A double dose of gobshite."

"I couldn't have put it better," I said.

The Hardmann brothers had built an empire of seedy nightclubs, striptease parlours, porn shops, and brothels in London. They'd expanded their business in Brighton a couple of years ago when they'd bought The Golden Kiss club on the seafront from the property racketeer Septimus Darke.

At the time, the rumour was that Darke didn't want to sell. He was a hard case who solved problems with violence. He'd tried to kill me when I'd exposed a bribery scandal. But he'd met his match with the Hardmann brothers. And knew it. I'd heard that Darke had handed over the keys to The Golden Kiss for less than half its market price.

I said: "Surely even Bernstein would have steered clear of the Hardmanns?"

Jessie said: "He got an offer he couldn't refuse."

"How did he come to know the Hardmanns?"

"Through another gobshite – Billy Dean, one of Bernstein's more scrubby clients. Dean does his act in the Hardmanns' clubs. He's the comic who fills in between the strippers. When the Hardmanns moved into Brighton, they needed a steady stream of girls for their clubs and brothels. Dean knew Bernstein had girls coming in every day looking for work. It wasn't long before the Hardmanns came calling with an offer that got pound signs dancing in front of Bernstein's eyes."

I thought about that. Bernstein had lost his meal-ticket client – Max Miller – two years ago. Yet it seemed he still had plenty of the folding stuff. He ran a Jag, wore a Rolex, ate at the best restaurants. He couldn't have financed that lifestyle from his diminishing string of down-the-bill performers. Unlike Darke, perhaps Bernstein hadn't wanted to refuse the Hardmanns' offer. But as the relationship developed, perhaps he'd wanted more. The Hardmanns wouldn't have liked that. And when they thought someone was a threat, they had a way of removing that threat – permanently.

I sat there wondering whether the Hardmanns could have killed Bernstein. There was a mystery man at Bernstein's office the morning he died. Could that have been one of the Hardmanns? Running Bernstein through with a sword would have been just the Gothic touch they'd have enjoyed.

Jessie said: "You're thinking what I'm thinking."

I said: "You don't know what I'm thinking."

I was thinking that if Jessie had killed Bernstein, the Hardmann story would be a great way to throw suspicion elsewhere.

Chapter 11

I left Jessie in the station buffet with the curly sandwiches and headed back to the *Chronicle*.

If what she'd told me about Bernstein and the Hardmann brothers was true, it would be a dynamite story. But you don't sling accusations of murder at gangsters without solid proof. And I still couldn't decide whether she was sincere or leading me up a garden path edged with nasty thorns.

So my morning had produced a lot of suspicion – but not a solid story. Figgis wasn't going to be pleased about that. Worse, I hadn't provided any copy for the paper's midday edition. I noticed the paper was already on sale at a newsagent as I hurried down Queen's Road.

It was just before one when I pushed through the swing doors into the newsroom. There was plenty of activity but no sign of Figgis.

Phil Bailey was pounding out a story on his typewriter.

"Seen Figgis?" I asked.

"Out at lunch," he said.

I nodded at Phil and headed over to my desk. Figgis would be back by half past one in time for the afternoon special edition deadline. That gave me just over half an hour to find a story and get some copy on his desk.

I pulled my telephone towards me and lifted the receiver. I dialled a number at Brighton police station.

The phone was answered after three rings by a man with a voice that reminded me of heavy cartwheels trundling along a country track.

"Didn't think I'd find you in your office?" I said. "Haven't you got a murder to solve?"

Ted Wilson said: "Tomkins has taken charge of the Bernstein killing himself. He's got me running around for him like a rookie constable. It's about time I jacked this job in. I'd have a better life as a traffic warden."

"Lots of fresh air and pleasant people to meet. Not to mention the *schadenfreude* of watching their tantrums when they come back and find you've ticketed their car."

"You make it sound irresistible. But you didn't call me to discuss my career prospects."

"Any new whispers on the Bernstein killing?" I asked.

"Not really. Tomkins is racing around but most of the time he's chasing his own arse."

"I'm guessing you haven't spent all your time acting as Tomkins' flunky."

"What do you think?" Ted sounded more cheerful. "You didn't hear this from me."

"Who are you?" I jested.

"And none of your 'police sources'."

"I'll source the information to '*Chronicle* enquiries'," I said.

Ted cleared his throat. "Well, you remember the receptionist at the office?"

"Sally Ashworth."

"Yes. She told us a mystery man went upstairs while she was signing for a registered letter. She saw the man leave wearing a raincoat about ten minutes later. Well, I suggested to Tomkins that we follow up that lead. He dismissed the idea – just a customer visiting one of the businesses on the upper floors."

"An insurance claims assessor and a chartered surveyor."

"That's right. I ignored Tomkins and interviewed the staff of both firms. Neither of them could place the man from his description."

"That's hardly surprising. The description was so vague it could apply to anyone or no-one."

"But here's the kicker. Last Friday both firms received phone calls from a man who wanted to make an appointment at eight-thirty on Monday morning."

"The day of the killing," I said.

"Yes. In each case, the two firms told the caller their office didn't open until nine-thirty. And, in each case, the caller made an appointment for later that morning."

"And didn't turn up," I said.

"You already knew?" Ted sounded a bit offended that I'd rained on his parade.

"No. But the bloke was obviously casing the joint. He was working out whether he'd be able to get upstairs without anyone on the top floors seeing him. Even if he knew the offices' regular opening hours, he couldn't be sure someone wouldn't be there early on the day in question. And he needed a clear run upstairs so he could use the backstairs down to Bernstein's office. In that way, he'd avoid close contact with Sally in the reception area downstairs. If he'd passed her, she might've been able to give us a more detailed description of him."

"Yeah! Sometimes I think we should change jobs."

"You wouldn't like it here," I said. "You'd end up swapping Tomkins for Figgis."

"Out of the frying pan into the fire?" Ted said.

"With Figgis, it would be an ashtray. But have you told Tomkins about this?"

"No."

"Because if you do, he'll accuse you of freelance enquiries and not following his orders."

"Right."

"So you want me to write the story in the *Chronicle* so the facts are out in the public domain and he can't ignore them?"

"Correct."

"Sneaky," I said. "But I can't help feeling I've been used."

"About time," Ted said.

The line went dead.

I pulled my trusty Remington towards me and started to type. Within five minutes, I had three hundred words which summarised what Ted had told me. I rolled paper out of the carriage, called Cedric over, and told him to take the copy up to the subs.

The story put another suspect – the mystery man - into the frame. But it didn't answer many of the questions I was left with after my morning's interviews. And it didn't help me to decide whether I could trust what Jessie O'Mara had told me about Bernstein and the Hardmann brothers. I needed confirmation from a second source. The obvious choice would be Billy Dean.

Still at least my story about the mystery man would put a grin on Figgis' face.

Or perhaps not.

As the happy thought had passed through my mind, he'd stepped through the newsroom doors.

He hustled across the room with a face like a gamekeeper's trap.

It was fair to assume he wasn't bringing me good news.

Two minutes later I was sitting in Figgis' office while he lit up a Woodbine.

He took such a long drag, the fag practically self-combusted. He blew out a long stream of smoke and relaxed a little as the nicotine hit his system. His cheeks sagged a bit but his eyes stayed hard.

I'd seen the signs before. He had news I wasn't going to like.

I said: "I've filed a new angle on the Bernstein killing." I filled in the details. "It could make a lead for the next edition."

"I'll take a look later."

Figgis' gaze strayed to a white envelope on his desk. It was sealed but lying upside down so I couldn't see the name of the addressee.

"I hope that's not my notice," I joked.

"No."

"So why am I sitting here?"

"Pope called me up to see him just before lunch."

"What did he want? A crash course in how to edit a newspaper?"

"Some hope of that. He wanted me to fire Sidney Pinker."

Figgis took another big suck on his gasper. Stubbed out the dog-end in his ashtray.

My jaw dropped and I swallowed hard. I couldn't believe it. Pinker had worked for the paper for more than twenty years. He'd sat in the end-seat in row C at the Theatre Royal so often, the seat had a permanent imprint of his bum.

I said: "You obviously refused." Glanced at the letter on the desk. "You didn't refuse."

Figgis shrugged. "Pope made it an order. He said having a theatre critic who was a suspected murderer was bad for the paper's image. Might lose us some of our readers among the county set."

"If he means those yahoos in the Cuckfield and Fulking Hunt he hangs around with, we'd be well rid of them. Besides, that sort wouldn't pick up a real paper like ours even if they were wearing surgical gloves. Most of them only get *The Tatler* so their moggie has something posh to line its litter tray. You need to speak to His Holiness again. Explain that if we sack Sidney now it'll make it look like we think he's guilty."

"I've already explained that," Figgis said. "Pope doesn't see how the police could get something as important as that wrong."

"I take it he's never met Tomkins then. Besides, I've already lined up a string of other suspects – all of them with more motive and opportunity than Sidney."

"But none of them were caught in Bernstein's office holding the sword that was sticking in him."

I pointed at the envelope. "Couldn't you forget to post it? Stick it in the post box without a stamp. That way, it sometimes gets returned to sender."

Figgis said: "His Holiness has ordered me to have it delivered by hand. This afternoon."

He reached for his cigarettes. But I reached across his desk and grabbed his wrist before he could reach them.

"Wait. I'm going upstairs to speak to Pope myself."

"No use. He's left for the day. Gone to his club in London."

"Let me take the letter," I said.

"You'll throw it in a bin."

"I promise not to. But what's the harm if I keep it in my pocket and forget to take it round to the cop shop for a couple of days? We could use the time to figure out a way to make Pope change his mind."

Figgis said: "I can't do that. Pope will be on my back this evening, wanting to know that I've had the letter delivered."

He shook a fag out of his packet and reached for his matches.

I sat there and glared at him. A thousand-watt stare of disgust and resentment. I was furious. Angry at Pope's heartlessness. Furious at Figgis' cowardice. I could feel my muscles tensing. I felt like grabbing Figgis by his red braces and hanging him from the picture rail.

But instead I grabbed the letter from his desk.

Figgis dropped the ciggie he was lighting.

He said: "Give that letter back."

"No."

"Don't be stupid. If you destroy it, I shall just write another."

"I'm not destroying it. I'm delivering it myself. The least I can do is be there for Sidney when he gets the news. He'll be devastated."

"I know you mean well, but I can't let a member of my news team do this."

"Why not?"

"Because it's unprofessional and will make us look like we're not serious about sacking Pinker."

"That's rubbish – and you know it."

Figgis stood up like a man who planned to tower over me. I'd be intimidated and give in. But he'd forgotten he was six inches shorter so sat down again.

He said: "Give me that letter or I'll have no alternative but to fire you."

I said: "I have a better idea. I resign."

I stormed out of the room, charged across the newsroom, and burst through the swing doors into the corridor.

Behind me, I could Figgis shouting: "You can't resign until I've had a chance to fire you."

I scuttled down the stairs. By the time I'd reached the door leading out into the street I was panting like a marathon runner. My forehead was damp with sweat.

I realised the letter had crumpled in my hand.

Suddenly, it felt like my own death warrant.

Sidney Pinker looked like someone had just slapped a coat of whitewash across his face.

His lips quivered. Tears rolled from his eyes across his cheeks. His nose was damp. Saliva dribbled from the side of his mouth. His hands shook. And he was breathing in great noisy gulps of air.

He fumbled in his pockets and said: "I've lost my handkerchief."

I reached for mine and handed it to him.

He wiped his eyes. Then blew his nose. It sounded like the foghorn which announces the Queen Mary sailing into port.

We were in an interview room at Brighton police station.

I'd handed him the letter five minutes earlier.

I could tell from the hunted look in his eyes he knew what it was. He ran it between his fingers, like a magician, as though he was trying to make it vanish.

I'd decided on my walk to the cop shop that there would be no easy way to break the news. I'd thought of trying to build him up with a few positive thoughts before I handed it to him.

But I couldn't think of any. I was now out of a job. And as soon as he opened the letter, he would be as well.

So when I'd walked into the room, I'd just handed him the letter and said: "It's not an invitation to a Buckingham Palace garden party."

Sidney finished wiping his eyes and nose and offered me the handkerchief back.

"Keep it," I said. "You deserve to get something out of this."

His lips twitched into a thin smile.

"More than twenty years I've served that paper, dear boy, and this is how they repay me. Where's the loyalty?"

"If you're looking for loyalty, Sidney, try dog walking. Newspapers have always been a rough game. Only adults can play."

"They think I'm guilty."

"It's just His Holiness. He's got as much backbone as an amoeba. He thinks that people will stop buying the paper because it once employed a murderer. But readers won't think that. Most people are fair-minded. They believe in innocent until proven guilty. Good old Magna Carta."

Sidney leaned forward eagerly.

"But you'll still write stories for the paper to help clear my name?"

I leaned back in my chair. It was one of the screwed to the floor ones.

I said: "There's been a little bit of a hitch in that department."

Sidney's eyes flashed with alarm. "Hitch?"

"Yes. I no longer work for the paper. I resigned."

"But why?" Sidney wailed.

"I believe the paper should stand by you. Help you clear your name. They can't do that if they kick you out."

"You resigned for me…" Sidney started to snivel again.

"That's enough of that. You've already made my only handkerchief soggy."

Sidney pulled himself together. "It was a noble gesture. But was it wise?"

"Probably not. But wisdom is often in short supply when you're angry."

"And hard cash is in short supply when you're out of a job."

"I'll freelance."

"The *Argus* won't employ you. Not after the number of times you've twisted Jim Houghton's tail."

"There are plenty of weeklies. I might even get some work from my first paper, the *Worthing Herald*."

We fell silent.

Sidney snivelled a bit. Rubbed his hands together nervously. Shifted uncomfortably on the hard wooden seat.

"I suppose this means you'll have to leave me to my fate, dear boy."

"Tomkins will never get the evidence to have you tried for murder."

"But innocent people do get convicted. I've read about it. Sometimes hanged."

"I've got good news for you. Today hanging for murder has been suspended for five years. The government is trying out a policy of abolition – but in my view, capital punishment will never come back."

"So I face a lifetime in prison. I'll have to wear those prison uniforms with arrows all over them. Not very chic is it? Rather *passé*, I'd say."

"Look on the bright side, Sidney. You'll be sharing the shower with the brawny types with big muscles who do bank jobs."

Sidney looked alarmingly interested "Mmmm. By way of introduction, I could always ask one to pass the soap."

I grinned. "Get a grip, Sidney. You're not going to end up in jail. You'll be out of here in a couple of days when Tomkins realises he hasn't got enough evidence to hold you."

"But what about you?"

"You know me. Fight the good fight. I may not work for the *Chronicle*, but I'm still a journalist and I intend to crack this story."

I stood up, gave Sidney an encouraging nod, and headed for the door.

Outside, Tomkins was lurking in the corridor. I expect he'd heard I was visiting Sidney. He'd probably had one of his elephant ears pressed to the door.

He saw me at once. His lips smeared into a lupine grin. He'd obviously heard the news of my departure from the *Chronicle*.

"Well, this is a great day for Brighton," he said.

"Is that because you've just announced your retirement?" I said. "No doubt the crooks are quaking in their boots. There might be some competent coppers to catch them now."

That wiped the grin off his face.

"I'm not the one out of work," he snarled.

"Neither am I. I've just changed the way I do it. I'm freelance now."

"You've got no independent status as a pressman."

"I've got my Press Card. Officially issued by the National Union of Journalists."

"A piece of cardboard. You don't have accreditation from a paper. So you're banned from the police station. And from talking to any coppers on the force. Including Ted Wilson. I know how you two are all chummy together. Well, that stops now."

He turned and stomped off down the corridor. Swivelled his head and said over his shoulder. "You're out in the cold now, Crampton."

Chapter 12

I stepped into the street and cursed Tomkins under my breath.

I dug deep into my four-letter-word vocabulary. Managed a six-letter one too. And seven-letters.

With that off my chest, I turned and headed towards the *Chronicle*. Then slapped my hand against my forehead in the "I'm an idiot" gesture.

I stopped so sharply a young woman pushing a pram crashed into my back.

I mumbled an apology and stepped aside.

I'd forgotten. I didn't need to head to the *Chronicle*. I couldn't head to the *Chronicle*. I no longer worked at the bloody *Chronicle*.

Tomkins had reminded me I was out in the cold. In the years I'd known him, it was the first time he'd said something that came close to being true.

I shuffled along the pavement to keep out of the way of people who bustled by me. Normally I'd stride along like I had springs in my heels. But now my limbs felt stiff and heavy. Perhaps it was a case of heavy heart, heavy body.

The street was busy for a dull November afternoon. Men in suits swung briefcases as they hurried to meetings. Young women hustled along with bulging shopping bags over their arms. A kid on roller-skates raced by.

I stood in a shop doorway and wondered what I should do next.

A big bloke wearing a donkey jacket and flat cap gave me a queer look as he sloped by.

I glanced in the shop window. The place was a corsetiere. The star item in the window was a big white thing with enough straps and buckles to tie down an elephant. According to the sales tag, it "shaped and firmed". If that was true, the shop was living off the fat of the land.

Metaphorically, that wouldn't be me now. Not now I wasn't picking up a salary from the *Chronicle*. I'd have to pay my own expenses, too. But money was likely to be the least of my worries.

I shuffled out of the doorway and headed down the street.

I glanced at my watch. It had been less than two hours since I'd walked out on Figgis. I'd spent most of the time trying to boost Sidney's morale.

Perhaps I should've spent more time on my own.

It wasn't surprising. I hadn't had time to consider the implications of becoming a freelance journalist.

But Tomkins' malicious comment had brought home to me just how precarious my position now was. For a start, I would be barred from the police press conferences. You needed proper accreditation to be admitted. Usually that meant working for a newspaper. It was possible for freelancers to worm their way in. But it was at the discretion of the officer in charge. Tomkins. He wasn't going to give me the time of day let alone a free pass to his press briefings.

Worse, Tomkins would now put a ban on Ted Wilson talking to me. In the past, Ted had usually ignored Tomkins. The fact Ted most often came up with the clues to solve a case meant Tomkins had to overlook his matey chats with me. But not now. Tomkins would have his spies out – and if Ted stepped out of line he'd be cut down to size. He'd end up directing the traffic around Seven Dials. So, unless Ted agreed to speak to me under top secret conditions, I could kiss goodbye to inside info on what the cops were doing.

And the trouble didn't end there. The *Chronicle* was a well-respected newspaper all over Sussex. Whenever I had a difficult interview to do, a mention of the paper's name opened doors. A freelancer wouldn't be welcomed so warmly. Or at all. The fish-and-chip tabloids had given freelancing a bad name. They'd employed seedy types who dug for dirt anywhere. They didn't care how many innocent people they hurt in the process. So freelancers were often treated with suspicion by the people they wanted to interview.

And then there was background research. The *Chronicle's* morgue was the best in Sussex. And what the morgue didn't hold in press cuttings, Henrietta Houndstooth held in her remarkable memory. Now I'd resigned, I'd be about as welcome in the morgue as an Egyptian mummy. That could be a serious difficulty on a story like the Bernstein killing. I'd have to think of a way to overcome the problem.

I'd been lost in thought as I'd walked. Now I realised I'd reached the seafront. Clouds heavy with rain hung over a grey sea. Towards the horizon, a cargo boat chugged through choppy waves. A couple of characters dressed in raincoats and sou'westers leant into the wind as they pounded along Palace Pier. They could have been heading for the theatre. Or the helter-skelter. Or the ghost train.

I spent a minute watching them. I wondered who they were and why they were there. But then I realised I was shutting out my troubles. I had to face up to them.

It was where I was headed that was important.

And I intended to write the scoop about who, how and why Danny Bernstein was killed. I didn't yet know which paper I'd write the story for. But when I'd cracked it, there'd be no shortage of buyers in Fleet Street for a sensational murder piece.

But there was one person's help I was going to need.

I headed to the phone box outside the pier.

Shirley Goldsmith gave me a basilisk stare and said: "You must have the brains of a deranged dingo."

"Be fair," I said. "I've heard some of those dingoes can be quite crafty. You need brains for guile."

We were sitting at the corner table at the back of the bar in Prinny's Pleasure. It was Shirley I'd called from the phone box outside the pier.

Shirl drained her glass of *chenin blanc* ("brashly fruity with an elfin wistfulness in the aftertaste") and said: "That plonk tastes like drain cleaner. I'll have a beer instead."

I signalled to Jeff behind the bar to bring new drinks.

Shirley said: "You should go back to Figgis and tell him you were only joking about your resignation."

"Give him the last laugh, you mean? That wouldn't work. He was taking orders from His Holiness Gerald Pope. Besides, it was a point of principle. Sidney Pinker is an innocent man."

"Yeah! I'll give you that. But there's no way you'll crack this story on your own. You've always needed the clout that being on a big-name paper gives you."

"But being a freelancer gives me more freedom. No Figgis for a start."

"And no pay cheque at the end of the week, too."

"But a big fee when I sell the story."

"If you sell it."

Jeff arrived with our drinks – half of lager for Shirley and another gin and tonic for me.

Jeff said: "I had a lovers' tiff once."

I said: "We weren't having a tiff."

"I could hear your raised voices over by the bar. Anyway, to get back to my tiff. It was with a girl called Gladys. She was chief bog washer in the public lavs down in the Old Steine. The first time I saw her, she reminded me of that *Cleopatra* film with Elizabeth Taylor and Richard Burton."

"She looked like Elizabeth Taylor?" I asked.

"More like Burton really – after one of his heavy nights out. Everything was going well. I took her for a slap-up meal – a plate of whelks at Vinegary Fred's seafood bar under the West Pier. Then I whispered sweet nothings in her ear. Well, one nothing actually – if you come back to my place, I'll take your knickers off with my teeth."

"*Ugh!*" Shirley said.

"Yeah! That usually gets a girl going. Anyway. She couldn't get back to my place fast enough. But that's when it all went wrong."

"Your false teeth came loose at a crucial moment?" I asked.

"No. I hadn't made the bed."

"Does it take long to tuck in a couple of sheets and plump up the pillows?" I asked.

"You don't understand. When I say I hadn't made the bed, I mean I hadn't put it together. A couple of days earlier, I'd bought a second-hand iron bedstead from Rusty Reg over at Fiveways. It was still in bits down in my yard but Reg had given me this special spanner thing that you used to screw the bits together. So I told Gladys that I'd get my tool out and we'd get it together. I think she must've misunderstood what I meant. She slapped my face and said, 'I'm not that kind of girl'. Then she stormed out. I wanted to see her again, but how could I? She worked in the ladies' lavs and I wasn't allowed in."

I said: "Why don't you go and mop down the bar, Jeff?"

"Sorry to intrude I'm sure," he said and walked off in a huff.

I reached over and took Shirley's hand. Gave it a little squeeze.

"We weren't having a tiff, were we?"

Shirley grinned. "Perhaps a small one. 'Thou and I are too wise to woo peaceably.'"

"I didn't know you'd read *Much Ado About Nothing*."

Shirley moved closer to me and said: "There are a lot of things you don't know about me, reporter boy. Tell me what you want to do."

So I told Shirley what I'd learnt about the Hardmann brothers from Jessie O'Mara. About how she claimed Bernstein pimped girls to their club with the help of Billy Dean.

I said: "I need to interview Dean, but he doesn't seem to go to the rehearsal rooms. So the only place I can do it is at the Hardmanns' club."

"The Golden Kiss? It won't be easy getting in there," she said.

"I have a plan," I said.

"I thought you might," she said.

Shirley gave me a hard look and said: "This is the last time I do something like this to keep your arse out of the fire."

It was just after nine o'clock that evening. We were sitting in my MGB. I'd parked a couple of streets away from the Golden Kiss.

"Sure, this is definitely the last time. Thanks, and by the way, you look terrific."

"I look like a tart. Isn't that what I'm supposed to be?"

"You're supposed to be an exotic dancer."

"A stripper."

I knew we wouldn't be able to con our way through the front door. The place always had a couple of beefy bouncers on patrol. So the plan was to sneak in through the stage door. Shirl would pretend she was a stripper turning up to her show. I suggested I could say I was her driver. But Shirl said the stage door keeper wouldn't buy that.

"I'll tell them you're my pimp," she'd said. "Safer for you, safer for me."

Shirl was dressed in a tight-fitting tee-shirt. It had a slogan printed on the front: *I wanted to burn my bra but I lost my matches*. Back at her flat she'd tried on some of her skirts but didn't think any of them were short enough. So she'd cut a couple of inches off an old denim number she'd bought in a Debenham's sale a couple of years ago. She was sitting in the passenger seat with the skirt riding high on her thighs.

She had a small pink vanity case on her lap.

I pointed at it and said: "Why do you need that?"

"All strippers have them."

"What's in it?"

"Make-up, hair curlers, powder puff, cosh…"

"Cosh?"

Shirley grinned. "To discourage unwanted admirers."

"I think it's about time we took our chances at the club," I said.

We climbed out of the MGB. Shirl shivered in the cold night air. I put my arm around her shoulder.

We walked briskly towards the Golden Kiss.

I said: "Remember, the first thing we do when we get inside is to check where the exits are. We may need to leave in a hurry."

"Yeah! And the second thing we do is to make sure the stage door keeper doesn't show me to the strippers' dressing room."

"Shouldn't strippers have an undressing room?"

"Seriously, I can't mix with the other girls. They'll spot me for a ringer within minutes."

I nodded. "That's fair. We'll go into the club and find a secluded table at the back somewhere. We'll order some drinks and keep our head down. After Billy Dean has completed his act, I'll slip backstage and try to interview him in his dressing room."

"While I sit like a wallflower?" Shirley said.

"I'll only be gone five minutes. I won't be able to risk more. Anyone who notices will think I've sloped up to the bar for more drinks. As soon as I'm back, we'll get the hell out of there."

The stage door of the Golden Kiss turned out to be in a mews which ran off the main street. It looked like the kind of modest back door you'd find on thousands of buildings in any town. Then I noticed it was covered with a steel plate and wired to an alarm.

I pointed at the wire. "They believe in their security."

Shirley flashed me a worried look. I took her hand and squeezed it gently.

I seized the door handle. No lights started to flash. No sirens sounded. So I opened the door.

I stood back for Shirley. "Strippers first."

Shirl tossed her head and flounced in swinging her hips in an exaggerated bump and grind.

We entered a small room lit by a harsh fluorescent tube that flickered. The walls were whitewashed. There was a stone floor. A small cubicle off to the right was fronted by a lift-up counter.

A notice on the counter read: "All artistes to report to stage door keeper."

As we paused to read it, an old geezer with a wrinkled face, a droopy moustache, and strangely sad puppy dog eyes appeared. He was wearing a worn-out tweed jacket with leather patches on the elbows. He had a grubby blue shirt, open at the collar and a flat cap. He carried a clipboard with a list of names on it. He glanced at the list and put the clipboard down on the lift-up counter.

He looked at Shirley through those sad eyes and said: "Name?"

This could be awkward. We hadn't reckoned that the performers would be checked in and out like prison visitors.

Shirley flashed a smile that could have illuminated the southern hemisphere and stuck out her chest. She pushed her breasts towards the old geezer.

The geezer said: "Put them away, darling. They don't impress me. I don't even notice these days. Not like the old times. We had that Sabrina here once. Cor blimey, hers came round the corner five minutes before she did. Name?"

I leaned over Shirley's shoulders and looked at the list.

"Clarice," I whispered in her ear.

"Clarice," Shirley said.

"Clarice," the old geezer repeated. He picked up his clipboard and consulted the list.

"Clarice," he said again. "Last name on the list. That means you're the final act. You don't come on until two. You're early."

"Punctuality is the politeness of princesses," Shirley said.

"Yeah! We ain't had no princesses in here. Not even that Margaret, and they say she likes a good night out."

"Probably likes to keep her clothes on," Shirley said.

"That's not what I'd heard," the old geezer said. "Anyway, the dressing room is down the corridor and round the corner to the left."

"Thanks," Shirley said.

We set off down the corridor.

"Hey," the old geezer called after us. He pointed at me. "Who's he?" he said.

"My pimp," Shirley said. "But don't worry – he's gay."

Shirley shot me a sly grin. We looked back to make sure the old geezer had retreated into his cubby hole.

Then we turned right – away from the dressing room and towards the club.

Chapter 13

"When the old geezer asked for my name, I thought my heart was going to stop," Shirley said.

We'd made it into the club. We'd bought drinks from the bar. We were sitting on a curving red banquette at a quiet table in an alcove at the back of the room. There was a lamp with a gold-covered shade on the table. It cast a pale yellow light and made our faces look ghostly.

At the far end of the room, there was a small stage lit by a couple of spotlights. A four-piece band was cranking its way through some old-time favourites. They started on Chattanooga Choo Choo. It sounded like it was stuck in the sidings.

I said: "I had to think fast when the old geezer brandished his clipboard with the list."

"How did you manage to read the names on it? From our side, all the writing was upside down."

"I learnt to read upside-down writing when I had to sub on the stone."

"Sounds like some weird sacrificial rite," Shirley said.

"It's what journalists do when they're making last-minute changes to a newspaper page which is set in metal type. The type is held in a frame called a chase. The printer – he's known as a stoneman – stands on one side of a metal-topped table called a stone. He's looking at the page the right way up. But the journalist has to stand on the other side and read it all upside down. So that's how I was able to read Clarice at the bottom of the list. I noticed he hadn't ticked off her name yet."

"If she's a regular here, the old geezer might know her by sight."

"He'd just told you he didn't even notice the girls these days."

"But suppose the real Clarice turns up?"

"She's the last act on – at two in the morning. If she's a

regular, she'll come in at the last minute. The old geezer was astonished you were so early. We've got a couple of hours leeway – probably all we need."

"I hope you're right."

"Let's enjoy ourselves while we're here," I said.

We hoisted our drinks – gin and tonic for me, a margarita cocktail for Shirley – and clinked glasses.

I sat back and looked around the place. A girl with long blonde hair and a slim figure stepped out from behind the bar. She wore a slinky black dress and leopard skin stilettos. She carried a tray with a bottle of champagne and two glasses. She tottered across the room. Sashayed between the little round tables. An old bloke at the bar lost interest in his whisky and turned around to ogle her.

Most of the tables were taken by couples. If you had an innocent turn of mind, you might have thought they were ageing uncles taking their young nieces for a night out. The men looked like they had too much fat, too much money, and too much time on their hands. The girls – bleached blonde hair, low-cut black dress, seamed stockings – looked like they'd come off a production line.

The men had whisky noses, bloodshot eyes, and hands that roamed around too much. The girls had pouty lips with smiles so cold they could've been beamed in from outer space. Of course, not all the men were the same. Not all the girls either. But they weren't entirely different. I was willing to bet the men all had the same thing on their mind. And the girls had the same fears.

It wasn't going to be easy for Shirley and me to fit in here.

Shirley had been looking around the place, too.

She said: "Ants have more fun than this."

"Yes. They do more work, too."

We fell silent. Read each other's thoughts and reached for our drinks.

The band's Chattanooga Choo Choo reached the end of the line. The house lights dimmed. A spotlight cast a pool of harsh white light on the stage. The band played a few chords which could have been Happy Days Are Here Again. Or possibly something I'd not heard before. It definitely wasn't the Hallelujah Chorus.

A stocky man bounced onto the stage. He had the build of a guy who sweats weights in a gym. He had wide shoulders and fleshy hips. He had a face which looked as though it had been set in a permanent grin since he was three. There was a wide mouth, shining eyes, bubbly cheeks. He had a full head of thick black hair which covered his ears and reached the nape of his neck. He wore a shiny suit in radioactive blue and black and white co-respondent's shoes. So this was Billy Dean.

Dean bounded up to the microphone centre stage and said: *"After that welcome I feel like I've just taken a cold shower. Mind you, after I've seen some of those strippers backstage, I need one. I share a dressing room with one of the girls. She asked me to help her take off her push-up bra. I thought this will be good. It was a frigging disappointment. It was like opening a packet of crisps. The thing was half empty."*

Someone at the back of the room tittered.

I whispered: "This is going to be grim."

Shirley nodded.

Dean gripped the mic stand and ploughed on. *"But, really, she's a nice girl. Eve her name is. Like the one who was naked in the Garden of Eden with Adam. I mean, can you believe that Adam? Alone in a garden with a gorgeous nude girl and all he wants is an apple. Personally, I'd have gone for Eve's pair. But, seriously, if there's a girl in the audience who has to dress half-naked to get a man's attention, here's my advice: don't. Be sophisticated. The rest of you girls see me after the show."*

Dean kept it up for twenty minutes. (I'm sure he'd find some smutty innuendo in that.) A few punters clapped, I expect out of sympathy. Dean didn't seem to care. He bounced off the stage as full of himself as he had been at the start of his act.

I shifted sideways on the banquette. "I'm going to speak to Dean while he's still on a high from his performance."

Shirley glanced anxiously at me. "Take care," she said.

"Don't talk to strange men while I'm gone," I said.

I headed across the room towards the door at the side of the stage.

The band started on the old Conway Twitty number It's Only Make Believe, which gave me some cover. I looked like a guy just trying to get out of the room before they reached the chorus.

The door had a sign which read: Private. Staff Only.

I ignored that, opened the door, and slipped through.

I found myself in a room lit by a couple of those red light bulbs photographers use in their darkrooms when they're developing pictures. To my left, some steps led up on to the stage. Ahead the room opened into an area behind the stage.

In the middle of the room a naked woman was crawling around on her hands and knees. She had curly blonde hair, large breasts which sagged towards the floor, and a mole on her left buttock. (I'm talking about a skin blemish not an underground mammal. I imagine there are limits even in a place like the Golden Kiss.)

She looked up as I stepped through the door and said: "I've lost one of my nipple tassels. It's come off."

I said: "Isn't that what it's supposed to do?"

She said: "Ha, bloody, ha. That's all I need – another frigging joker in the show."

"If you ask me, you've already got one too many."

"You can say that again. Anyway, aren't you going to help me look for the tassel?"

"Too busy I'm afraid."

She gave me a big fat saucy wink "What about meeting up after the show instead?"

"I'm already with a girl."

"I don't mind waiting in the queue."

I pointed under a chair. "Is that the tassel?"

The woman grinned: "You're right. I'd never have spotted that."

I left her scrabbling under the chair and headed round the back of the stage.

I found Billy Dean's dressing room along a small corridor. At the far end of the corridor there was a door with a green Emergency Exit sign above it.

I knocked once on Dean's dressing room door and walked in. Dean was sitting in a broken-down armchair. Stuffing burst from a split in one of the arms. The springs sagged at the side. The cover was faded and grey with dirt.

But the chair didn't look as bad as Dean. Out of the spotlight, the bounce had faded. His face was red and blotchy. He was slumped in the chair with his belly hanging over his trouser belt. He'd taken off his jacket, unfastened his tie, and loosened his collar. His trouser buttons were undone.

He was holding a tumbler half full with a colourless liquid. Could have been gin. Might have been vodka. Certainly wasn't water. He was on the point of raising the glass to his lips as I came through the door.

He gave me a warm welcome. "Who the frigging hell are you?"

I said: "I was in the audience for your act and thought I'd come round for an autograph."

Dean's eyes became less truculent. He shuffled in the chair to sit up straighter. His free hand rummaged south and fumbled with his trouser buttons.

I said: "I'd never heard that one about the actress and the bishop before."

"Which one was that?" Dean said as he looked around for somewhere to park his glass.

"The one where the bishop says, 'I can't wait for the second coming' and the actress says 'I'd be satisfied with the first one'."

Dean put his glass on the dressing table next to his sticks of make-up.

"Yeah! That's a good one. I don't remember telling that one tonight."

"I'm a big fan of your act. I may have heard it another time. Say, tell me, where do you get these gags? Does your agent help you think them up?"

"Nah! Old Danny Bernstein's got about as many laughs in him as a hearse load of pallbearers. Besides, he's dead now."

"Murdered, I hear. Any idea who killed him?"

"Could have been hundreds of people. Thousands even. Old Danny knew how to rub up people the wrong way."

"Including you?"

"Nah! I knew he was an old bastard, but he was an old bastard who got me work. Made me money."

"I suppose the police interviewed you. Did they ask for an alibi?"

"Nah! But I'd have told them I was back at my place in bed. I'd had a skin-full the night before. Not a good audience."

I winked a little innuendo. "In bed alone, I suppose."

Dean reached for his glass and lowered the tide line with a big gulp. "Nah! I'd had a bit of luck as I was leaving that night. Ran into Gertie the Gobbler. She only does late shows when most of the punters have quit, on account of she's got an arse the size of the Isle of Wight. And not as pretty. Anyway, as I say, I'd had a skin-full and was in no mood to be choosy, so I invited her back to my place for a cocktail. Get my drift?"

"She was with you all night?"

"Couldn't say. I passed out on the floor when we got back to my place. Last thing I saw, she'd raided my fridge and was gobbling the last of an old roast chicken. I'd had it in there for a couple of weeks. She'd gone when I woke up in the morning. Food poisoning probably. Anyway, didn't you say something about an autograph?"

I started to pat myself down in the way people do when they think they've missed something.

"I seem to have forgotten my autograph book." I produced my reporter's notebook. Flipped it open to a blank page.

"Perhaps you could sign here," I said. I took out my pen and handed it to Dean.

He stood up, shuffled over to the dressing table. He rested the book on the table and focused on the page.

Dean sat down on the stool beside the dressing table and pulled the notebook towards him. His mind was preoccupied with what he was going to write. It was time to ask the loaded question.

I said: "I suppose Terry and Tommy will be sorry about Bernstein's death."

"Who?" Dean said. His mind was elsewhere. He'd started to write some convoluted dedication.

"Terry and Tommy Hardmann. They did a lot of business with Bernstein, I hear."

Dean finished writing and handed the notebook and pen back to me. His mind wasn't elsewhere now. His eyes focused on me hard. He'd started to wonder who I was. Whether I really was a fan. There wouldn't be many of them. Possibly any of them.

He said: "You don't want to hear too much about Terry and Tommy Hardmann. They're not the kind who like people hearing about their business."

We fell silent. My mind raced. I couldn't decide whether to push it. But perhaps it was best to leave Dean thinking I was a fan. If he knew I was a journalist, he'd clam up and tell me nothing. If he worked it out later, he could tell the Hardmanns. I could do without them on my tail. So I decided to leave a false trail behind me.

I looked at what Dean had written in my notebook. I couldn't read it properly. But I said: "I'll treasure this. Wait 'til I show it to my colleagues in the accounts department at the Water Board."

Dean grinned. "They'll be dripping with jealousy."

I nodded.

Dean had relaxed. "Dripping… Water Board… Get it?"

I forced a laugh. "Hilarious," I lied. "I'll remember our meeting for a long time."

At least that bit was true.

I headed back front-of-house feeling irritated by my meeting with Dean.

I hadn't learnt as much as I'd hoped. But, at least, I now knew he'd had no credible alibi for the time of Bernstein's murder. But none of them did. Dean hadn't provided any new information about the Hardmanns either. I wasn't narrowing the field. I was as far as ever from nailing the true killer. So Sidney would have to sweat it out in the cop shop's cells for a little longer.

I stepped back through the door into the club. The band was playing something from *Oklahoma*. Or it may have been *Seven Brides for Seven Brothers*. I get them mixed up. It sounded like the band had the same problem.

I hustled between the tables back to the alcove.

Came to a sudden stop. Gawped at the table. Swallowed nervously. Approached cautiously.

Shirley had been joined by two men.

One had a bruiser's face with deep-set eyes and a pencil moustache above thin lips. He had slicked-back hair. He wore a double-breasted dinner jacket with a red carnation in his button hole. He looked like the kind of man who enjoyed nothing more than pulling the wings off butterflies.

The other one looked exactly the same. I mean like they'd been cast from the same mould. Like they were identical twins.

There was a large ice bucket with a bottle of champagne on the table. It hadn't been there when I'd left.

Shirley's eyes flashed a warning as I stepped up to the table.

But I was already on red alert.

As I approached, the one I'd spied first, rose from the banquette and extended his hand. "I'm Terry Hardmann," he said.

The other one got up and stuck out his arm. "I'm Tommy Hardmann."

"We saw this little lady sitting all alone, so we guessed we ought to extend some old-fashioned hospitality," Terry said.

"We bought a bottle of champagne for her," Tommy said.

"I told you I don't want your champagne," Shirley said. "It makes me fart like a jackaroo who's had a double helping of bean stew."

Terry smiled at that. And Tommy smiled in exactly the same way.

I smiled in a different way. The way that says thanks for the drink but don't try anything.

"We're leaving now," I said.

"Well, that might be a little difficult," Terry said.

"If you look over towards the door, you'll see two large gentlemen. They wouldn't like you to leave just yet," Tommy said.

I clocked them straight away. They were a pair of bouncers. They looked like gorillas in dinner jackets. They radiated trouble.

Terry said: "You see, Old Jim, our stage door keeper, told us Clarice, one of our strippers, checked in early for her act. Except she wasn't Clarice."

Tommy said: "And she had a man with her - a gay pimp, Old Jim said. But Ditzy Dora said she saw a man with the same description backstage while she was hunting for her missing tassel."

"So we thought we'd better investigate," Terry said.

"And now we have a proposition to put to you – all civilised like, over a glass of champagne," Tommy said.

I forced a confident smile and said: "That's very kind of you.

Perhaps another time."

Terry's eyes opened in a cold stare. "We insist you hear us out."

"It's quite simple," Tommy said. "As the little Missy here came in as a stripper, we thought everyone ought to have the chance to see her perform as one."

"So she's going on as the next act," Terry said.

"In your dreams, bozo," Shirley said.

"Oh, I think you'll want to give a good show," Tommy said.

Terry's tongue flicked lizard-like across his lips. "Because if we enjoy it – if we see everything we want and I do mean everything – we won't kill your boyfriend."

Shirley gasped and looked at me. Her eyes had filled with terror. I held her gaze. Tried to make her feel strong. I shifted my gaze slowly to the ice bucket with the champagne, then slowly back to her. I gave the tiniest of nods.

Shirley had composed herself. She knew what was going to happen next. She was ready.

Terry said: "You're a lucky man to have a girl like this."

Tommy said: "And in a few minutes everyone here is going to see how lucky."

"I wouldn't bet on it," I said.

I grabbed the champagne bottle and swung it at Terry's head. I missed but the bottle hit his shoulder. The champagne fizzed into his face.

Tommy turned to his brother. But he should have focused on me. I leant across and tipped the ice bucket into his lap.

He sucked in a long "*Ooooh!*" as enough ice to sink a small boat froze his nether regions.

"This way," I shouted to Shirley

But she'd already grabbed her vanity case and leapt off the banquette.

We left the Hardmanns fumbling with the bucket and bottle as we raced for the door at the side of the stage.

Chapter 14

As we reached the door, there was a crash on the other side of the room.

Glasses broke and crockery shattered. The Hardmanns had overturned the table as they'd scrambled off the banquette. They yelled at the bouncers over by the main door.

The two oafs stared at one another looking for answers. But neither of them had a clue what had happened. But they would. And then they'd come after us.

No time to lose.

I grabbed the handle and yanked open the door.

Beside me, Shirley screamed: "Move it!"

We hustled through the door and slammed it after us. There was a bolt at the top. I shot it to lock the door.

I said: "That should hold them up for a few seconds, but not for long."

"I hope you know the way out of here." Shirley's words came between pants of breath.

"There's an emergency exit at the back of the stage," I said.

It was the one at the end of the corridor where Dean had his dressing room. I'd seen the emergency sign when I'd been to interview him.

We sprinted round to the back of the stage.

The stripper who'd lost her tassel was standing there. She had them both on now. She was waiting for her cue to go on.

Her eyes widened in shock as we raced by.

Shirl's arm stretched out.

There was a sharp intake of breath followed by *"Ouch!"*

We ran on and Shirl waved one of the tassels in my face.

"A souvenir of my night as a stripper," she yelled.

We skidded around the corner leading to the emergency exit. I could see the green exit sign ahead of us.

We were both breathing heavily when we reached the door.

Behind us we could hear the stripper screaming: "I can't go on only half dressed. It ain't professional."

A couple of gruff voices mumbled something. It sounded like the bouncers had got through the door. I'd bet the Hardmanns weren't far behind them.

The exit door had one of those bars you push to open. I gave it a hefty shove but it didn't shift. Shirley joined me and we pushed down hard. Something cracked and the door swung open.

We rushed out into a cobbled yard. There was a manhole cover in the far corner. The yard was lit by a light fixed by a bracket to the building's wall. The yard was surrounded by a 10-foot brick wall. The wall was topped with shards of broken glass embedded in concrete. The sharp bits stuck up like deadly daggers. The only way out of the yard was through a sturdy wooden gate. It was secured with a large padlock.

We'd raced into our own trap.

I glanced around the yard. There were stacks of crates with empty beer and wine bottles.

I said: "Let's stack these against the door. It will buy us a minute or two to figure a way out."

Shirl started to speak. Realised this was no time for debate.

We set to work like a pair of navvies. Bottles rattled as we heaved the crates in front of the door. We crashed the crates down on top of one another. In less than a minute, we'd built a wall of crates five feet high. We reinforced it with a second layer.

By the time we'd finished, I reckoned the combined weight of the crates and the bottles had to be half a ton. Enough to hold up a couple a bouncers. But for how long?

"What now?" Shirley said.

"Perhaps we can build a staircase of more crates and climb up," I said.

"The glass on the wall will cut us to ribbons," Shirley said.

I paced around the yard like a caged tiger.

The wall of crates started to rattle. Behind them one of the crates shifted and toppled backwards.

It crashed to the ground and the bottles exploded into fragments.

A volley of swear words came from behind the crates.

One of the bouncers said: "That's it. I'm forcing my way through. I'll smash the frigging lot."

Then Tommy Hardmann said: "No you won't. The brewers give us money back on these bottles. Dismantle the pile carefully. Don't worry about the runaways they can't get out of the yard. They're rats in a trap."

Rats in a trap.

Of course, there was a way out. The way the rats go.

I hustled over to the corner of the yard where I'd seen the manhole cover.

I called Shirley over.

"Help me heave this up," I said.

"Where does it lead to?" Shirley said.

"The sewers."

"*Ugh.* I'm not going down there."

"It's quite safe. The corporation even runs guided tours for tourists around Brighton's sewers. They're famous."

"I'm wearing heels."

"Don't worry. You won't be stepping into anything you shouldn't."

The manhole cover had a ring in the centre. Shirley put down her vanity case. We both grabbed the manhole ring and heaved.

The cover shifted up a couple of inches and clanked back shut.

Behind us, we heard Tommy's voice shout: "Shift those crates, you lazy oafs."

One of the bouncers said: "Your trousers are all wet."

The other one said: "Looks like you've pissed yourself, boss."

Tommy yelled: "Just move the frigging crates."

Terry yelled: "Just move the frigging crates."

Tommy said: "I just said that."

Terry said: "So did I."

At the manhole cover, Shirley and I breathed in deeply, puffed out our cheeks, and heaved on the ring.

The cover came loose with a clump and a clank.

I peered down the hole. There was a shaft built out of bricks. A vertical metal ladder was fixed to the edge of the shaft by angled brackets.

I said: "It's dark, but we'll take our chance. I think there are lights further on in the part they use for tourist visits."

"Don't need them," Shirley said.

She opened her vanity case. "Don't have a cosh, but I do have this," she said.

She handed me a torch.

I shone the torch down the shaft. It was about twenty feet deep.

I said: "You go first with the torch. I'll toss the vanity case down to you when you're at the bottom, then I'll come down."

Shirley lowered herself into the shaft. I watched her blonde hair bob from side-to-side in the torchlight as she clambered down.

She looked up when she reached the bottom. I dropped the vanity case. She caught it like Richie Benaud pouching a catch on the boundary.

I lowered myself into the shaft. Realised that I wouldn't have the strength to haul the cover closed behind me.

There was no time to worry about that now.

Perhaps Tommy and Terry would call off their goons when they saw where we'd gone. After all, they had a club to run with paying punters.

The punters would be worried about what had happened. They'd fear that trouble would have the Old Bill paying a call. And the people who patronised the Golden Kiss were not the sort who wanted attention from the cops.

So I figured that Tommy and Terry would hurry back to calm their punters. Free drinks all round.

Besides, Tommy badly needed to change his trousers.

And Terry would have champagne soaking through his shirt.

Shirley was shifting nervously from foot-to-foot when I reached the bottom of the shaft.

I gave her a hug and kissed her. "Fancy meeting you here," I said.

"Yeah! I go to all the best places."

We were standing in a thin tunnel, not more than the width of a single person. It was built out of bricks and had a curving roof, like the arch in a church. The tunnel ran off into the dark in two directions. To the right, it sloped away gently. To the left it rose uphill.

Shirl said: "Which way, mastermind?"

"The Golden Kiss is on the cliffs to the east of the Old Steine. That's where we'll find an exit. And the Steine is down in the valley. So we head downwards to the right."

There was a scuffling sound at the top of the shaft. I looked up and the light darkened as a figure leaned over.

"Look out!" I shouted.

I pushed Shirl into the tunnel. A brick shattered into shards on the ground right where we'd been standing.

"Looks like the Hardmanns' goons are under orders to follow us," I said. "We'd better lose them fast."

The metal ladder vibrated against the wall as heavy feet descended.

"Let's beat it."

Shirl led the way with the torch and we hustled along the tunnel.

Behind me, I heard heavy boots land on the floor.

A gruff voice shouted up the shaft: "It's dark down here, Den."

An angry voice yelled back: "Do I have to do everything, Bert? I'll get a torch."

I tapped Shirley on the shoulder. "Quick! Turn the torch off before they see the light."

The torch died and we stood immobile in the dark.

I whispered in Shirl's ear: "If Bert and Den don't see our light, they won't know which way we've gone. Besides, it'll take them a few minutes to find a torch of their own."

"Why don't we finish this farce and lend them ours?"

"We can keep going in the dark by feeling our way along the walls."

"Until we end in the shit."

"You've got the wrong idea about sewers. You could eat a three-course meal down here."

"Yeah! Just like back home when I take afternoon tea and biscuits in the dunny… I don't think."

"Just keep moving," I said.

Something scuttled between my legs.

Shirl let out a little "*Eeek!* Was that what I think it was?"

"It's just a rat. Stop moaning. If we were in New York, we'd have alligators to worry about."

"Yeah! I just don't know how lucky I am."

But Shirley started to edge forward. I followed close behind.

After fifty or so yards, the tunnel curved around a bend.

I said: "I think we can risk the torch again. Bert and Den won't be able to see the beam now."

Shirl flicked on the switch. She ran the beam over the tunnel. Up ahead, it broadened out into a small chamber. We hurried into it.

The roof was higher and there was some metal machinery in the middle of the floor. It was rusted up and looked as though it hadn't been used for years. The place had a musty smell like sweaty socks had been left to rot in a damp corner.

We looked around. Three more tunnels ran out of the chamber

– one on the left, one straight ahead and one to the right.

"Crossroads," I said.

"But no signpost to tell us which way to go," Shirley said.

I held up my hand and put a finger to my lips.

We strained our ears. Close by water dripped with a rhythmic plop. Somewhere down one of the tunnels a motor – probably a pump - was running. But the sound was distorted in the chamber. The echo made it difficult to tell which tunnel the sound came from.

Shirley shone the torch around the chamber. Two sets of green eyes shone out of the darkness from the right-hand tunnel. They disappeared as the beam reached them. The scuttling sound receded as they disappeared into the dark.

"I'm not going down that one," Shirl said.

"Let me have the torch."

She gave it to me and I went over to the right tunnel and shone its beam as far as it would reach. The tunnel sloped gently upwards. The green eyes had vanished.

I trotted round to the other two tunnels. The one straight ahead sloped gently downhill but the left-hand tunnel fell away on a sharper gradient.

I said: "I think we should take the left tunnel."

Shirl said: "I think we should go straight ahead."

"The left tunnel slopes faster. It could get us out more quickly."

"Or leave us up to our necks in crap. Straight ahead follows the route we've taken so far."

"I vote left," I said.

"I vote straight ahead," Shirley said.

"So we go left."

"No, the vote was tied."

"You want a recount?"

"I want to sock you on the schnoz."

We fell silent.

132

Way back in the tunnel we'd just come from, a man grunted in pain.

A voice said: "I've twisted my ankle, Bert."

"Keep quiet, Den."

"But it hurts. And I've got green slime from the walls on my jacket. The boss will kill me."

"I'll kill you if you don't shut up."

I looked at Shirley. She stared at me.

I said: "Okay, straight on."

At the same time, Shirl said: "Okay, left."

We hurried across the chamber and disappeared into the left tunnel.

I led the way with the torch.

The floor was slick with green mould. We had to step slowly. We made sure each foot was firmly planted before we moved the next one.

Shirl said: "Jeez! We'd be better on skis. Four-inch stilettos don't make it down here."

I whispered: "We better move quietly. The bouncers could be in the chamber soon."

Shirley closed up behind me.

She said: "They won't know which tunnel we've taken."

"Sure. There are two chances they'll make the wrong choice to one they get it right."

"I still don't like those odds."

I nodded.

After about a hundred yards the gradient levelled out. We made better time.

I held up my hand to listen. I couldn't hear any footsteps coming up the tunnel behind us. I stared into the darkness ahead. There wasn't a glimmer of light.

I said: "I think we've thrown them off."

"Great. Now let's get out of here."

We picked up speed on more level ground. We curved round

a bend. And stopped in our tracks.

The tunnel forked in two directions. To the left, it fell away gently. To the right, it started to rise again.

I said: "We should go left."

We stood silent and listened. The sound of dripping water echoed from the left tunnel.

Shirl said: "Give me the torch."

I handed it to her. She shone it into the tunnel.

"I've got a bad feeling about this. The floor is moving."

I stepped nearer to look.

"Shine the torch closer to the floor," I said.

Shirl moved forward, stooped down. She ran the beam from the torch across the floor. It was shifting about randomly. Then the floor started to move towards us.

"Cockroaches," I said. "They're attracted by the light from the torch."

Shirl jumped backwards.

CRUNCH!

"*Yeuk!* I've impaled one on my stiletto. It's wriggling up the heel. Get it off."

"Shine the torch on it," I said.

The stiletto had sliced through the roach's crusty shell but its legs were still waving. I knelt down while Shirl lifted her leg. I grabbed her shoe and flicked the roach hard on its shell. It slid off the stiletto and fell onto its back.

Shirl said: "There's no way I'm wading through a sea of roaches. We'll take the right fork."

"I agree."

We hurried into the right tunnel and plodded up hill. Shirl led the way with the torch.

She said: "How far do these tunnels go?"

I said: "I've heard there are forty-four miles of tunnels in the sewer system."

"Jeez! I hope you know where we are."

"We're walking up hill slightly, so I guess we must be heading towards the Queen's Park area of town. We'll find a turning off to our left soon, so we can head back to the Old Steine and find a way out."

But after two hundred yards, the tunnel turned through a dog-leg to the right. We were heading back the way we'd come.

I said: "I have a feeling this is going to lead us back to the chamber with the machinery."

"We're going round in a circle."

"Sure, we should have taken the left fork with the roaches."

"No way."

Fifty yards on, we came to an alcove set in the wall. There was a sturdy metal door in the alcove. I tried the handle. It was locked.

I said: "We'd best head back to the chamber and try another route."

Shirl said: "*Ssssh!* There's a light ahead."

We stood as still as statues and strained our ears.

Bert's voice echoed down the corridor. "We've lost 'em."

Den's voice said: "We'll go on another hundred yards, then turn back. We'll tell the boss they got away."

"He won't like that."

I whispered: "We'd better turn back."

"I'm not going back to those roaches," Shirley said.

"Let's try and hide ourselves in the alcove. If we switch off the torch and press ourselves in as deep as possible, they'll pass us by."

We hustled back down the tunnel. We could hear Bert and Den's feet clump closer.

We pressed into the alcove against the metal door.

Bert and Den's footsteps were only ten yards away now.

Bert said: "If we catch them, we'll do them and leave what's left for the rats."

Den said: "The boss will like that."

"So will the rats."

"Swing that torch about. We need to see more up ahead."

The beam moved up and threw a shard of light into the alcove.

When Bert and Den were closer, they couldn't miss us.

My heart thumped in my chest. My mouth was dry. My hands were damp. And so was Shirl's when she pressed hers into mine.

We forced ourselves tighter against the door.

But it was hopeless. The alcove wasn't deep enough to hide us.

The beam of light widened.

I whispered to Shirl: "Let's get ready to rumble."

She gave my hand a confident squeeze. What a girl!

But we couldn't hide any more. Our backs were pressed as hard as we could on the door.

The best method of defence was attack.

It was fight or flight. And flight was no longer an option.

The adrenalin surged through my body like I'd just knocked back a treble brandy.

Then the door behind us swung open.

And we tumbled into space.

Chapter 15

We screamed with terror, like a couple of pilots pushed out without a parachute.

Our arms and legs flailed wildly as we fell.

Our yells echoed off the walls. The echoes of the echoes filled the space with a blur of noise. We must have sounded like the screaming inmates of Bedlam.

And then we landed. We bounced into the air and fell back again.

I shook with relief. I was alive and uninjured. No bones broken. No cuts. And if there were going to be bruises, what the hell? It was better than becoming raspberry jam on the floor.

My eyes flicked back and forth as I searched for Shirley.

She was beside me, also uninjured. But both of us were winded and panting like we'd just gone ten rounds with Muhammad Ali.

We had landed on a huge straw-filled palliasse.

We'd fallen ten feet and were in a large room with a vaulted ceiling held up by cast-iron columns. The walls were covered with brown and blue tiles. Light fittings had been screwed into the tiles at regular intervals around the room. Each fitting was held in place by a metal grille.

We rolled together as the weight of our bodies created a dip in the palliasse's centre. We looked at one another with the kind of wild surmise old Cortez was supposed to have had when he first gazed upon the Pacific. But that was only John Keats' version of the story and he wasn't there. For all I know, Cortez might just have shrugged his shoulders and said: "I've seen better."

I gazed at Shirley. She gazed at me. We grinned at each other. They were the grins people have when they're alive and realise they shouldn't be. We were in danger of becoming a bit manic after this experience. Hysterical laughter was only an inch below the surface. It could bubble up at any minute. Then we'd lose control completely.

I couldn't think what to say. So I put my arms around Shirley. She put her arms around me. And we kissed – a long lingering smooch which could well have gone further.

Would have gone further if a voice with a soft Irish lilt hadn't said: "Now, now, not in front of the children."

We broke our embrace and stared upwards.

A man was clinging to a metal ladder which ran up the wall towards the door we'd just fallen through. The man had a head of unruly red hair and a bushy beard. He had piercing blue eyes and a pointy nose. He had chubby red cheeks. He was dressed in a flowing green smock that came down to his thighs and brown trousers. The trousers were tied at the knee with string. He wore a pair of those short wellington boots which come up to mid-calf and which always fill up with water when you're wading through snow.

He'd just finished closing the door. Now he reached under the smock to a pocket in his trousers. He pulled out a large key and locked the door.

Shirl nudged me and said: "Who's the leprechaun?"

I said: "I don't know, but he's just saved us from a beating."

The leprechaun replaced the key in his pocket and shinned down the ladder, as agile as a circus acrobat.

He walked over to us and perched on the edge of the palliasse.

He said: "They say pride comes before a fall, sure they do. You had the pride and I provided the fall."

I said: "Who are you?"

He held out a hand. "Darragh Mahoney at your service."

I shook: "Colin Crampton."

Mahoney nodded towards Shirley: "Who's the colleen?"

Shirl's eyes flashed. "I'm not a colleen, I'm a Sheila. And the name's Shirley Goldsmith, cobber."

Mahoney grinned. "We don't get many girls down here. Especially not ones wearing stilettos longer than their skirts."

Shirl tugged down the hem of her denim. "I was pretending to be a stripper."

"Why pretend?" Darragh said.

This was getting out of hand. So I said: "Who are you?"

Mahoney said: "You've heard that old saying: the luck of the Irish. I'm the one who provides it down here. I like to think of myself as king of the underground kingdom. But I'm really just the sewers' head of security."

"Did you know we were behind that door when you opened it?" I asked.

"Do you think I floated up the Liffey in a matchbox? Of course, I knew. Just as I knew you were being hunted by bad people."

"How did you know that?"

"When you've been here as long as the stones have stood in Knocknakilla, you know when something is wrong. When someone opens a manhole cover, you can sense a change in the air. And if you know how to listen, you can hear the sounds vibrate along the walls as clear as if that fine Mr Marconi were sending them. And him being Italian, too, and not of the favoured race."

Shirl slid off the palliasse, hitched her skirt down a bit more, and said: "I guess we should thank you. We were in a tight corner and you saved our arses."

Mahoney took rather too close a look at Shirley's and said: "And well worth the trouble, too."

I said sharply: "The trouble is that those two goons are still roaming around the tunnels. I'm not sure how we get out of here without the risk of running into them again."

Mahoney hurried across the room to a wooden panel which held the ends of a dozen tubes each stopped with a thick cork.

He said: "These are speaking tubes. They help me hear what's happening in different places underground as clearly as if a fair colleen were singing Danny Boy in front of me."

"Are they like the speaking tubes they have on ships?" I asked.

"Yes, and installed long ago. That would be in the days when that fine Queen Victoria had put on so much weight they could have rolled her down Parnell Street in Dublin like a barrel."

Mahoney removed one of the corks and stuck his ear to the tube.

He shook his head. "As peaceful as a baby's dream."

He tried another tube. Listened for a moment. Then beckoned me over.

I put my ear to the tube. I could hear a low threnody of wind, but above it the sound of voices. I could make out two voices – Bert and Den's. Their voices were raised in anger.

I stepped aside and let Mahoney put his ear to the tube again. He grinned. "Fighting like Kilkenny cats," he said. "They're in the junction chamber under Madeira Place."

"Is that bad?" Shirley asked.

"It will be. Worse for them than if that black-hearted scoundrel Lord Randolph Churchill's sock suspenders snapped while he was making a speech in that fine House of Commons."

He moved to another tube and took out the cork. He beckoned us over.

"We can be as cunning as a Tipperary tinker," he said. "If we speak into the tube it carries the sound to the other end. Talk now and they will hear it in a tunnel near to them."

Shirley and I stepped up to the tube.

"I wonder where we are," I said into it loudly

"I think we must be lost, whacker," Shirley shouted.

"I do hope those goons don't find us," I yelled down the tube.

Mahoney put his ear to the tube and listened. He drew his eyebrows together in a serious frown.

"Has it worked?" I asked.

"No... yes. I can hear running feet. They've reached the tunnel connected to this tube."

He crossed the room. Pulled a lever on a control panel.

He said: "They won't stay in the sewers now."

"What have you done?" Shirley asked.

"Further up the hill, there's a holding tank. It would be a terrible place to be, right now, that's for sure. Three thousand gallons from the good people of Brighton – curry suppers and all - and not yet flowed out to sea."

"And you've just released it," I said.

"Sure as there are no snakes in Ireland, I have to let the natural flows take place. It's too bad our friends are now standing right in its path."

I said: "I hope they won't drown."

"Goodness no. It'll be much worse than that. You could fillet all the fish in the Irish Sea and then shovel all the horse shit from Leopardstown races and still not smell as bad as our two friends will in ten minutes time."

"They won't move in decent company for weeks," I said.

"Those whackers wouldn't know decent company if it bit their knackers off," Shirley said.

Mahoney's brow wrinkled in a frown. "There's you talking of decent company, and me not even offering you the hospitality of the house. You'll take a draught of the Liffey water before you go?"

He led us across the floor to an area on the far side of the room. Three or four chairs were grouped around an electric fire whose bars burnt bright red. A worn old Wilton carpet on the floor attempted to make the area look homely. A standard lamp threw a mellow glow over the rug.

He gestured at the chairs and we sat. He crossed to a small cupboard and took out some bottles and glasses. He poured three creamy glasses of Guinness.

He handed round the drinks.

He raised his glass in a toast. "Confusion to our enemies," he said.

Shirley and I chorused the words together and drank.

"That's good," I said. I waved my arm around at the room. "What is this place?" I asked. "And why is the door high up in the wall? And why have you got a palliasse on the floor?"

Mahoney put down his glass and threw up his hands.

"More questions than a priest in a confessional. But I can tell you what it was then and what it is now," he said. "When those Victorian gentleman with their fine silk top hats built these sewers, this was a holding chamber."

"To hold what?"

"Water. When the town has a soft day with the blessing of God's gracious rain, the water has to go somewhere."

"Along the gutters and down the drain," Shirley said.

"But where does it go when it's in the drain?"

"Search me," Shirl said.

Mahoney grinned. "I may take you up on that kind offer another time. But to answer your very fair question. It goes into the storm drains and these very fine sewers. But those clever Victorian gents knew they couldn't allow rainwater to overwhelm the natural flows. By the blessing of the good Saint Patrick, no. Our friends up the tunnels will now be feeling as mucky as a shamrock under a fresh cowpat. So the engineers set to work and built this fine chamber to hold the sweet rain until it was a fit time to let it out into the sea. The rainwaters came down the tunnel you walked through and when they threatened to overwhelm the natural flows, the doors opened and the waters rushed into here with a force that would have shocked that good Noah with his ark."

"But not anymore?" I asked.

"No, there's a big new holding tank. Bigger than that great St Paul's cathedral in London town, I'm told."

"But why the palliasse?" I reminded Mahoney.

"Oh, we can't have people falling ten feet to the floor. The place would look like Dublin's fair city after the Easter Rising, sure it would."

I downed the last of my Guinness.

I said: "We have a lot to thank you for – and not just for the drinks."

"It's been a pleasure to help a young gentleman with such a fine countenance." He nodded towards Shirley. "And the lady – even though she'd make a priest say a hundred Hail Marys just for the pleasure of looking at her."

"Can you show us how we can regain the world above ground?"

"It would be a pleasure. And you'll pop out of a manhole in the Old Steine like the Devil and his wife.

"Jeez, that guy had more chat than a Wagga Wagga washerwoman," Shirley said.

We'd climbed out of the manhole cover in the Old Steine just as Mahoney had predicted. Nobody took a second look at us. As if seeing a couple of people coming up from the sewers was part of the natural order of things. Perhaps it was in this part of town. After all, enough tourists did it.

We were walking back to the street where I'd parked the MGB.

I said: "Yes, he was certainly a classic example of the stage Irishman. I haven't heard so much paddywhackery since I saw *The Playboy of the Western World* at the Theatre Royal."

"Playboy? Not that magazine with nude bunny girls?"

"No, this was a play by an Irish playwright called John Millington Synge. It's a serious play but not all the Irish like it because it shows them as caricatures."

"So what's your point, mastermind?"

"He was just too Irish."

"He was just pleased with our company. Can't be much fun spending your life in a sewer."

"But did you notice, most of his Irish references were to traditions or things that had happened years ago? He never mentioned anything about today's Ireland."

"Why does that matter?" Shirl asked.

"Because I think he hadn't been there. At least, not for many years."

"And what was all that cock and bull about the palliasse? The simple way to stop people falling through the door is to keep it locked."

"Yes. And he did have a comfy set-up round the electric fire with Guinness on tap. Almost like it was a home from home."

"You think he lives there?" Shirley said.

"For the time being, I think he does. Just behind the cupboard I noticed a sleeping bag. It was rolled up tight, so I guess he thought we wouldn't see it."

"So he wasn't the security guy in the sewers?" Shirley said.

"I don't know," I said. "If he wasn't, I can't think what he was doing there."

We passed a couple of drunks staggering towards their next pub.

"Hey, did you see the way that guy looked at me?"

"He's drunk," I said.

"And you're saying I wouldn't be worth a look if he were sober?"

"You're worth a look drunk or sober." I jumped into the MGB before Shirl could answer back.

She climbed into the passenger seat and tugged down the hem of her skirt.

"I guess strippers wear a long coat to cover their assets when they go out," she said.

I fired the ignition, put the car into gear, and we took off towards Shirley's flat.

When I pulled up outside, I leaned over and kissed her.

I said: "I'm bushed and I've got an even busier day tomorrow."

Shirley kissed me – a real gold standard plonker.

"Don't you want to finish what we started on the palliasse?"

she said.

"Well, if you put it like that..." I said.

It was two hours before I left Shirley's flat.

And I felt like I could conquer the world. But perhaps after a good night's sleep.

It was gone one in the morning by the time I parked in the mews behind the Widow's lodging house. The Widow would be long abed in her winceyette jim-jams and snoring like a gored bull.

So I breezed through the front door and headed for the stairs.

The Widow shot out of her parlour before I could get a foot on the first tread.

She said: "What time do you call this?"

"Time you got a watch."

The Widow stepped closer. I could smell the Horlicks on her breath.

She said: "Don't get sarcastic with me."

"There was no-one else around."

"As it happens, you're wrong. You've had a visitor."

"I'm not at home."

"You are now. And so is your visitor."

I gave the Widow a stern stare. Had she been slipping Drambuie into her bedtime drink again?

I said: "Which visitor?"

"Your cousin from the United States. As you're so late and she's near family, I said she could wait in your rooms. She's up there now."

The Widow turned on her heel and stomped back into her parlour.

I looked up the stairs wondering what the hell had happened now.

I didn't have a cousin in the United States.

Chapter 16

I pounded up the stairs and barged into my room.

My so-called cousin was sitting in my best chair. She had poured herself a gin and tonic and cut a slice off my last lemon.

She was about my age, had blonde hair, and an hour-glass figure. Her face was a little too thin to get her on the front cover of *Playboy*, but the rest of her would have looked good on the magazine's fold-out centre spread.

She looked up as I charged in and grinned.

She said: "Hi, I'm your long-lost cousin." She spoke with a strong New York accent.

I said: "Sure you are. You've got everything I look for in a long-lost cousin except one thing."

"What's that?"

"You're not lost."

Her lips pulled a disappointed moue. "Don't be like that."

She stood up and stuck out a petite hand. "I'm Mary-Lyn Monroe."

"A close relation, no doubt, as well as being a long-lost cousin."

I didn't want to look like a dog in a manger, so I took her hand and gave a brief shake. It was soft and limp. (Her hand, I mean, not my shake.)

"No, I ain't related to the late, great Marilyn. Although I guess I might be if I traced my family tree far enough back."

"Except her real name wasn't Monroe. It was Norma Mortenson."

"Sure it was, honey. But I was saying my Pa was called Monroe. He worked in a steel yard in Newark, New Jersey. He wanted to call me Mary but my Ma, who used to be a croupier in the Lucky Casino in Atlantic City, wanted to call me Lyn. Apparently, they decided to settle the matter on one spin of the ball on the roulette table. If it came up black, I'd be Mary. If it was red, Lyn."

"And it came up as a big fat zero. So your parents decided to use both names."

Mary-Lyn smiled showing a fine set of teeth. "You're a clever guy. Maybe we can do business."

"And maybe we can go to bed. It's nearly two."

Mary-Lyn winked. "Hey, maybe we can and all. If we do the deal I'm offering, maybe we can seal it with more than a handshake." She double winked. "Know what I mean?"

I crossed my room and poured myself a stiff gin. Topped up with tonic. Added a slice of the lemon Mary-Lyn had cut.

"I was suggesting we might go to our respective beds."

"Now there's a problem there. I just blew into town this evening, and I still need to find myself a hotel."

"You could try the Beauregard on the seafront."

The guest house was run by Mrs Blagg, the Widow's crony. It was about time the bedbugs had someone new to bite.

"Well, that's real kind, Colin." She raised an eyebrow. "It is Colin isn't it?"

"It was the last time I checked my birth certificate."

Mary-Lyn crossed to the table and freshened her G and T. "Let me cut to the chase."

"I wish you would before you drink all my gin."

"One of your guys is in the slammer on a phony charge. Am I right?"

I nodded thoughtfully. She seemed to know a lot for someone who'd just blown into town.

I said: "My colleague Sidney Pinker should be released in days."

"Yeah! That's what they all say. But the cops seem made up with the idea that your Pinker croaked a guy called Danny Bernstein. Right?"

I nodded again.

"Well, I bet you didn't know this."

"Try me?"

"Bernstein made a trip Stateside last year."

That had my attention.

Mary-Lyn said: "Apparently the guy was looking to see if he could break into the entertainment business in Atlantic City. Those casinos need that bit extra to hook the punters. So they put on shows. Singers, funny men, jugglers, strippers. It's classy stuff. The agencies who supply the acts make good dough. Bernstein wanted a slice of the action."

"Which he didn't get."

"Worse than that. He got the wrong kind of action."

"You're talking the mob?" I asked. "The Mafia."

"Here's the crack. While he was in Atlantic City, Bernstein became too fond of the little steel ball."

"He played the roulette tables?"

"Like he was Nelson Rockefeller. But he ended owing a lotta money to a lotta people. Then he skipped town before they could put the squeeze on him."

"Let me guess," I said. "Those lotta people have hired you to get the money back."

"You've just hit a home run, my friend."

"As I'm on a winning streak, let me make another guess. You were behind the anonymous phone calls to my landlady yesterday."

"Made the calls before I quit New York. Just checking out the lie of the land, honey."

I drained the last of my gin and tonic and put my glass down.

"Well, it's an interesting story, Miss Monroe, and I should be able to get five hundred words out if it. Thank you and good night."

Mary-Lyn sat down again in my best chair.

She said: "I ain't finished yet. I hear you could be looking for work."

"I've got plenty," I lied.

"That's not what I'd heard. The scuttlebutt is you got canned from your job."

"I've decided there are more opportunities for freelance work," I said stiffly.

"And so there are. Team up with me, and we get a twenty-five per cent commission on the money we recover. My clients reckon Bernstein must have his loot stashed somewhere."

"I'm a journalist, not a debt collector."

"Sure. But you find out things. You could tell me and I'll pay big money. I read your articles. You know who's screwing who in this town."

I thought about that for a minute. A lot of things didn't add up here. Mary-Lyn said she'd just blown into town, but she knew what had happened to Bernstein and the fact Sidney was in jail. She knew about me and claimed to have read my articles in the *Chronicle*. And she knew I'd recently quit the paper.

Mary-Lyn took a slurp of her gin and emptied the glass.

I said: "Let me pour you another."

I crossed to the table and collected the gin bottle. Moved back to the chair. Feigned a trip on the carpet. And made sure a good shot of gin drenched Mary-Lyn's blouse.

She shrieked. "Goddam it, can't you pour it into the glass."

"I'm really sorry," I said. "There's a dry towel in the bathroom. You can mop yourself down."

Mary-Lyn stood up and stomped off to the bathroom. "Yeah! Like I don't need a complete change of clothes."

Mary-Lyn slammed the bathroom door behind her. I dived to the side of the chair and grabbed her handbag.

I opened it and rummaged inside. There was an airline ticket from New York. She'd arrived in Britain two days ago – not today, as she'd claimed. There was a compact, a lipstick, and a brush thing. And there was a hotel key. For room 636 in the Majestic Hotel. Posh and expensive. Way out of the Beauregard league.

I made a note of the room number and thrust the key back in the bag. I put the bag back at the side of the chair.

Mary-Lyn stomped back into the room.

"Jeez! I stink like a distillery."

"Perhaps you should find a hotel and change," I said.

"Yeah! But you think about what I've said. We could be a team – you and me."

She grabbed her bag and stalked out of the room.

I had a good sniff to see if I could smell the spilt gin. But the only scent that reached my nostrils was like a sweet honey carried on a summer's breeze.

It could have been her perfume.

Or it could have been trickery.

When I finally climbed between the sheets, I couldn't get to sleep.

Too many mysteries were chasing around my mind. I tossed and turned on the lumpy mattress to try to make sense of them.

This all started with a murder and a theft – of the Blue Book. I now knew for certain that Sidney hadn't killed Bernstein. There were just too many other suspects with a real motive. So if Sidney hadn't killed Bernstein, he couldn't have stolen the Blue Book.

Yet I still couldn't nail the true killer – and neither could the cops. All of the comedians had a motive – and none of them had an alibi for the time of the killing. Only one of them – Peter Kitchen – had a history of violence. But I didn't attach too much importance to that. Giving a heckler a slap wasn't in the same league as running through a theatrical agent with a sword.

More likely candidates as killers would be the Hardmann brothers. They'd built their criminal empire through violence. Murder, too. None had ever been proved because the bodies weren't usually found. But I couldn't rule them out. Perhaps one of them had been the mystery man.

Normally, I'd be able to eliminate the suspects one by one. But not this time. To make the whole thing more mind bending, the evening's fun and games had produced two new mysteries. I couldn't figure out what Darragh Mahoney was doing in the sewers. If he was a true Irishman, I'd whack myself over the head with a shillelagh.

To top it all, the appearance of my so-called long-lost cousin, Mary-Lyn, posed fresh questions. I was willing to bet she wasn't who she said she was. But who was she? Could she have been hired by one of the suspects to find out what I knew? Did she hope to undermine my investigation? Was she going to steer me onto the wrong track?

I didn't have an answer for any of the questions. But I did have a decision. I would find out who she really was in the morning.

The only thing I hadn't yet worked out was how.

At eight o'clock the following morning I was standing in a phone box opposite the Majestic Hotel.

I had a plan of sorts. It was dangerous to the point of crazy. If it had gone wrong when I worked for the *Chronicle*, it would have got me fired. But I didn't work for the *Chronicle*. And if it went wrong, I wouldn't fire myself. I might even give myself a promotion. Unless I was in jail.

My plan was to get into Mary-Lyn's room and search it while she was having breakfast in the restaurant. I reckoned I'd be able to find out what she was really up to.

I'll admit there were one or two holes in the plan.

After a late night, she might sleep in. She might order room service.

But I was about to plug those holes. I hoped.

I picked up the telephone and dialled the Majestic's reception. I asked to be put through to room 636.

The telephone rang. It rang seventeen times before the

receptionist came back on the line.

"I'm afraid Miss Monroe is not in her room at present. May I take a message?"

I replaced the receiver.

So the room was empty. Or, perhaps, not. Mary-Lyn could have been in the shower. But I couldn't keep throwing up difficulties.

I scooted across the road to the broad marble steps which led up to the hotel's grand entrance.

I avoided them and slipped round the corner to a less imposing door. It was the one which servants used to bring in the luggage when gentlemen travelled with a valet and ladies with their maid.

I barged through the door and hurried down a short corridor to the backstairs. I was pretty sure Mary-Lyn would take the lift. She didn't look like a backstairs kind of girl.

I had a little rest on the fourth floor, got my breath back, and then attacked the summit.

If you've watched as many Hollywood private eye movies as I have, you'll know that getting into a hotel room without a key is a cinch. You find an obliging chambermaid and then pretend you've locked yourself out. Or dropped your key down the lift shaft. Or given it to your wife, who's unexpectedly walked out on you.

So, on the sixth floor, I pushed through the doors from the backstairs and looked for a chambermaid.

But, like waiters, there's never one about when you need one. Well, I said my plan had a few holes.

I was in a corridor with doors off to the rooms on either side. There was a thick carpet which sighed with pleasure when you walked on it. At the far end of the corridor, there was a lift. The lights above the door showed the lift was on the ground floor.

There was a large laundry basket parked half-way down the corridor. It was a big wicker job which pushed along on casters.

Perhaps a chambermaid would appear in a few moments with some dirty laundry to put in it.

Trouble was, I didn't have a few minutes. If Mary-Lyn was at breakfast, she might just be polishing off her last slice of toast and marmalade. She could be heading back to her room.

The door to room 636 was a few steps along from the laundry basket.

I walked over and tried the handle.

Locked.

There were more holes than I'd expected in this plan.

I stood there and wondered what to do next.

And then the lights above the lift door flashed. The lift was coming up from the ground floor. It passed the third floor.

It could stop at the fourth. Perhaps the fifth. Wouldn't necessarily come on to the sixth. It might be full of other guests. All standing ramrod stiff and staring at the floor, like people do in lifts. Not necessarily Mary-Lyn. But, then, I was loitering in the corridor and I'd look suspicious - even to other guests.

I had to retreat or find a way to hide.

I hurried back to the laundry basket and climbed in. The thing creaked as I lowered myself over the side. And there was a strong smell of starch as I plunged among the bedding and lowered the lid.

I heard the ping as the lift reached the sixth floor and the doors opened.

I lifted the lid an inch and peaked.

Two men stepped out of the lift. The doors closed behind them and the lift started down.

The men walked towards me and my eyes popped. I couldn't believe it.

On the left was Gino, the small guy who'd tried to use my head for baseball practice outside the Last Laugh club.

On the right was Willis, the guy with hands like baseball mitts.

They strode confidently along the corridor. Like they knew where they were going.

They stopped outside room 636. Gino knocked on the door.

They waited. Looked at each other like they hadn't expected the door to stay shut.

Willis hammered on the door. It shook on its hinges.

He said: "The broad ain't at home."

Gino said: "She's the boss to you."

"I thought you were the boss."

"Only when the broad ain't around."

Willis' brow wrinkled in confusion.

He said: "Do you think she's having breakfast?"

"Could be."

"Be awesome if she eats Korn Krunchies for breakfast."

Gino looked puzzled. "Why awesome?"

"Because of those TV ads we have back home."

"Which TV ads?"

"The ones where you get those girls dressed as chipmunks singing 'Eat Bekker's for breakers'."

Now Gino was irritated. "What is this?"

"Don't you know, boss. It's because Brandenburg J Bekker makes the Korn Krunchies."

At the mention of Brandenburg J Bekker, Gino's posture tensed.

"I told you not to mention that name," he said.

"Korn Krunchies?"

"No. Brandenburg J Bekker. We do not know that name. Understand?"

Willis scratched his head. "But we do know it. It's why we're here."

Gino shook his head in despair. "Come on, let's try the breakfast room."

I lifted the lid of the laundry basket and watched as they sloped back down the corridor. They climbed into the lift, the doors closed, and the lift descended.

A chambermaid came out of a room with a bundle of bedding in her arms. It piled up in front of her face.

I ducked down under the laundry.

She walked to the basket, lifted the lid, and tossed it in. Didn't see me lurking in the bottom, partly hidden by a pillowcase.

The basket started to move. Its casters squeaked. The basket creaked. The chambermaid was singing Don't Let Me Be Misunderstood. Didn't sound a bit like Nina Simone.

I lay doggo under the soiled sheets and decided to spring out of the basket as soon as it stopped. As soon as the chambermaid went into another room.

And then the basket tipped sideways. I sprawled on my side.

And suddenly I was sliding down.

Down.

Down.

Like I was on the longest helter-skelter in the world.

Chapter 17

If you're ever leaving a hotel in a hurry, I don't recommend the laundry chute.

It's a long way down and dirty linen doesn't make great company. By the time I'd reached the bottom I was tangled in a mass of sheets and pillowcases.

I'd been buffeted from side to side until it felt my bum was on fire.

I shot into a large hopper and sank into a pile of linen. And then a heap of sheets and towels landed on top of me.

I lay there winded, wondering what the hell would happen next.

I scrambled about in the heap of linen and somehow got my head in the air. I grabbed the side of the hopper and heaved myself free of the tangle.

As I appeared above the top of the hopper, a young woman wearing jeans and a kind of tabard arrangement, turned round and looked at me.

She had mousey hair tied up under a scarf. She was heaving wet linen out of a washing machine.

Her eyes turned into saucers and her jaw dropped. Her mouth worked to say something but no words came out.

I hauled myself up onto the side of the hopper, swung my legs over, and jumped to the ground.

"I was looking for a sock I'd lost in bed," I said.

She nodded, but her jaw still hung loose.

"The laundry basket tipped over while I was looking," I said by way of explanation.

I smiled at her and headed for the door.

I had opened it when she said: "Did you find it?"

"Find what?"

"The sock."

"Must still be up there," I said.

I stepped outside and closed the door behind me.

I crossed the road and sat in one of the prom's shelters looking out to sea. A stiff breeze was coming in from the south-west. The sea was grey and heaved in a swell. Waves sploshed noisily on the shingle and tossed spray into the wind.

A couple of seagulls circled above the water.

I had a lot to think about. It was clear that Gino and Willis were Mary-Lyn's hired help. I'd first had the pleasure of meeting them on Monday, two days earlier. But Mary-Lyn had pitched up at my rooms only last night.

There was one explanation. Mary-Lyn knew that I was investigating Bernstein's death – and she wanted me stopped. She had a Yank's desire for simple and permanent solutions. So Plan A. Gino and Willis had been despatched to do the business. But Shirley had foiled plan A.

So Plan B. Mary-Lyn had decided on a more subtle approach. Softly, softly, catchee monkey. If she couldn't knock my head off – I could still feel the swish of Gino's baseball bat - perhaps she could blow it with the thought of making big money. Especially as I was now without gainful employment.

Well, I'd scotched Plan B. What would she try next? Did she even have a Plan C? I had no idea, but I'd need to be extra vigilant in watching my back.

What I couldn't figure out is how an American breakfast cereal magnate came into the picture. Was Brandenburg J Bekker one of the hard types who were owed money by Bernstein? Perhaps Bekker had loaned Bernstein dollars which he'd frittered away in the Atlantic City casinos.

My stomach rumbled. Thinking about breakfast reminded me that I hadn't yet had any.

Ten minutes later I walked into Marcello's.

The breakfast rush was in full swing. A couple of beefy

builders in overalls and hard hats scoffed bacon sandwiches. A nurse dipped a toast soldier into a boiled egg. A bank manager type in a grey suit and striped tie picked the bones out of his kipper. The red stripes in his tie matched the veins in his nose.

I walked up to the counter. Ruby, Marcello's assistant, was standing by the griddle frying bacon. She used a pair of tongs to turn the rashers.

She winked at me and said: "Your usual order? A bacon sandwich – but no sauce 'coz you've already got enough?"

I said: "Do you stock Korn Krunchies?"

"You gone weird or vegetarian or something?"

"None of the above. I just felt like something different for breakfast."

"You've been watching those adverts."

"Bekkers for Breakers? No, but I've heard about them."

Ruby put down the tongs and leaned on the counter.

She said: "Well, you can forget Korn Krunchies. I'd rather eat the cardboard box they come in."

"But I'd heard they were popular."

"Yeah! But mostly with kids. You see each box comes complete with a little plastic animal."

"What for?"

"They're for the kids to collect. There's a set of six – lion, tiger, antelope, hippo, giraffe and wildebeest. For kids, having a full set is a huge status symbol. But there's a catch. There are roughly an equal number of the first five animals. So the law of averages says you'll get them after buying a dozen or so packets of Korn Krunchies. But you won't have the wildebeest. They're very rare. I've heard rumours there's only one wildebeest for every ten thousand packets. So kids go crazy if they don't have the full set. They nag their mums to keep buying more Korn Krunchies until a wildebeest pops out of one."

"Sneaky marketing," I said.

"Yeah! But I hear that Bekker guy who runs the company has

made zillions."

I nodded. "You know, you've talked me into a bacon sandwich after all. But make sure the bacon's hot."

Ruby grinned. "As hot as me?"

"I'm not sure I can handle that."

Ruby laughed and made the sandwich. I took it to a table near the front of the café.

I took a bite of the sandwich and chewed thoughtfully. From what Ruby had told me, Bekker was a shrewd tycoon.

But aside from the fact he'd thought of a sneaky way to sell his cereal I knew nothing about him. If I could find out more, perhaps I could make a link with Bernstein.

Normally, that would be easy. I'd waltz into the morgue at the *Chronicle* and plead for Henrietta's help. Even if she had nothing about Bekker in the *Chronicle's* morgue, she'd know people who had.

I was now banned from the *Chronicle's* building. But there was one way I might dig out the facts I needed.

Jeff Purkiss leaned on the bar and said: "It's not often you're in here as soon as the doors open."

I was in Prinny's Pleasure. I'd perched on a bar stool and ordered a gin and tonic.

I said: "I'm meeting someone."

"Man or woman?" Jeff asked.

"Mind your own business."

"So it's a woman."

"There's a fifty per cent chance of that."

"Is it your girlfriend Shirley?"

"No."

"So it's a bit on the side."

"No, she's not a bit of the side. Nobody would describe the woman I'm meeting as a bit on the side."

At that moment, the pub's double doors opened and Susan

Wheatcroft, the *Chronicle's* business reporter, appeared. She stood framed in the doorway - all seventeen stone of her, and proud of every ounce. Her frizzy brown hair had been blown about by the wind. Her cheeks were pink from the cold. She was wearing a huge cape arrangement which rested extravagantly over her shoulders like a giant bat and flowed down to her knees. She had a large brown handbag looped over her left arm.

Susan spotted me and her eyes lit up with a smile. She hurried across the bar grinning with pleasure.

She greeted me with a kiss on both cheeks, just like the French. I returned the compliment.

She said: "Great to see you, honeybunch." She nudged me in the ribs. "And just because I kissed you like the continentals, doesn't mean I wouldn't prefer a proper snog."

I laughed. "It's good of you to come."

"Now that I'm here I'll have what you're drinking, but twice the size," she said.

We took our drinks to the corner table at the back of the bar. We clinked glasses and drank.

Susan said: "The newsroom has changed since you left."

I said: "I only quit yesterday. Hardly any time at all."

"Figgis is in a foul mood."

"He's always in a mood."

"This is the worst one ever, honeybunch. He sits in his office smoking and growls at anyone who comes near him."

"It wasn't a good time for me to call you then?" I said.

"It didn't matter. But you understand why I couldn't talk on the phone."

"Too many twitchy ears in a newsroom."

Susan nodded and had a good pull at her drink.

I said: "I badly need some help on a story I'm working on."

"Is this to do with Sidney Pinker?"

"Yes. But I can't yet figure out what the angle is. That's why I need your help."

I told Susan about Brandenburg J Bekker. I said: "I need to know more about him. But I can't go into the morgue."

Susan chuckled. "And you'd like me to do it for you?"

"I'd be eternally grateful," I said.

"Eternal gratitude. Now that sounds like a deal I could go with," Susan said. "What exactly do you want to know?"

"I need to know more about how Bekker came to set up his breakfast cereal company and whether he's ever had any connection with Brighton. Or with Danny Bernstein. Or Max Miller," I added as an afterthought.

Susan took out a small notebook and made a couple of jottings.

I said: "If you find a connection, I want you to follow it up in the files and find out as much as you can."

"Henrietta in the morgue will want to know why I've suddenly taken an interest in this guy."

"I'm on good terms with Henrietta. You can tell her what you're doing. She'll help you out and keep it to herself."

"And if others stick their noses in?" Susan asked.

"Tell them you're researching background for a feature on the breakfast cereals market. After all, you are the business reporter."

Susan made a couple more notes.

She said: "This won't be easy."

"I know. And it gets worse. I need the information this afternoon."

Susan put the book and pen back in her bag. She looked at me. Her eyes were sad. The edges of her lips turned down. Her double chin sagged lower than usual.

"Of course, I'll do this. But will you come back to the *Chronicle*? We all miss you." She took a last sip of her drink. In a tiny voice, she said: "I miss you."

I leant forward and kissed her on the cheek. "Consider that a down payment on a proper snog."

Susan brightened up and smiled. "You'll need a bigger

payment than that for what I've got in mind."

She stood up. "Meet me back here at five."

She wrapped her cape more tightly around her and stomped towards the door. She looked like a vampire queen on the hunt for a neck to bite.

The door closed behind Susan and an icy chill descended on the room.

I felt goose bumps rise on my back and I shivered. I buttoned my jacket and folded my arms around myself. I hadn't felt like this earlier. But seeing Susan reminded me what I'd left behind at the *Chronicle*. I'd loved life in the newsroom. Susan had been one of my many friends there. Now I'd see them from time to time around town, but I'd be the outsider. I'd be the one who wasn't in on all the latest gossip. I'd be the one who didn't know which hot stories the newsroom was chasing.

But there was no going back. I'd cut myself loose and I had two choices. I could drift aimlessly like an old rowboat caught on the tide and carried out to sea. Or I could set a determined course for the horizon and discover what was over it. I only hoped it wasn't an iceberg.

The trouble was my horizon analogy was a bit like the Bernstein case. When you're in the middle of an ocean, the horizon isn't only what you see ahead. It's what you've left behind. And what you've never encountered on either side.

The harsh reality was that so much had happened, I felt lost. I couldn't make the connections between Bernstein's murder, the missing Blue Book, the Laugh-a-thon comics, the Hardmann brothers, Mary-Lyn Monroe – and a breakfast cereal zillionaire. It was like heading into a maze where there was only a way in – but no way out.

I needed some help. And, at the moment, the only person who could provide it was locked in a cell.

I drained the last of my gin and tonic and headed for the door.

***

I had a bit of badly needed luck when I reached Brighton police station.

Tomkins had left for a Rotary Club lunch where he was the guest speaker. I couldn't think of anything more likely to bring on a mass attack of indigestion.

I called in a final favour from Ted Wilson. He had Sidney Pinker brought up from the cells. He locked us in an interview room and told me I had fifteen minutes. I doubted a quarter of an hour would be enough time to unravel this puzzle.

Sidney looked thin and pasty-faced as he was brought into the room. Stubble sprouted on his chin and his hair had tangled.

He sat down on the chair screwed to the floor and said: "Now I know how Oscar felt, dear boy."

"Oscar?" I queried.

"Oscar Wilde. He was in jail, too, you know. Reading Jail. He wrote a poem about it. 'I never saw a man who looked, With such a wistful eye, Upon that little tent of blue, Which prisoners call the sky.'"

I said: "There hasn't been any blue sky all week. This is November."

"There's no poetry in your soul, dear boy. You don't know what it's like here. Last night, the duty officer brought me a bowl of soup that was like washing up water. And it had a fly in it. I said, 'What's this fly doing in my soup?'"

"And he said, 'I think it's the breaststroke.'"

Sidney scowled. "How did you know that?"

"It's the oldest joke in the book and you gave him the feeder line. It was probably in Max Miller's Blue Book."

Sidney managed a thin grin. "He'd have accentuated the breast part when he told it."

"Yes. A laugh a minute. But not for me. This case has lost me my job – and I'm nowhere near coming up with answers or even a story. I need you to delve deeper. I must know more about Bernstein. For a start, did you ever hear of him having anything to do with a Yank called Brandenburg J Bekker?"

Sidney pulled a puzzled frown. "The man behind Korn Krunchies?"

"Behind them, in front of them, in them for all I know."

Sidney shook his head. "No."

He fell silent. He scratched his head, tugged his right earlobe, looked hard at the blank wall.

"I've just remembered something else about Bernstein." He tugged his left earlobe.

"Well, what is it, Sidney?"

"You know how he fell out with Ernie Winkle over the ownership of the Blue Book?"

"Yes. What about it?"

"Well, about three weeks ago, I was having a drink with a few nice boys in Fancy Nancy's. Dirty Denis said he'd heard a rumour that Bernstein had been seen a few times at the Last Laugh."

"Ernie Winkle's club. I thought the two never met after they'd fallen out over the Blue Book."

"Not according to Denis who heard the rumour from Bruce the Boxer."

"Flyweight, no doubt."

"Actually, the boxer bit is a nickname." Sidney leaned towards me and winked. "It's a reference to his underwear. Shorts. Silk, I can personally confirm. Anyway, it was Bruce who'd seen Bernstein coming and going from the club when it was closed."

"How did Bruce manage that?"

"He runs the small newsagent's just on the other side of the street. It's the one with the special magazines in the back room. But you wouldn't be interested in them. Anyway, Bruce wasn't in the back room when he saw Bernstein. He actually saw Ernie waving him off one day. Very pally they looked together."

I thought about that for a moment. When I'd interviewed Winkle, he'd not told me that he'd recently been seeing Bernstein.

Could the pair have been negotiating about the ownership of the Blue Book? If they were, it looked like the talks were going well.

At least, until the Blue Book was stolen and Bernstein killed.

I said: "Both Bernstein and Winkle knew Max Miller, didn't they?"

Sidney nodded.

"Could it have been shared memories of him that brought them together?"

Sidney shrugged.

I said: "How much do you suppose the Blue Book is worth?"

Sidney thought about that. "Hard to say," he said. "Could be thousands. It could provide a comic with a stage act that would keep him in bookings for years. Then there's the publicity. Not to mention radio and TV spin-offs."

"But Miller never tried to sell it," I said.

"Why should he? He'd already earned millions."

"But he only left £27,000 in his will."

Sidney moved closer, like someone who's got a secret to impart. "Max was always very careful with money. People who've come from poverty often are. I've heard rumours that Max squirreled money away in safety deposit boxes. There could be thousands of pounds out there undiscovered, even two years after his death."

"He was a bit of a miser, then?"

"Not at all. Big-hearted Max. He bought that big house out at Ovingdean – Woodland Grange. That woman, Mrs Van der Elst, who ran the anti-hanging campaigns, used to live there. Anyway, when the Second World War broke out, Max lent the Grange to St Dunstan's. No rent – absolutely free. They used it as a hospital for soldiers who'd been blinded in battle. Thousands of veterans were grateful for what Max did."

I sat back and thought about that. There was something about what Sidney had said which stirred a memory. But I couldn't recall what it was.

And then the door rattled as it was unlocked. Ted Wilson stuck his head round.

He said: "You've had half an hour. Tomkins will be back soon. Best for all of us if he doesn't find you here."

I stood up and nodded at Sidney.

"Don't give up," I said. "If you feel a bit down, think of old Oscar. A spell in clink didn't stop him entering the literary giants' hall of fame."

Sidney looked up and dabbed his eyes with the handkerchief.

"I'm not sure even that is worth what I'm going through."

Chapter 18

An hour later, I met Shirley for lunch.

We sat on a bench in a shelter on the seafront and ate fish and chips wrapped in newspaper.

The bench was hard, the shelter was draughty, and our moods were sombre.

Grey clouds scudded across the sky. The tide was up and waves broke with a noisy roar on the shingle.

An old boy wrapped against the cold in a duffle coat walked by. He had a cocker spaniel on a lead. The dog was straining for a run on the beach.

Shirley said: "This newspaper is all soggy and it's sticking to my chips."

I said: "You've put on too much vinegar."

"*Yuk!* You really know how to show a girl a good time."

"Get used to it. This is the freelance life. No more expense account lunches."

"So next time we'll be huddled in a shop doorway eating stale cheese sandwiches?"

"Who said anything about there being cheese?" I said.

Shirley looked at me and grinned.

She said: "Perhaps we'll end up dressed as tramps and stroll along the prom singing that movie song, We're a Couple of Swells."

"What? With me as Fred Astaire and you as Judy Garland? I don't think we're ready to play the hobo yet."

Shirley ate a last chip and screwed up her newspaper.

"You will be if you can't make it as a freelance."

"I'm on a great story now. If I can crack it, I'll make some serious money."

Shirley took my arm. "Why don't we walk and talk?"

We stood up, tossed our chippy papers into a waste basket,

and strolled towards the West Pier.

"I've had an idea," she said. "Why don't we move up to London?"

I looked at Shirl open-eyed. "What's brought this on?"

"I've been thinking about it for some time. My modelling work down here is going well, but the big opportunities are in London."

"I thought you liked the location fashion shoots around Brighton."

"I do, but you don't make it big in fashion unless you can crack the London studios. I think I'm ready to try that now. I didn't mention it before, because I knew you were committed to the *Chronicle*. But now you're footloose there's no reason we shouldn't both go to London. That's where the glittering prizes are in journalism, too. A cocky bastard like you would soon land a top job on a Fleet Street paper. Probably be editing it within five years."

I laughed. "Thanks for the vote of confidence. But I need to crack the Bernstein murder first."

"And spring your theatre critic friend from the can?"

"No-one else will."

"If you do get him off, he won't thank you."

I stopped, turned to face Shirl. "No, he won't. Most people complain when you knock them down but don't thank you when you pick them up. I expect Sidney is no different. But you shouldn't do the right thing just to win gratitude. You should do it so you can look yourself in the bathroom mirror of a morning and know you're looking at a decent human being."

Shirley leaned forward and kissed me gently on the cheek. "You really are crazy. I guess I must be a girl who goes for crazy."

"I've always hoped so," I said.

Shirl glanced at her watch. "I've got to run. I'm due at a shoot in a studio in Hove this afternoon."

"Let's meet this evening," I said. "I'll come to your flat at seven."

We embraced and kissed. And for a moment, the wind seemed to drop and the waves grow quiet.

And then, with a toss of her head and a "See ya!" Shirley hurried off along the prom.

I watched her go, until she crossed the road and turned into a side street.

I wondered how much she wanted to go to London. And whether I should follow her.

But I would have to think about that later. I was due to meet Susan Wheatcroft at five o'clock. She was going to tell me what she'd discovered about Brandenburg J Bekker in the *Chronicle's* files.

I wondered whether I'd be able to take it all in. I bummed around town most of the afternoon in a daze. Shirley's idea about moving to London had taken me by surprise. I'd thought it might happen one day, but I felt I had unfinished business in Brighton. There were still stories here that I wanted to tell. Had wanted to tell, I should say, because the *Chronicle's* columns wouldn't be open to me now.

There was always the *Evening Argus*. But I didn't think Jim Houghton would take kindly to me straying onto his turf. So perhaps that only left the London papers. It would be a big step. Perhaps I had to take it. But first I had to crack the Bernstein story. Or was it the Winkle story? Or the Hardmann brothers? Or Mary-Lyn? Or Bekker? There were so many twists and turns in this I simply didn't know which would lead me to the truth.

But perhaps Susan had found some information that would throw new light on the story.

When I reached Prinny's Pleasure, Jeff was behind the bar.

He was foraging in his left ear with the wrong end of a teaspoon.

I said: "Have you ever thought that kind of activity might be one of the reasons you never have any customers?"

He said: "What kind of activity? And, anyway, I do have customers. You're in here."

You can't win against that kind of logic.

So I said: "Give me a gin and tonic. And make sure that spoon goes nowhere near it."

Jeff poured my drink and I took it to a table near the door.

Susan bustled in a couple of minutes later. She hurried over to my table. She looked hot and flustered, like she'd just had a steamy session in bed with Steve McQueen, her latest object of lust.

She sat down and said: "When you hear what I've got to tell you, you'll owe me a big one, honeybunch."

I said: "You can have any drink on me – double or treble."

Susan winked. "Who said anything about a drink?"

I grinned: "In that case, I may need to ask Shirley's permission."

Susan mock-pouted. "Why should she have all the fun? Anyway, I would like a noggin. Make it a pint of best beer."

I called over to Jeff to bring the drink.

Susan said: "You'll be surprised by what Henrietta and I turned up about your Bekker guy in the morgue."

She reached into her handbag and pulled out a bunch of yellowing press cuttings.

Jeff arrived with Susan's drink. He put the glass on the table and said: "I like a girl who can put away a pint."

She winked at him: "I can put away more than that, honeybunch. The question is: have you got it?"

Jeff blushed and retreated to the bar.

I smiled. "Don't embarrass the kiddies," I said. "Now, what have you got for me?"

Susan frowned a bit, compressed her lips, put on her serious face. "It wasn't easy, even with Henrietta's help. We looked under Bekker. Nothing. Then we tried Korn Krunchies. Zero.

We even tried breakfast cereals. Zilch. We were going to give up when Henrietta suggested that, as we were looking for a connection between Bekker and Max Miller, we should try under Miller. Apparently, if a cutting is filed under the name of a famous person, but other people are mentioned, it isn't always filed under their names as well."

"I believe Henrietta once mentioned that to me," I said. "It's because the other names are usually onlookers rather than news-makers in the event which the item covers."

Susan hoisted her glass and took a good long pull at it. Replaced the glass, wiped her lips with the back of her hand.

"You've got it, honeybunch. But Hen hit the jackpot."

Susan flourished a cutting from among the bunch she'd laid on the table.

"Look at this," she said.

I took the cutting and stared at it. It showed a photo of Max Miller sitting next to a sturdy young man in a US Marines uniform. There was a strip of medal ribbons on his tunic. The golden oak leaf on his epaulette showed he held the rank of major. The guy had the kind of face which once would have been strong with high cheeks and square jaw. But now it looked ravaged. As though he'd been through long hardship. Or some ordeal.

He was wearing dark glasses.

The caption below the picture explained why.

"Everybody's favourite comic Max Miller shares a joke with Major Brandenburg J Bekker, US Marines, during a visit to Woodland Grange, St Dunstan's, near Brighton. Major Bekker has received treatment at the hospital after losing his sight in the battle for Omaha Beach on D-Day. Max talked with the hero for half an hour during one of his regular morale-boosting tours of St Dunstan's. Major Bekker told the *Chronicle*: "St Dunstan's is just the best place ever – and Max the perfect tonic for a guy who's been through some tough times. They've given me more than I can ever repay."

I handed the cutting back to Susan.

I said: "So Miller and Bekker knew one another from the war."

"There's more," Susan said. She flourished a second cutting. "This one's about three months later."

She handed the cutting to me. It showed Bekker and Max Miller sitting at a table. The caption read: "War hero Brandenburg J Bekker and everyone's favourite Cheeky Chappie Max Miller entertain each other with some brain teasers. Major Bekker said: "Max and I love to test each other with riddles and puzzles. Max always wins. He's a real clever guy.""

I said: "It looks like they met regularly and became friends. I wonder whether those meetings continued after the war."

Susan cocked her head to one side while she considered that. "Could be," Susan said. "There were no more cuttings of Bekker and Max together. But I did get this."

She rummaged in her bundle of cuttings. She pulled out four pages cut from a glossy magazine.

She said: "So what did the poor blinded major do after the war? He went and launched the most popular breakfast cereal after cornflakes in America. Lot of other places, too."

She handed me the magazine pages.

I said: "These come from *Fortune* magazine."

"Yes. The American business monthly. I know a guy in the magazine's London bureau. I once did him a favour. He's what they call over the pond a real stand-up guy. Although he was lying down when I did the favour."

I grinned. "I won't pry into that."

"I called him and he biked the cutting down. One good turn deserves another, eh?"

I skimmed down the pages. It was a profile job of the man and his works. The story told how Bekker had returned penniless from the war – and blind. But he was determined not to let his blindness stand in the way of making a success of his life.

He had an uncle who was a farmer in Kansas. The uncle was complaining the US Department of Defense had cancelled its contract for corn now the war was over. He had tonnes of the stuff sitting in a silo. Bekker found a way to turn it into a breakfast cereal. News of the blind veteran hero spread in the papers – and Korn Krunchies became the number one breakfast for other veterans and their families. Within two years, Bekker was a millionaire. Within three, a multimillionaire. After ten years, he had so much boodle, he'd set up his own philanthropic foundation. It was rumoured the foundation had funded scores of projects to help the blind. Rumoured because Bekker was shy about his charity work and donations were often anonymous. Sometimes he made them through third parties.

I put the cutting on the table. "Did he make donations to St Dunstan's?" I asked.

Susan shrugged. "Don't know."

"Remember what he said about St Dunstan's in the *Chronicle* cutting: 'They've given me more than I can ever repay.' Perhaps he decided he wanted to repay. But if his donations were anonymous nobody would know, including St Dunstan's."

"Well, even if he did, they won't be getting any more."

"Why?" I asked.

"Because Bekker died two years ago."

Susan pulled a cutting from *The Times* out of the bunch. It was dated the fifth of May 1963. It recorded that Bekker had died the day before, the fourth of May.

Susan said: "After Bekker died, his company was bought by one of those faceless corporations. His foundation was dissolved last year. My stand-up lying-down guy told me."

Susan picked up her glass and drained the last half-pint in a couple of swallows.

I nodded at her empty glass. "Another?"

Susan giggled. "No, I'm meeting someone later. And I think he might need careful handling."

"Be gentle with him."

"Aren't I always, honeybunch?"

And with that, Susan gathered up her things and bustled out of the pub.

I idly swirled the lemon around in my gin and tonic while I thought about what Susan had discovered.

Fact one: Max Miller had met Brandenburg J Bekker. Theory: Miller and Bekker had developed a deeper friendship founded on their personal experiences of blindness. I recalled Cilla at the Last Laugh had told me that Max had been blinded for three days in the First World War. Fortunately, he recovered his sight. But the experience had seared him for life.

Fact two: Bekker was a rich man and gave money anonymously to charity, sometimes with the aid of other people. Theory: Bekker used Max to funnel money to St Dunstan's. Perhaps he'd sent money to Max to pass on anonymously to St Dunstan's shortly before he died. But wait a minute. There was something about the date of his death that was also important. It was just three days before Max had died on the seventh of May 1963.

Fact three: Max had a reputation for keeping money in safety deposit boxes. Theory: Bekker had given Max money to pass to St Dunstan's – but Max had died before he could do it. The money was still sitting in a deposit box.

Conclusion: Somehow Mary-Lyn Monroe had learnt about this and was on the trail of the cash. But was she the only one? Did the Hardmann brothers know about it as well? And what about the five comics? Evelyn Stamford had told me that Max dropped by the office to jaw with Bernstein over a bottle of whisky. Could Max have dropped a hint to Bernstein about his role as a conduit for donations? If he had, and the Hardmanns knew about the money as well as Mary-Lyn, Bernstein could have been the source of the leak. Perhaps Billy Dean learnt about it and passed the information to the Hardmanns.

It all made a kind of sense although I couldn't prove any of it. But it didn't explain why Bernstein had been murdered. And it didn't provide a reason for stealing Max Miller's Blue Book if the real target was the cash.

Just as important, it didn't provide the proof I needed to spring Sidney Pinker from the cells.

And it didn't give me the hard facts I needed to write the kind of story I could sell to a national newspaper for big money. Anything I wrote now would sound like a crazy conspiracy theory. If I wrote a story like that, I'd look like a charlatan rather than a serious reporter.

I drained the last of my gin. I couldn't think of any way to make my theories stand up. But Ernie Winkle had known Max Miller better than most people. Perhaps he'd heard something.

It might be hard to make him talk.

But not as hard as persuading Shirley to come on a second visit to the Last Laugh club.

Chapter 19

The lights outside the Last Laugh were out when Shirley and I pitched up, shortly after eight.

A seagull had splattered the display case with the picture of Ernie "Mind your manners" Winkle.

The place looked more like a funeral parlour than a palace of fun.

I tried the front door. It opened and we stepped into the foyer. The place was empty and felt cold. There was no-one behind the glass window of the ticket office.

Shirley gave a little shiver. "Jeez! Winkle should call this place the Last Hope," she said.

I'd had a tough time persuading Shirl to come. But I'd explained my theory about Bekker using Max Miller as a funnel for an anonymous donation to St Dunstan's. I'd said Ernie Winkle might know more and I hoped to force the truth out of him.

Shirl had just arched her eyebrows in disbelief.

"Let's try in the auditorium," I said.

We pushed through a pair of swing doors. The lights were on but no-one was at home. There wasn't going to be anyone to groan at Ernie's jokes.

Cilla was behind the bar. She'd sold us the tickets on our first visit.

She flipped the pages of an old *National Geographic* magazine.

She looked up as we approached the bar. "Didn't think I'd see either of you back here. Not after the barney and break-up you had last time."

"We made up outside," I said.

"With the aid of a fire extinguisher," Shirley added.

Cilla's face lit up with a grin. "You're not the pair who saw off those two Yankee hoodlums? Left the street knee deep in foam."

Shirley and I held hands and took a mock bow.

"We scarpered before any blue flashing lights appeared." I put on a Chicago gangster's accent. "Me and my moll split before the cops could put on the bracelets."

We ordered drinks and Cilla did the honours.

I said: "Is Winkle doing his act tonight?"

"If he does, I'm going back to the ticket office," Cilla said.

"Yeah! His jokes are about as funny as finding a cane toad in your dunny," Shirley said.

"Winkle was always weird but these last few days he's been stranger than ever," Cilla said.

"Strange? How?" I asked.

"He sits in his dressing room all day long. He thumbs through a dictionary. He bought a second-hand encyclopaedia from a bookshop. He's scribbling stuff on bits of paper then ripping them up and throwing them away."

"He's thinking up some new funnies," Shirley said.

"No. He's past that. It's as much as he can do to remember the old jokes."

I said: "Is he in his dressing room now?"

"I expect so," Cilla said. "Where else would he be?"

"Let's pay him a visit," I said to Shirley.

"You're not allowed back stage," Cilla said. "I'm supposed to stop you. But I guess I just didn't notice."

She reached for her magazine and turned a page.

We crossed the auditorium and stepped through the door next to the stage. The lighting guy who'd been there on my last visit wasn't around. Perhaps it was his night off. Or perhaps he'd quit.

We found Winkle in his room. He was sitting on a stool in front of his dressing table staring at himself in the mirror. He had a glass of scotch in front of him. Papers and books were scattered across the top of the table.

Winkle shifted his gaze as we stepped into the room and our

images were reflected in his mirror.

He swivelled wearily on the stool like a man who's too tired to be bothered about anything.

He said: "You were here before. I never forget a face. But in your case I'm prepared to make an exception."

"As Groucho Marx said," I added.

Winkle grunted. "Clever bastard, aren't you?"

"I try," I said.

Winkle spotted Shirley and brightened up. Switched on his cheesy grin. "Who's the doll?"

"Not one that's ever gonna climb into your pram," Shirley said.

"An old man can dream."

"Yeah! Keep it that way."

"Anyway, why are you here?" Winkle asked.

I idly picked up one of the books on the dressing table at random. It was *Brewer's Dictionary of Phrase and Fable*.

I flipped through the pages. The corners of lots of them had been turned down.

I said: "What do you need this book for?"

Winkle had a swig of his scotch. "What's it to you?"

I moved away from the dressing table and Winkle's gaze followed me. Shirley slipped behind him. Silently, she started to look through the books and papers.

I said to Winkle in a voice intended to get his full attention: "I just thought it might provide a clue about why you lied to me last time we met."

His piggy eyes watched me as I turned *Brewer's* pages.

"My whole frigging life has been a lie," Winkle said. "I promised myself I was going to be a top-of-the-bill comic and look what happened to me. I played second fiddle to Max Miller and ended up in this shithole."

"And then to add insult to injury, Danny Bernstein inherited Max's Blue Book instead of you."

"A travesty." Winkle took another pull at his scotch.

"And you fell out with Bernstein, never to speak to him again."

"I cheered when I heard he was dead. They could hear me as far away as Eastbourne."

"Except it's not true, is it?"

Winkle frowned and his eyes darkened. "What do you mean? It's a documented fact that Bernstein got the Blue Book."

"But it's a lie that you cut your contact with him. In the days before his death you met him here."

Winkle bristled. "Where did you get that idea?"

"From a witness who saw both of you together. And full of mutual bonhomie, I'm told. Not a cross word."

Behind Winkle, Shirl's hand slipped silently under a pile of loose papers.

"Why should I want to meet a man who'd cheated me?" Winkle whined.

"Because he needed your help. And if his plan came off, you'd never have any financial worries again."

Winkle had rouged his cheeks as part of his stage make-up. But the colour turned a pasty pink as the blood drained from his face.

Shirl's hand slipped out from under the papers.

It held a small blue notebook.

"Now that's what I'd call a Blue Book," she said.

Winkle spun round. He jumped up. Took three steps towards Shirley, but she put out her left arm and pushed him away. He staggered backwards and jostled against me.

I grabbed his shoulders to steady him. Then I forced him down on to his stool.

He sat hunched forward, grasping his hands together like he was praying for his last breath.

I said: "If this is what I think it is, you're facing a murder charge."

"It's not the original Blue Book. I promise. I bought that

notebook in W H Smith's. It was my little bit of revenge to get one that looked just like Max's. But open it. You'll see it's not Max's. It's all in my writing."

Shirl handed it to me. I opened it. I read it for a few seconds. I looked at Winkle: "You copied this from somewhere else."

Winkle said: "I copied it from the Blue Book that Bernstein found in the cigar box. Danny kept the original for himself."

I glanced at Shirley. "It's a message from Brandenburg J Bekker. One of the last he must have sent. Certainly the last to Max Miller."

I read:

Hi Max,

Guess you didn't expect me to visit your dear old Blighty again.

But there was something I had to do. I was gonna tell you, but I guess you were out of town when I was here – and I gotta fly back to the States for a big deal.

So here's what I wanted to say. I wanna give those great guys at St Dunstan's one million dollars. Yeah! You read aright – a big one. But I don't like a lotta fuss, so I want you to sneak the cash over the line for me.

You can do that, can't you? Of course, you can.

I've just had a thought. You remember those riddles we used to play on each other when you visited me while I was recovering in St Dunstan's. I seem to remember you were great at solving them – you took a buck or two off me in those days.

Well, it's more than a buck now. I've left a bearer bond for one million dollars – your bank manager will tell you what it is – in a safe place in Brighton. You solve the riddle and find it before the end of May and I'll double the money I'll donate to those great St Dunstan's guys. Yeah! I'll make it two big ones. If not, well I guess I'll have to spill the beans on where the bearer bond is, you old lame brain!! (Only joking!)

You'll find the clues below. Yeah! I thought them up myself. I'm not such a dullard. Can't be with $39 million smackaroos in the bank.

I know you're a busy guy and don't open letters in case they're from the revenue service. Me, too! That's why I got my confidential secretary to write all this in a Blue Book, just like the one you used on stage. Thought that would get your attention!! I know it's not the original, but we both know the little secret about that!

Well, that's all for now old friend. I guess we'll meet up for a beer next time I'm over the pond.

See ya!

Your old pal, Brandie.

I said: "Why did Bernstein show this to you? I thought you'd both fallen out."

Winkle shrugged. "And for a million dollars we'd fallen in again. Bernstein asked me to meet him at his office. It was supposed to be confidential but that assistant of his, Evelyn something or other, saw us. So we met here after that."

"What did Bernstein want with you after all these years?"

"He needed my help to understand what it all meant. He'd tried for months to solve the puzzle, but had to admit to himself that he'd never do it alone. He needed help. He realised I knew Max better than anyone else after all those years touring with him. I've been trying to figure out the riddle for days. But I'm no nearer to a solution."

Shirley said: "My old Pa used to tease me with riddles when I was a kid. 'The more you take, the more you leave behind. What am I?'."

"Footsteps," I said.

"You already knew the answer."

"I didn't. But let's not argue. This riddle is much more complex – and there's a million dollars for solving it."

"Read it," Shirley said.

I did:

My first is in value but not there in dearth
My second is first in words and in worth
My third is in under but not in above

My fourth is in front when it comes down to love
My fifth is the drink that we all like to pour
My whole is my hiding place within the store
When there think of Caesar, the Rubicon's hero
But remember in Rome there is never a zero
The first of four numbers you'll find there in Mary
And the rest, of course, follow right from the Dairy

I turned to Winkle. "What stopped you solving this?"

"Well, Bernstein and I got it that the answer in each of the first five lines is a letter – and the letters spell out where the money is. But we couldn't make it work. I mean, if you look at the first line…"

"*My first is in value but not there in dearth,*" I read.

Winkle nodded. "Well, there are three letters in the word 'value' but not in 'dearth', V, L and U. But when you get to the second line, the trouble starts."

"*My second is first in words and in worth,*" I read.

"Yeah! We figured the first letter in words and in worth is W. No argument about that. But that means the full word has to start either VW, LW or UW."

"And you couldn't think of any words that did that?"

"Nope. It didn't make any kind of sense. I guess we'd just hit the buffers, brain-wise. Now, you look a clever guy. Help me crack the riddle and we'll split that bearer bond. Seventy per cent to me, thirty to you. What do you say?"

He grinned at Shirley. "There might even be a little loose change left over for you, sexy pants."

Shirley said: "Watch your mouth, cheapskate. If we crack the riddle, we're keeping all the cash – for St Dunstan's."

"You've got to crack all of it first," Winkle said. "Besides a bearer bond belongs to anyone who has it. Bernstein checked it out. You got the bond, you get the cash. But you lose that bond – no matter how - and it's gone for ever. It can't be replaced."

"He's right," I said. "Bearer bonds are like a shadow in the world of high finance. They're there – and then they're gone."

"Yeah! But we ain't got the bond," Winkle said. "Bernstein and me couldn't even figure out what those last four lines were all about."

"They're more difficult," I said. "But with a bit of effort I think Shirley and I can solve the first part."

"I sure hope so," a familiar voice said behind me. "Because then I won't need to shoot this dame."

I spun round.

Mary-Lyn Monroe stepped into the room. She pushed Cilla in front of her. Cilla's hands were bound behind her back with a stout cord. And Mary-Lyn was pointing a neat little Luger – the ladies' gun of choice - at Cilla's head.

Gino and Willis moseyed into the room after them. They were carrying heavier pieces. And they had them pointed at Shirley and me.

I said: "I wondered when my long-lost cousin would turn up again."

Mary-Lyn smiled. Let her tongue flick lightly over her top lip while she thought about that.

She said: "Shut it. When I want you to say something, I'll kick your ass."

"A polite query is normally enough to get my attention."

Mary-Lyn sighed and turned to Winkle. "A broken-down old funny man like you wouldn't want an employee shot." She pushed Cilla towards Winkle.

Cilla sobbed: "Please, Ernie."

He looked at her with lizard eyes. "You're right. I wouldn't want an employee shot. Cilla, you're fired."

Cilla's eyes opened wide, like she couldn't understand what had just happened. Then tears welled up and ran down her cheeks. She struggled, but her hands were tied together too tight.

Shirley moved towards Winkle. "You dickhead – you've got

the grace of a brown-eyed mullet. I ought to kick you in the…"

Winkle clapped his knees tightly together.

Gino clicked off the safety catch on his Beretta.

Willis laughed: "That dame's got balls of fire."

Mary-Lyn screamed: "Cool it, sister. You're gonna get your tits in a wringer."

I shouted: "Shall we all calm down?"

They all looked at me like I'd just delivered the Gettysburg Address.

I said: "Let's all assess the balance of power in this room, shall we?"

Mary-Lyn said: "There ain't no balance of power here, smart-ass. Me and my boys got the guns in our right hands."

"Willis is holding his gun in his left hand."

Mary-Lyn shot him an angry glance. "Is that true, dumbo?"

"Yeah, boss. It just happens that way. I'm left-handed."

Mary-Lyn raised her eyebrows. "Jeez! I hire a tough guy and he comes with a defect."

I said: "You have the guns, but no matter how many bullets you fire, they won't solve the riddle. You need help for that."

Mary-Lyn had a mocking look in her eyes. "And where am I gonna find that, wisenheimer? As if I didn't know."

"Shirley and I will solve the riddle for you."

I glanced at Shirl. Her eyes popped and she shook her head.

"You're not getting any of the dough," Mary-Lyn said.

"That's my money," Winkle whined.

"Shut up," Gino said.

I said: "We'll do it in return for you telling us how you found out about the Blue Book."

Mary-Lyn grinned and turned to her tough guys. "Now he's negotiating. Like he's at the United Nations. Like he's a regular Dean Rusk."

She turned back to me: "Well, let me tell you, big shot, I call the plays around here."

"Have it your own way." I handed Mary-Lyn the Blue Book open at the page with the riddle.

Her brow folded into a cute little crinkle as she read the words. Her left eyelid drooped as her brain tried to make sense of it.

Then she handed the book to Gino. "What's that all about?"

Gino said: "It ain't Italian, boss. I can tell you that."

"I know that," Mary Lyn said testily.

She thrust the book at Willis. He looked at it with blank eyes.

"There ain't no pictures," he said.

"Of course, there ain't pictures, you moron. Who do you think wrote it – Walt Disney?"

I said: "How's the solution coming along, Mary-Lyn?"

She said: "Okay, big brain. What do you want to solve this crap?" She waved the Blue Book at me.

"I want to know how you found out about that book. It was private between Brandenburg J Bekker and Max Miller before Danny Bernstein accidentally came by the original. The one you're holding, by the way, is a copy."

Mary-Lyn turned to Gino and grinned. "Do you think the boy is old enough to know?"

"I reckon he might colour up when you tell him," Gino snickered.

"Don't tell me," I said. "Let me solve it, like the riddle. Bernstein met you when he visited Atlantic City."

Mary-Lyn nodded. "You're smart."

"Bernstein would have been frustrated after he'd spent a long day and failed to interest anyone in his string of tired music hall acts. We already know what he was like from the way he ran his agency. He'd look for some female company. But from what I've heard, there's not that much respectable female company to be had around the casinos of Atlantic City."

"So he turned to a tart," Shirley said.

Mary-Lyn scowled at Shirley. "Working girl."

"Prostitute."

"Lady of the night."

"Whore," Shirley said.

Mary-Lyn clicked the safety-catch off her Luger. She stared at Shirley like she wanted to plug all six shots into her.

She said: "For that, you're gonna work with your clever-dick boyfriend and solve the riddle. And then, to celebrate, I'm gonna shoot you."

Chapter 20

Shirley grabbed for me and I put my arms around her.

I hugged her tight. She buried her head on my shoulder.

"Shooting the messenger is a sure-fire way not to get any messages," I said. "What do you want – revenge or the money?"

Mary-Lyn held up her hands. "Okay, I get it. I guess if I get the money, I might can the payback."

I said: "It's getting hot in here."

Shirley released my hug and glanced at Winkle. "And it stinks like a dingo's do-do," she said.

Winkle fanned himself with a paper tissue. We all wrinkled our noses.

"Why don't we all move into the auditorium?" I said. "More room for everyone and we can have a drink while we solve the riddle."

"Yeah, and we can get up-wind of the funny guy," Gino said.

Mary-Lyn stepped forward. "Okay, we move but remember my boys will have their guns trained on your every step."

We shuffled towards the door.

I hung back so that Mary-Lyn went through first.

Shirley whispered: "Are you really going to help these dingbats loot that cash?"

I whispered to Shirley: "I'm playing for time."

Mary-Lyn swung round. "No whispering. What did you say?"

"I said, 'I'm committing a crime'."

Mary-Lyn laughed. "Consider it a career move."

We pushed through the door into the auditorium. Shirley and I chose two seats on a table at the side.

Mary-Lyn ordered her goons to untie Cilla so she could serve drinks. We all put in our orders.

Mary-Lyn sidled up to the table as I opened the Blue Book.

She said: "Right, Einstein, let's see if you really do know how many beans make five."

I said: "The opening line – *My first is in value but not there in dearth* – looks simple. Winkle and Bernstein worked it out for themselves. It could be one of three letters – V, L or U. But they didn't know which and they couldn't work out how to whittle the three letters down to the right one. They got even more confused when they thought the answer to the next line – *My second is first in words and in worth* – was W, the first letter in words and worth. But it's not. They missed a subtle clue."

Mary-Lyn pulled up a chair. "Amaze me."

"The clue mentions words, plural, not word, singular. If it were singular, the answer would be W, the first letter. But if it is words, plural, it can't be W because not all words begin with W. In fact, the letter that makes the first words in the dictionary is A."

"Same for worth," said Shirley.

Mary-Lyn looked doubtful.

"Anything that's really bonzer – that's worth something - gets an A grade. Get it, sister?" Shirley explained.

Gino and Willis had been at the bar with Cilla collecting the drinks. Now they crossed the room towards us. Cilla carried a tray while Gino and Willis covered her with their guns.

Mary-Lyn turned to her goons. "Hey, guys, we've got a real double act here – George Burns and Gracie Allen – 'cept the dame ain't as dumb as Gracie."

Cilla put the drinks on the table. I hoisted my glass and took a good pull at my gin and tonic. Shirley sipped her lager. Mary-Lyn wrinkled her nose at a vodka martini.

Winkle piped up: "Make sure you take the money for those drinks, Cilla."

She said: "Do it yourself, tightwad. You fired me."

Mary-Lyn licked her lips and sneered: "The drinks are on the house."

Willis gulped half a pint of beer and wiped his hand over his mouth. "Gee, thanks boss."

Mary-Lyn said: "Okay, refreshment time over. What's next?"

I said: "We now know the second letter is A. When we've discovered the third, fourth and fifth letters we can go back to the first and decide whether V, L or U start the word. But the next line – *My third is in under but not in above* – presents a similar problem to line one. Only one letter in under is also in above – E. Which leaves us with U, N, D and R. We'll come back to that when we have more letters."

"Not as smart as you think," Mary-Lyn said.

I grinned. "I get by. And the next line – *My fourth is in front when it comes down to love* - is easy to decipher. It's L, the letter that's at the front of the word love."

Shirley said: "*My fifth is a drink that we all like to pour* – and it isn't a vodka martini. It's tea. Get it – T!"

Mary-Lyn looked baffled.

I said: "So we're now certain about the second, fourth and fifth letters in the word. They're A, L and T. We just need to fill in the first and third from the choices we've got. And the answer is obvious – isn't it?"

I looked at them. Mary-Lyn's brow had buckled into a puzzled frown. Gino scratched his head. Willis stared at the ceiling. Winkle was trying to work out how much the drinks had cost him.

I said: "The word is Vault."

"Like that crazy game they play at the Olympic Games with a pole?" Gino said.

"No. As in a creepy place underground where you're likely to run into Count Dracula," Shirley said.

"Gee, that's the guy who needs to see a dentist real bad," Willis said.

Mary-Lyn held up a hand. "As in a bank vault. Where they keep the money."

"We can't break into no bank vault, boss." Willis said.

"We'll need Jelly Jonah to blow the door off," Gino said.

"He's in Brooklyn. I think," Mary-Lyn said. "Or he might still be in Sing Sing after he screwed up that Bank of America job."

"Yeah!" said Gino. "Big blooper. He blew the windows out of the Pentecostal church next door by mistake."

"And they were having a prayer meeting at the time," Willis added.

I stood up to stretch my legs. Strolled around the auditorium a bit while the rest of them chattered. It was taking up time which was just what I wanted.

"Where do you think you're going?" Mary-Lyn called after me.

"Just taking a breather," I said. "You're all miles from the truth."

"Spit out what you know, smarty pants."

"The vault we want isn't in a bank. It isn't even in a Pentecostal church." I had everyone's attention now. "The sixth line of the poem tells us where."

"My whole is my hiding place within the store," Mary-Lyn read. "What the holy crap does that mean?"

"It means the vault is in a store – a department store."

"Hannington's," Shirley helpfully added.

"You mean a joint like Macy's has got a vault?" Willis said.

"Why not?" I said. "Hannington's has a lot of wealthy customers. Some of them want to rent a deposit box to keep items they've bought in the store – jewellery, for instance. Others might just rent a box for their private use. I guess Brandenburg J Bekker was one of them."

"Okay, we'll do the rest at Hannington's," Mary-Lyn said.

"You mean we're gonna bust into the store now?" Gino asked.

"You think I'm gonna stand in line tomorrow morning with a load of broads looking for a new shade of lipstick?"

She pointed at Winkle and Cilla. "Tie them up and lock them

in that shithole of a dressing room. The cleaner can find them in the morning."

"We don't have a cleaner," Winkle wailed.

"Then you better get to know each other real well," Mary-Lyn said.

"*Ugh!*" Cilla said.

I winked at her. "I'll send a rescue squad," I whispered.

Mary-Lyn stood up and stomped around like a general giving orders.

"Move your asses," she said. "I've got a deposit box to bust into."

Gino and Willis motioned their guns at Shirley and me and we headed towards the door.

"What are we going to do now?" Shirley whispered.

"I guess that depends on Julius Caesar," I said.

Shirley rolled her eyes and shook her head.

Shirley and I were driven across town in the back of an old Bedford van.

It had once been painted white, but had turned grey. Its engine sounded like an old bear with a bad cough. And the inside smelt like it was used to transport dead badgers.

But it was everything Mary-Lyn needed – anonymous, private and easy to steal.

Gino drove while Mary-Lyn navigated from the passenger seat. Willis crouched in the back with his gun trained on us. He had his finger on the trigger. I hoped he had the safety catch on or he could loose off a shot when Gino swerved round a corner.

The clock on the Chapel Royal sounded two as we parked in East Street, fifty yards from Hannington's. As the engine died, Mary-Lyn and her hoodlums began an argument about how to break into the store.

The hoodlums wanted to bust through a door. Mary-Lyn preferred a subtle approach.

She said: "These places always have a night watchman. We'll need to put him out of action. He'll have an office near the back door."

"How do you know that, boss?" Willis asked.

"'Coz I've ripped off more stores than you can count on your fingers and toes. Don't do it now. Jeez! Why have I hired morons?"

"What's the plan?" Gino asked.

"I'll sidle up to the door, like I'm a street girl looking for some action. When I've got his attention on my outstanding assets, Willis will wing in from the side and sock him so he has a nice long sleep."

"What do I do?" Gino asked.

"You stay in the van and make sure these two don't lam out of there."

Mary-Lyn and Willis climbed out of the van and disappeared round the back of Hannington's.

The plan must have worked, because Willis was back in five minutes. Gino and Willis harried Shirley and me out of the van. They hustled us up a dark alley and through a back door into a large storeroom. It was lit by low-watt bulbs hanging from loose flex. The place was lined with metal shelves stacked with brown cardboard boxes.

To the right of the back door, there was a glass-walled office. It was furnished with a desk and a chair. There was a cup of coffee and a half-eaten sandwich on the desk. The door was open and I stuck my head in. The room was warm from an oil heater burning in the corner. This would be where the night watchman would hang out during the witching hours.

For the moment, he was in the storeroom with his hands and feet tied and a handkerchief gag around his mouth. He was propped up against a pile of boxes. He looked at us with dagger eyes. I'd put him straight later. I hoped.

In the meantime, I said: "Where's Mary-Lyn?"

Willis said: "She's looking for the safety deposit boxes. She's a real smart lady."

"If she's that smart, she can decode the rest of the riddle herself," I said. "We'll be on our way."

"Stay where you are." Mary-Lyn appeared from behind a stack of boxes. She had a shit-eating grin on her face, like she'd just been handed an Oscar and was lapping up the applause.

I said: "Don't tell me – you've found the safety deposit boxes."

She said: "I can sniff out anything."

Shirley said: "With a nose like that, I'm not surprised."

Mary-Lyn snapped: "Do you want a bullet in the fanny?"

Shirley said: "They don't all make as big a target as yours."

Mary-Lyn's eyes flared. She raised her Luger.

I said: "Fire that and you'll have the cops here within minutes."

Mary-Lyn shot Shirley a dirty look: "You'll end as pussy food," she said.

"Seems you already are," Shirl said.

Mary-Lyn knew she'd lost the verbal battle. She stomped off through the store room. The hoodlums hustled Shirl and me after her.

We clumped down some stairs and pushed through a strong steel door. We entered a dark windowless room.

Mary-Lyn threw a switch and long fluorescent tubes hanging from the ceiling flooded the place with light.

A bank of more than a hundred safety deposit boxes, stacked five deep, lined one side of the room. The other side had a set of cubicles where box owners could pore over the contents in privacy.

Willis gawped at the row of boxes and said: "Gee, boss, how long is it gonna take us to open this lot. I said we'd need Jelly Jonah."

"Shut up, dope," Mary-Lyn snapped. "We ain't opening them all. We're opening only one. The one with the bearer bond."

"Which one is it?" Gino asked.

Mary-Lyn waved her Luger carelessly at me. "This guy's gonna tell us. Unless he wants his mouthy girlfriend perforated like a five-cent stamp."

I said: "If I decode this, you let us go unharmed. Agreed?"

Mary-Lyn grinned. Like one of those spiders that eats its partner after mating. "Now he wants to do a deal," she said.

She walked over to me. Looked me in the face. I looked back. Her face was twice as tough as mine. But then in my job I didn't spend as much time lying on my back and looking at the ceiling.

"You put that bearer bond into my hand and you and miss slut-face walk out of here on both feet," she said.

"Spoken like a true con-woman," I said. "But we accept."

I shared a glance with Shirley. She raised an eyebrow and shrugged. It didn't seem like we had much choice. Shirl had had her fun with Mary-Lyn. But it looked like we were the losers.

Right now, we had to focus on walking out of this alive.

"So which of these boxes have we gotta bust into?" Mary-Lyn asked.

"Clever old Bekker gives us that clue in the seventh line of the poem," I said. *"When there think of Caesar, the Rubicon's hero."*

Willis piped up: "I got that one, boss. It's Caesar's Palace in Vegas. Won three hundred bucks there once."

I ignored him. "We're talking about Julius Caesar, the Roman bloke who shouldn't have gone out on the Ides of March. But years earlier, when he was a guy on the make – he faced a big choice. He could march on Rome with his legion and seize power. Or he could do what the senators back home had ordered. They wanted him to disband his victorious troops so he didn't pose a threat to them. Instead, he marched the legion to the very boundary of Italy – the river Rubicon. If he crossed that river with his legion, there was no turning back."

Mary-Lyn tapped her foot impatiently. "Jeez, what is this? A sophomores' history seminar? I want the frigging box number."

"The story tells us. Because Caesar crossed the Rubicon in

49BC. You want box 49."

Gino slid across the floor to the box like a lizard swimming in its own slime.

"This is the box, boss," he said. "But it's got one of those four-number locks on the front. We gotta get the combination."

Mary-Lyn rounded on me. "Well, what is it, big brain?"

"You've got to remember that this poem was written for an audience of one – Max Miller."

"You telling me that only this Miller guy could understand the whole poem?"

"That's what Bekker intended. It's like a private code. If only the sender and the receiver understand it, no-one else can crack the secret."

"Looks like you're walking outta here horizontal after all."

"If I were horizontal, I wouldn't be walking. But I think there might be a way to get the answer. Max had a song that he sang at almost all his shows. It was called *Mary from the Dairy*. The seventh line of the poem tells us the first digit in the code is in the word Mary."

I quoted from the Blue Book: "*The first of four numbers you'll find there in Mary.* And the final line provides the other three digits in the words *from the dairy*."

"That Bekker guy don't know 'rithmatic," Willis said. "There ain't no numbers in words."

"Aren't there?" I said. "Remember we've been asked already to think of Caesar. The Romans used letters to denote numbers – V stands for 5, X stands for 10, L stands for 50, for example."

"None of those get us anywhere in Mary," Gino said.

Mary-Lyn was quiet. But she was interested. She'd stopped tapping her foot on the floor.

I said: "The M in *Mary* stands for 1,000. Then in the words *from the dairy*, another M adds another 1,000, the D stands for 500 and the I stands for 1."

"So where does that get us?" Mary-Lyn asked.

"Suppose we add them all together," I said.

Willis put his gun on the floor and started counting on his fingers.

"Pick your piece up, clown." Mary-Lyn commanded. "Leave brain work to those of us with brains."

"So what's the answer?" I asked her.

"Er…"

"It's 2501," I said.

Gino moved to the deposit box. He twiddled the rotors on the number lock 2, 5, 0, 1. He heaved on the handle. The box rattled in its casing. Wouldn't shift.

I moved over and tried it. The thing was locked solid.

"Looks like you and your little tart will be leaving horizontal, after all," Mary-Lyn said.

She checked the bullets in the magazine. "Two each and three to spare," she said. "You're just about to go from hero to zero."

Hero to zero.

I clapped a hand against my forehead. "Of course! The sixth line of the poem. *But remember in Rome there is never a zero.* The Romans may have been great road builders and invented underfloor central heating, but they never came up with a character for zero. We need to exclude the zeros in the four numbers we've got."

I flipped the page on the Blue Book and scribbled the four numbers down – 1,000, 1,000, 500, 1. Then I crossed out all the zeros and looked at what was left – 1151.

I handed the Blue Book to Mary-Lyn. "That will open the box," I said.

Mary-Lyn spun the rotors, then pulled on the handle. The box opened with a gentle hiss.

She reached in and pulled out a single sheet of paper. Her brow wrinkled as she studied it. Her lips moved as she silently mouthed the words.

She looked up and grinned. "One million smackeroos. And

all mine," she said.

She turned to Willis, but pointed at me and Shirley. "Now shoot them," she said.

Chapter 21

"If there's any shooting to do, my brother will oblige," a familiar voice said.

We all spun round and gawped.

Terry and Tommy Hardmann loomed in the doorway. Terry Hardmann held a vicious looking pistol. It had a long barrel, like an anteater's nose.

Tommy Hardmann toted a machine gun. It was one of those old-fashioned ones with a circular magazine underneath the barrel. Edward G Robinson had one in that nineteen-thirties film *Little Caesar* I'd once seen on TV. It looked like a serious piece.

Or perhaps Terry had the machine gun and Tommy the pistol. After all, they were identical twins.

Either way, they outgunned Mary-Lyn's raggle-taggle army.

Mary-Lyn's eyes blazed with fury. She looked like she wanted to say something. But her hand holding the bearer bond whipped behind her back. She wouldn't be able to hide it from this pair for long.

The Hardmanns advanced further into the room.

I said: "Let me guess. You turned up at the Last Laugh after our party was over. You discovered Ernie Winkle and Cilla tied up in the dressing room. You persuaded them to tell you what had happened and where we'd gone. What I can't work out is how you found out about the bearer bond."

Tommy looked at Terry and giggled.

Terry said: "Shall we tell him?"

Tommy snickered: "I think we could answer, er... a gentleman?"

Terry chuckled: "Yes, a gentleman."

"And does this gentleman have a name?" I asked.

"Several," Terry giggled.

"But we're not telling," Tommy cackled.

The pair couldn't contain their merriment. At least, someone was having a good time.

"Oh, I get it," I said. And I did. "You both know Bruce the Boxer, the man who saw Bernstein visiting Winkle at the Last Laugh. No doubt you're regular visitors to Bruce's back room with the special magazines. He would've been keen to ingratiate himself with a couple of gangsters like you. After Bernstein was killed, Bruce told you about the visits. I expect the mystery has been nagging at your nasty minds for days. No doubt last night's ruckus at the Golden Kiss spurred you to put the squeeze on Winkle this evening. Pity Mary-Lyn got there first."

While I'd been delivering this speech, Mary-Lyn had edged closer to the deposit boxes. Gino slid forward, but Terry saw the movement and waved him back with the barrel of his gun.

Willis said: "Hey, boss, are these guys on our side?"

Mary-Lyn ignored that and said to Tommy: "What do you want?"

Terry said: "I want that bearer bond you're holding behind your back."

"We can negotiate," Mary-Lyn said.

"Okay," Terry said. "Here's my final offer. Give me the bond within ten seconds or I'll shoot you."

Mary-Lyn pouted her lips. Lowered her eyelids like she was a regular Mata Hari. She hitched up the hem of her skirt and thrust out her breasts.

She said: "Shoot me, honey, and you'll lose out on the fringe benefits."

Terry glanced at Tommy: "We could shoot her later."

Tommy said: "Don't fall for her tricks."

"Try mine, instead," Shirley said.

Tommy hadn't noticed Shirl had crept up beside him.

Shirl puckered up her lips and tossed back her blonde hair. She moved so close to Tommy he had to move his machine gun.

She said in a low husky voice: "I like a guy who fires more than blanks."

Tommy coloured up. He said: "Ain't you the bint we met at the club?" He glanced at Terry who was staring at Mary-Lyn. "Hey, perhaps we could have one each if we shoot these other guys. We could take the bond later."

Shirl ran her hand softly up the back of Tommy's head.

"I like a man who plans ahead," she said. She was right in front of Tommy now.

And then her right leg moved in a blur. There was a wet squelch as her knee connected with Tommy's crotch. And he buckled over.

His finger squeezed the machine gun's trigger and a volley of shots bounced off the floor and ricocheted around the room. And then something jammed and the magazine fell off. It clunked on the floor and rolled away.

We'd all dived for the floor as the gun's blast echoed. It sounded like a thousand pneumatic drills had hammered through the walls. The bullets singed off the boxes and dinged around the cubicles. And then one hit a fluorescent light. It shattered and glass rained down on the room.

I stuck my head up to see where Shirley was. She'd taken cover behind Tommy.

The other lights flickered. And then they died. The room was plunged into a blackness so dark it could've been the end of the universe. The place where all light ends.

And then the roar of the echoes faded as though they'd been drawn away to another world. A heavy silence descended on the room.

But the silence lasted only for seconds. Because Tommy moaned. Then there was a guttural choke in his throat - like slugs sliding down a slimy drainpipe. There was a plop and a squelch as Tommy's vomit hit the floor.

"*Yuk!*" Shirley said.

On the other side of the room, Willis said: "My leg hurts, Gino, I think one of those bullets hit me. Gino, are you there…?"

Gino didn't reply.

To my left, there was a rustling sound. Mary-Lyn was moving. I couldn't see anything, but I sensed she'd stood up and was moving across the room.

Terry still had his anteater pistol. I hoped she didn't bump into him. If that pistol went off in the dark, there was no knowing who it would hit.

I slithered along the floor and bumped up against the safety deposit boxes. I stood up and felt along the boxes until I came to the opened one.

I felt inside. There was a single sheet of paper in the bottom of the box. In the dark, I couldn't see what it was. But Mary-Lyn must have missed it when she grabbed the bearer bond. Silently, I slid it out of the box, folded it, and slipped it into my pocket.

Mary-Lyn still had the bond. I had to get it back.

At the far end of the room, the door opened. A pencil of yellow light filtered through the opening from outside. The silhouette of Mary-Lyn slipped through the door.

With a glimmer of light, I could see a moaning hump on the floor. Tommy. Shirl crouched behind him. Across the room, Willis sat and held his ankle. A short body lay near him. Gino. Perhaps he was dead, perhaps unconscious. My gaze flicked around the room.

No sign of Terry Hardmann. He must have slipped outside, too. Perhaps while I was searching for Shirley.

Terry would also be after Mary-Lyn. He'd want the bearer bond as badly as Shirley and I did.

I crept along by the deposit boxes and whispered to Shirley. "Are you okay?"

Her hand reached out for mine and we moved towards the door.

As we reached it a flatulent gurgle, like a blocked drain

had just overflowed, rumbled through the room. Tommy had thrown up again.

In the morning, Hannington's manager was going to need a very large bucket and a very large mop.

Shirley and I slipped through the door and found ourselves in the corridor.

At the end, we could see the stairs which led up to the storeroom on the ground floor.

For a moment, we stood and looked at one another. We were both breathing fast. Our faces were flushed. Our lips were compressed and our eyes were set hard. We both knew we had a job to do.

We had to recover the bearer bond.

I said: "The only way out is through the night watchman's door. Mary-Lyn will make for that."

"But what about Terry Hardmann?" Shirley asked.

"I didn't see him in the room, so he must've got out somehow."

"He couldn't have got out before Mary-Lyn left or we'd have seen light as the door opened."

"He must've slipped out immediately after. I was concentrated on finding you."

"We need to move like we're invisible," Shirley said. "I didn't like the look of that pistol Terry had."

"Me neither. But he's not after us – he wants the bond."

"That doesn't mean he won't plug us. Have you seen the way he looks at people? It's like he's trying to melt them with a death ray."

"Perhaps you should stay here," I said. "Keep an eye on Willis. Help Tommy to find his balls – if he still has any."

"Forget it, you crazy bastard. I'm coming with you."

We slipped silently down the corridor and slunk up the stairs like a pair of ghosts.

We arrived back in the storeroom. The lights were still low

and the place was silent. We crept behind a pile of boxes and listened. We strained our ears. Nothing.

"What would Mary-Lyn do?" Shirley whispered.

I put my mouth to her ear. "She'd know the only way out was through the night watchman's door. The shop's front doors are all tightly locked and she couldn't break through them. They open onto the street. Even at this time of night, there'll be people about."

"So she'll head for the watchman's door."

"But Terry knows she has to do that. Remember, he came in that way. If he was close behind her, she might not have had time to make it to the door. If I were Terry, I'd stand sentry-go on the door and wait for her to appear. She's got to get out before the store opens in the morning and staff find the chaos in the vault."

"Perhaps she's hiding in the hope that Terry will come looking for her. Then she could give him the slip and make it to the back door."

"I think we should look for Mary-Lyn in the store. Remember she still has the bond and we don't want it to fall into Terry's hands."

At the far end of the storeroom, there was a set of double doors. We ran on tip-toe towards them and pushed silently through.

We were in the crockery department. The place was illuminated by low nightlights. There were shelves loaded with cups and saucers. There were willow pattern plates to hang on the wall. There were thick white plates for a wife to sling at her old man if he complained about his dinner. There were soup tureens as round as Buddha's belly. There were bulbous teapots and slim elegant coffee pots. There was a little brown jug which reminded me of the song.

But there was no sign of Mary-Lyn.

We crept forward and the air became heavy with musk as we

reached the perfume department.

Shirley pointed at a big square bottle. "That Chanel No 5 is great," she said.

"Would you really buy a perfume from someone who couldn't get it right the first four times around?" I said.

"*Ssssh!*" Shirley said.

We headed towards ladies' fashions. We crept behind a rail holding party dresses for the Christmas season. There was a red one in taffeta, a blue one with frilly lace, and a green one in some kind of heavy velvet material. I had no idea what they'd look like on a partygoer, but they made great cover.

I poked my head above the rail and peeked around the store.

"Can you see anything?" Shirley whispered.

"Mary-Lyn's not over by the jumpers and cardigans. Not enough room to hide."

I turned my head slowly and surveyed the department. Nothing moved among the tweed skirts. All was silent on the slacks and trousers front.

And then there was the tiniest twitch. Behind the winter coats. The hanger holding a thick brown number with a fake fur collar slid ever so slowly half an inch to one side.

It would have been the perfect cover if Mary-Lyn hadn't moved the coat to get a better view.

She'd have heard us come in. She wasn't sure where we were. But now we knew where she was.

I ducked down behind the Christmas dresses and signalled to Shirley where Mary-Lyn was hiding.

Shirley whispered: "Has she got her gun?"

"No. She dropped it when Tommy's machine gun fired. We need to trap her so we can grab the bearer bond without damaging it. You creep round to the right and hide behind those blouses. I'll sneak left and crouch behind the hats and scarves. When we're ready, I'll signal like this." I stuck two fingers in my mouth a showed how I would blow a whistle. "Then we charge in."

"The noise will attract Terry," Shirley said.

"Sure. But we'll leave Mary-Lyn scrabbling on the floor. It'll take a few minutes for Terry to confirm she's lost the bond. We'll scarper up the stairs to the next floor. Terry will expect us to go down. But we'll find the backstairs and make it to the back door into the alley."

"Jeez! It sounds risky," Shirley said.

"Can't go wrong," I said.

"As General Custer said when he pitched up at the Little Bighorn."

But she leaned forward and gave me a kiss that had me wishing we could head to the bedding department for a lie down.

We unlocked our embrace and crept silently in opposite directions.

I crawled past a row of skirts. There was a thin carpet on the floor that was rough to touch. Worse, it made a low sibilant hiss every time I moved my knees. There was nothing I could do about that.

I reached the hats and scarves. They were arranged on a stand. I crouched down behind it. Looked cautiously around the edge and saw one of the blouses shake ever so slightly.

Shirley was in position.

I put my fingers in my mouth and blew. The whistle pierced the air.

Shirley and I arose from our hiding places like a pair of devils who'd leapt from the underworld. We charged towards the winter coats.

But I'd not taken more than five steps before a stand of bras and panties to my left toppled over and Mary-Lyn galloped towards the storeroom. She must've heard us move and changed her position.

She flicked a contemptuous glance in my direction. She

shoved rails of skirts and jackets aside as she raced towards the door.

"After her," I yelled at Shirley.

But Shirl was already pounding towards me. Mary-Lyn reached the door to the storeroom and barrelled through it.

Shirley and I reached it two seconds later and shoved the door open. We raced through and came to an abrupt halt.

We couldn't see Mary-Lyn anywhere.

But we could see Terry Hardmann.

He was standing in front of us. He had the anteater gun in his hand.

And it was pointed right at us.

It didn't look so funny now.

Terry's eyes were dark, like little chips of coal. His nose had wrinkled and his lips had curled into a snarl.

He looked at Shirley like he wanted to dismember her limb by glorious limb.

He said: "You hurt my twin brother. He's vomited up his dinner. Course by course. In reverse order. First the cheese and biscuits. Then the apple crumble and custard. Then the pork chop with apple sauce and broccoli."

Shirley said: "Don't tell me. He's waiting for the French onion soup to reappear before he complains to the chef."

Terry said: "My brother and I do everything together."

Shirley said: "Fair enough, whacker. Step forward and I'll kick you in the balls. Stand by for the gastronomic novelty of a four-course meal in reverse."

Terry clicked off the safety catch on his gun.

He said: "I want to shoot you. But I want something even more. I want to kill you slowly so that I get all the pleasure from it."

I said: "You're mad. But you're sane enough to know you came here to pick up a million-dollar bearer bond, not to hurt us."

"Who says I can't have both?"

"You have to find Mary-Lyn first. She has the bond," I said.

"I'll find her."

I gestured at the piles of boxes. "You'll never do it. While you're looking behind one pile, she'll bound out from behind another and slip out of the door. You'll still be chuntering about what Tommy's going to bring up next. Perhaps teatime's cucumber sandwiches."

"I don't have to search for Mary-Lyn myself."

I made an ostentatious show of looking around. "I don't see anyone to help you. You can't rely on Tommy. He'll spend the next week searching for what's left of his balls."

Terry grinned in a way that showed a full set of his top teeth. It was the kind of grin you'd use if you wanted to advertise poisoned toothpaste.

He reached into his pocket and pulled out a white mouse. "Meet Michelmore," he said. He cradled the wee beastie in his hand. He kept the gun in his other hand trained on us.

I'd never seen anything like this before. "Do you usually walk around with a mouse in your pocket?" I asked.

"Michelmore helps me with girls. Girls don't like mice. They hate Michelmore 'coz I've trained him to run up their legs. It was fun training him. Not for the girl with the leg, of course."

"You're a sick bastard," Shirley said.

"I'm a man who likes girls to do what he says. A girl will do anything to stop Michelmore running around her room. Or her bed."

He put the mouse on the floor. It did a couple of circuits of Terry's feet as a warm-up routine. Old Robbie Burns might have found the beastie tim'rous. To me, Michelmore looked like a little bundle of trouble with a long tail.

"Go find the naughty lady," Terry said.

Michelmore raced off among the boxes. We heard its feet scurry as they scratched the floor.

And then there was a scream. A pile of boxes toppled over. Mary-Lyn sprang from behind them.

"*Yeeeeouw.*"

Her shriek cut through the storeroom's air.

She raced towards the night watchman's room. She moved like an Olympic sprinter. Which was impressive as Olympic sprinters don't race in a figure-hugging skirt, stockings, suspenders, and four-inch stilettos. Although who knows what they do in private?

Mary-Lee reached the office three yards ahead of Michelmore. But he slipped through the crack as she slammed the door.

Terry turned and rushed towards the office. We followed.

Inside the office, Mary-Lyn shrieked again.

"*Yeeeeouw!*"

She jumped on the chair. She clasped the bearer bond to her chest.

Michelmore circled the chair. He was looking for the best chair leg to climb.

Terry pushed open the office door. He yelled: "Give me that bond and Michelmore comes back to me."

"No," screamed Mary-Lyn. "You'll have to take it from me – dead or alive."

I pushed forward to reach Terry. I wanted to pull him back. To break his neck. To stamp on his foot. To do anything that would stop this.

Shirley shouted: "Stop the bastard."

"I'm trying."

But Terry raised the gun before I could reach him.

He fired once. Mary-Lyn's eyes popped in surprise. Then blood welled in her chest. Her eyes disappeared into the top of her sockets.

And she tumbled from the chair.

She hit the oil heater which toppled sideways.

Pooooooouuuf!

We felt a blast of heat as the thing exploded into flame.

Mary-Lyn was dead on the floor as the fire licked around her body.

But she had dropped the bearer bond as she fell.

It floated on a wave of hot air that rose from the burning oil.

Terry pushed forward but the heat was too intense. He reached out as the bond drifted towards him.

But then the tank in the oil heater exploded. It forced him back.

The bond floated like a feather.

But now it was on fire.

Little blue flames flickered along its edge. The paper wrinkled and began to curl. Black blotches bloomed like ink blots.

And then the bearer bond flared into a fireball.

Within seconds a million dollars had turned into ash.

It drifted like a lazy autumn leaf to the floor.

Terry turned on us. A dark fury burnt in his eyes.

"You have spoiled my evening," he said. But he made it sound like we'd ruined his life. Perhaps we had.

He raised the gun. "I'm going to kill both of you," he said. "Which of you wishes to die first?"

"Me," Shirley and I answered together.

So this was how it was going to end. Dead in a burning storeroom. *Gotterdammerung* with a box of brassieres (C-cup) stacked nearby.

And a trained mouse.

Shirley and I held each other tight while Terry took aim.

Shirley whispered in my ear. "I love you."

I started to say…

A gunshot filled the storeroom with a roar so physical I felt it could crush me.

But I was still alive. The bastard had killed Shirley first.

I turned to kiss her for the last time ever. The last time before her body went limp in my arms.

But her body wasn't limp. And as I turned to kiss her, she turned to kiss me.

Together, we looked at Terry. A carnation of red blood bloomed on his chest. His eyes were blank. His jaw had dropped open. And he swayed on his feet like a Saturday night drunk. Michelmore had climbed onto his shoulder.

Terry's arm dropped to his side. His fist went limp. The anteater gun clattered to the floor.

Then his legs folded under him. His body hit the ground. A gout of blood pumped from his chest. His neck twitched, like the whole process had been an irritant he'd rather forget.

And then he lay still.

Michelmore scampered away into the depths of the storeroom.

Shirley and I held one another. We were both shaking. We couldn't understand what had happened.

We turned our heads. Darragh Mahoney stepped towards us. He'd lost his red hair and his beard. The smock and the trousers tied with string had gone. He had a crew cut and a clean-shaven square-jawed chin. He was dressed in a smart grey suit, white shirt and preppy tie. He was replacing a small gun in a shoulder holster.

He pointed to the back door that was wide open.

He said: "Sure as they say in Dublin's fair city, never bolt your door with a boiled carrot."

Chapter 22

"But it's not a fine thing the watchman's den is on fire," I yelled.

Mahoney and I grabbed fire extinguishers from the wall, pulled out the pins, and poured foam onto the flames.

By the time the last of them had died, we could hear sirens in the distance.

The cops swarmed in seconds later. They'd been alerted by a passer-by in the street who'd heard gunshots. They found three dead – Mary-Lyn, Terry Hardmann and Gino.

Willis was whisked under police guard to the Royal Sussex Hospital with a broken ankle. Tommy Hardmann was taken to the police cells. They had to carry him as he still couldn't uncross his legs. By now, he was probably throwing up last Tuesday's breakfast. I hoped it wasn't Korn Krunchies.

We'd untied the night watchman. He was furious about the wreck of his den. Apparently, he'd had two ounces of Ship's Shag tobacco in there. He'd looked forward to smoking it.

Now, two hours later, Shirley and I were sitting in an interview room at Brighton police station. Darragh Mahoney sat opposite us.

Except that he wasn't Darragh Mahoney. He flipped open a leather folder to reveal a metal badge in the shape of a shield topped by an eagle. The folder identified the holder as Devlin O'Rourke, a special agent of the United States Federal Bureau of Investigation.

I said: "What's an FBI special agent doing in Brighton?"

Shirley looked more impressed than I cared for. "Is it true what they say about that J Edgar Hoover?" she asked.

O'Rourke smiled. "One question at a time. I'll tell you as much as I can – after tonight's shenanigans, it's gonna come out anyway – on one condition."

"What's that?" I asked.

"You don't identify me. I have to work undercover. Name me and I'm finished in that line of work. And I love it."

I nodded. "Agreed."

O'Rourke grinned. He slipped back into his Mahoney character. "You're a fine upstanding Englishman, to be sure."

He turned to Shirley. "And as for Hoover, it's true about the women's clothing – but not the crotchless knickers."

"Yikes," Shirl said. "That's wild."

"Can we keep to the point?" I said.

O'Rourke settled back in his chair and looked more serious. "Since the nineteen-twenties, the Bureau has battled organised crime. We've closed down some big-time racketeers in our time. But they're like weeds. You pull some out and others sprout. That's bad enough, but they sprout in a different strain. Your typical mobster used to confine himself to a single city. He'd run illegal gaming joints, perhaps push some drugs, pimp a string of prostitutes. Very lucrative. But then some got greedy. Being a big shot in one city wasn't enough for them. They had to go state-wide. And now the sharpest are thinking even bigger."

"They want to go international?" I asked.

"You got it. They see General Motors and Coca Cola everywhere and think: why ain't we gotta slice of that action? But there's a problem. If you're in let's say Atlantic City, all you know is New Jersey. You want to run your rackets in Brighton, England you don't know anyone in town."

"So you have to look for partners," I said.

O'Rourke gave me a thumbs up. "Sure. Now there's a mobster in Atlantic City called Vittorio Mirandola. He's vicious but he's smart. We believe he's offed at least fourteen people, including three rivals who tried to muscle into his patch. But we've never been able to nail him. Mirandola has a wife, seven children and three mistresses. But what he really craves is respect. Not from decent people like us. No, from rival hoodlums, the kind of guys who're snapping at his heels. He reckons he wins that respect by

showing he's got the cojones to take his business worldwide –
just like General Motors."

"But why Brighton?" I asked.

"Sure," said Shirley. "London is the obvious choice if you
want to run rackets."

"You might think so," O'Rourke said. "But the competition is
tougher. And if you're the new boy on the block, you don't want
to start with a knock-back. That's not the way to win respect."

"So the Hardmann brothers in Brighton fitted the bill as
partners," I said.

O'Rourke nodded. "A deal between mobsters starts off like a
deal between legit businesses. If both have something the other
one wants, it makes sense to work together. And Mirandola
wanted in to Britain."

"What did the Hardmann brothers want?" I asked.

"Guns."

"We've already seen a couple of those," Shirl said with a
shudder.

"Yes, I saw the cops here bringing them in earlier. Antique
pieces, but deadly. Mirandola wouldn't have started with
his best merchandise. He'd want to see if he could trust the
Hardmanns before he rolled out the ace gear."

"What did Mirandola want from the Hardmanns?" I asked.

"The chance to take part in their rackets. He wanted to lord it
around New Jersey that he was the guy with the connections. The
guy to see when you wanted some action across the water. But
then it all got leery. You see, Mary-Lyn worked for Mirandola.
I might say worked her ass off. She was top-of-the-range pussy
– rented out for five hundred bucks a night. This guy Bernstein
fancied some tail." He nodded at me. "You know how it is – guy
in a strange town, time on his hands."

Shirl nudged me in the ribs. "He'd better not know how it is."

"I'm a one-girl guy," I said.

"Sorry, miss," O'Rourke said. "Anyway, it seems that there

was some pillow-talk. Bernstein wants to impress the girl. Show he's not some out-of-town schmuck. He's a big-timer. And suddenly Mary-Lyn knows about the bearer bond and the million dollars. She wants a better job in Mirandola's outfit. Something that doesn't involve lying on her back. A standing up job. So she takes a grift to Mirandola. She'll blow into Brighton and reacquaint herself with Bernstein. She'll work him as only a professional girl can and get the low-down on the million bucks. Then she'll croak the guy and make it back home in triumph."

"And Mirandola went for that?" I asked.

"Sure. He thought it was a gas. He makes a million bucks, less what he pays to Mary-Lyn – unless he offs her after the job to save himself a bill."

"Except by the time Mary-Lyn reached Brighton with her goons, Bernstein was already dead. So she had to work out how to find the bearer bond without his help – not that he'd have given it."

"Her goons would have persuaded him," O'Rourke said. "But even with Bernstein dead, Mary-Lyn thought she could scoop the cash and win her spurs with Mirandola. Trouble is, of course, if the Hardmanns find out they're being screwed, then we got a mobsters' fight on our hands. Welcome to World War Three. And that 'special relationship' your Harold Wilson talks about between our two great nations gets flushed down the toilet. So the Bureau sent me to Brighton to stop the scam. Got the thumbs up from a big cheese in some hush-hush government department in London to work undercover."

"But why the Irish act in the sewer?"

"I gotta keep out of the way. A Yank in this town would stand out like a buffalo on the beach. Besides, it seems the cops have raided the Hardmanns' joint three times looking for guns. Came up nix. I reckoned they were hiding them in the sewers – easy access from that hatch in their backyard. You found that. And they'd been using the tunnels to get around town unnoticed.

Did tonight. That's how I knew they were coming this way. Anyway, some big wheel in London had a word with the sewer guys down here and told them I was a mad Irish professor doing research on underground insects. Guess you saw the 'roaches."

"Nearly came a gutser with them," Shirley said.

I said: "We have to thank you for saving our lives tonight."

"Yeah!" Shirley said. "You're a bonzer guy, even if you are a bit mad."

"So I guess that wraps it up," O'Rourke said. "Leave the clearing up to the local cops."

"I have one more question," I said. "Did you find out anything about who killed Bernstein?"

"Can't help you there," O'Rourke said. "But I don't think it was the Hardmanns. I'd been riding them pretty hard and I think I'd know if they'd offed Bernstein."

He stood up, a sign our meeting was over.

"I guess you'll have to solve that one yourself," he said.

I was awoken the following morning at half past six by someone hammering on my bedroom door.

The Widow called out: "Are you awake, Mr Crampton?"

"No."

"This is important."

"So is my sleep. I didn't get to bed until four."

"Have you got any girls in there?"

"The Dagenham Girl Pipers. Would you like me to get them to play Scotland the Brave?"

"Not now."

"Then why are you hammering on my door?"

"Because there's a man here to see you."

"What about?"

"He didn't say."

"What's his name?"

"I forgot to ask."

"What does he look like?"

"I couldn't see very well. He was smoking this smelly cigarette and blew smoke in my eyes."

Figgis.

"I'll take it from here, Mrs Gribble."

I heard the Widow's footsteps as she clumped down the stairs. I levered myself out of bed.

Figgis didn't normally make house calls at six-thirty in the morning.

But I already had a good idea what this one would be about.

Fifteen minutes later I'd showered and dressed and opened the front door.

Figgis was standing on the doorstep. His hair looked thinner than usual. There were black circles under his eyes. His nose was red. He had the stub of a Woodbine stuck to his bottom lip.

I said: "What are you doing out here?"

Figgis peeled the fag-end off his lip and flicked it into the gutter.

He said: "The old witch wouldn't let me in. Had the temerity to suggest I smelt like I'd spent the night asleep in a blast furnace. She can talk. As soon as she opened the door, I got a whiff like she'd stuffed a box of moth balls up her arse."

I said: "Come into the hall. I'll take responsibility. Perhaps your rival aromas will cancel each other's out."

Figgis pulled his grumpy face, but stepped inside.

I said: "What do you want?"

Figgis looked at the hat stand, then at the fading print of Holman Hunt's *Light of the World* on the wall. Evidently didn't find inspiration from either of them so he studied his feet.

I said: "Out with it."

"Well, it's like this. You know I've got a generous nature and I don't like to see an old friend make a fool of himself."

"I didn't realise you had a friend."

"I'm talking about you," Figgis said testily.

"I see. I didn't realise I'd entered your pantheon of old friends."

"I've always had a high regard for you," Figgis said.

"Well, thank you for coming round to tell me. But did you have to make it so early?"

"There's a reason." Figgis cleared his throat. "If you'd like to withdraw your resignation, I'll generously overlook the difficulty you've caused the paper and reinstate you at your old salary."

At the far end of the hall, the telephone rang. The Widow barged out of the kitchen, glared at us, and answered it.

I turned my attention back to Figgis and said: "No doubt that's very generous of you. But, if you remember, I resigned because the paper refused to let me pursue the story to free Sidney Pinker."

"We might be willing to think again about that."

"Willing?"

"All right, we have thought again. Pope's changed his mind."

"When did this happen?

"About half past four this morning when the duty reporter called him and told him it looked like the *Evening Argus* was going to scoop us on the Hannington's story."

The Widow bustled up the hall.

She said: "Do you mind if I interrupt?"

"Yes," Figgis said.

"No," I said.

"There's a Mr Albert Petrie on the telephone for you, Mr Crampton." She turned to Figgis. "And I thought I told you to wait outside."

Figgis ignored that and said: "Petrie is the news editor of the *Daily Mirror*. What's he want?"

I said: "An exclusive, I expect."

I walked up the hall, picked up the receiver and said: "Colin

Crampton."

I spent three minutes on the phone, sometimes listening, sometimes talking. All the time watching Figgis' reaction at the end of the hall.

Finally, I put down the phone and re-joined Figgis.

"Well?" he asked.

"Albert Petrie has offered me one thousand five hundred pounds for an exclusive about the Hannington's caper. That's almost half what you pay me in a year."

Figgis said: "I'll raise your salary five hundred pounds if you come back today."

"Make it a thousand," I said.

"I can't do that."

"Yes, you can," I said. "Because I bet Pope has told you he'll fire you if you don't get me back on the paper."

Figgis frowned. I'd never seen him so put out. "How come you know so much?"

"It's obvious, isn't it? The biggest crime story for months and the *Chronicle* hasn't got a crime reporter. It'll have to rely on agency copy while Jim Houghton on the *Argus* uses all his many contacts in the cops to deliver a sensational piece. The *Chronicle* and *Argus* normally sell about the same number of copies each day. But today the *Argus* will sell twice what the *Chronicle* shifts."

Figgis fidgeted irritably. He stuck out a leathery hand. "Very well, a thousand more – as long as you're at your desk in the *Chronicle* in half an hour."

I took the hand and shook. "Good to be back," I said.

Figgis grunted as he stomped out of the front door.

The Widow emerged from the kitchen. She hurried up the hall.

"Did I do it right, Mr Crampton? I called the hall phone from the extension in the kitchen, then came through to answer it in the hall as though it was an outside call."

I grinned. "Yes, you were very convincing when you said Albert Petrie was on the line. Even I believed you – and I'd told you to say it when we planned this little trick last night."

"How did you know Mr Figgis would come round?"

"He had to. It was the only way he was going to get a scoop into the paper."

"Did you get your job back?"

"Yes, I start in half an hour."

"At a big salary increase?" the Widow asked.

"Afraid not," I said.

There was no point telling the Widow I was a thousand quid a year richer. She'd only want to put up my rent.

I met Shirley for a celebration lunch after the busiest morning I'd ever had at the paper.

I'd hammered out a front-page lead which appeared under the headline THREE DEAD IN FAILED STORE HEIST.

I'd written another piece on page two with the headline: HOW THE CHRONICLE FOILED A $1M STING.

I'd added a story for page three with the headline: HANNINGTON'S BLAZE DRAMA.

I handed Shirley a copy of the midday edition. She read the first few paragraphs on the front page.

She said: "They're great stories but I can't believe we were really there."

I said: "I should never have led you into something so dangerous."

Shirley grinned: "Try and stop me, whacker."

We were in English's seafood restaurant feasting on lobster Thermidor and champagne. Figgis would find the bill on my expenses at the end of the week. Shirley and I deserved a bonus.

I forked up some lobster and said: "Despite what happened last night, there's still unfinished business."

"Your guy Sidney Pinker, you mean?"

"Yes, he's still in jail. I called Ted Wilson this morning. He told me the cops don't have any evidence that the Hardmann brothers or Mary-Lyn and her goons were behind Bernstein's killing."

"So that still leaves Sidney holding the can?"

"He was holding the sword. And it was sticking in Bernstein at the time. That's the problem."

"So who do you think did it?"

I shrugged. "It could be the mystery man. But no-one has been able to identify him. Or it could be any of the five comedians. None of them have an alibi. Or it could be more than one person – if the cops are right about it being a two-person job. Trouble is, by tomorrow the comics could be anywhere. The Laugh-a-thon takes place this evening. Ted told me they're having a dress rehearsal at the Last Laugh club this afternoon."

Shirley finished her lobster. She picked up her glass and sipped some champagne.

She said: "How do they judge a Laugh-a-thon. Do the comedians stand there telling jokes until there's only one man standing?"

"One of them is a woman," I said and lifted my champagne glass.

"Woman or man – what difference does it make?" Shirley said.

I sat there with my champagne poised half way to my lips.

Woman or man?

Of course it made a difference.

I gawped at the glass like it was the looking-glass in Alice's adventure and I could see a different world on the other side.

And as in *Through the Looking-Glass*, I stared at a world in which logic was reversed. In which people could arrive before they appeared. Where they could make time run backwards. It was a world where people could wear clothes they didn't have. And walk through doors that were always bolted.

I put down my glass.

I just stared like I was looking through a peephole into the past. Random images flashed in my mind. I saw Danny Bernstein arrive at his office. I saw a cigar box lying on the ground. The scene cut to a sword dripping with blood.

I should have worked this out before. All the clues had been there.

Shirley looked hard at me. She could see I was lost in my thoughts. "You know, don't you?" she said.

I nodded. "Yes."

"Will it save Sidney?"

"I think he'll have the last laugh, after all. But I'm going to need Ted Wilson's help. And I've got to bust in on the Laugh-a-thon rehearsal."

"Go now," Shirley said. "We'll catch up later."

I leant across the table and kissed Shirley. Then I hurried from the restaurant.

Chapter 23

The rehearsal for the Laugh-a-thon had started by the time I reached the Last Laugh club.

There was no sign of Ted Wilson, but he had other work to do before he joined the fun.

I walked into the auditorium. Billy Dean and Jessie O'Mara were leaning on the bar. Teddy Hooper had slumped on a chair at the back with Percival Plonker on his knee. The pair were arguing with one another.

Evelyn Stamford sat at a table covered in papers in the middle of the auditorium. She was making notes on the different acts.

Peter Kitchen was on stage trying out his material.

"As I was saying, the trouble with political jokes is that too many of them get elected. I mean, take Harold Wilson for example. He's always got that pipe stuck in his mouth. He thinks if he makes enough smoke people won't be able to see what he's doing. I think if Harold Wilson is the best a general election can produce, we should abolish democracy. Everyone in favour raise their hands. Yeah! I didn't think that would get much of a response. I was going to be apathetic, too – but I couldn't be bothered. Anyway, let's take a tough line on repeat offenders. Don't re-elect them. Never mind, things aren't as bad as you think. They're worse..."

I left him to it and made my way backstage.

Ernie Winkle was in his room. He held a glass with two fingers of whisky. Actually, it looked more like the whole fist. He took a good pull at the whisky and let out a contended sigh.

He glowered at me as I stepped into the room.

I said: "I guess being trussed up like the Christmas turkey makes a guy thirsty."

Winkle gulped the rest of the whisky. "Yeah! I was ecstatic about that. Two hours before the fuzz turned up to untie me."

"How's Cilla?"

"How should I know? After the cops had got the ropes off us, she slapped my face, raided the till behind the bar for her back wages, and cleared off."

Inwardly, I gave a little cheer. Cilla struck me as the kind of girl who'd cut herself a determined path in life. She was too good for Winkle's deadbeat club.

I said: "At least you had a tale to tell your fellow comics today."

"Yeah! They thought that was hilarious. Now they all know I had a copy of the Blue Book. Thanks to your paper, they think I was in league with Bernstein to screw St Dunstan's out of a million quid. They don't know whether to hate me or pity me. But they made it clear they don't want me in the competition. I've had to pull out."

"Worst of all, the bearer bond got burnt," I said.

Winkle pulled a rueful smile. "I suppose that's what you call hot money."

"Too hot for you," I said.

I left him pouring another slug of scotch and headed back to the auditorium.

Kitchen had finished his act. There was a hiatus while the others milled around and argued about who should perform next.

Evelyn scribbled notes at her table. She looked like someone who longed to be elsewhere. Like on a sinking ship. Or trapped down a coal mine.

I walked up to her, pulled up a chair, and sat down.

She had a face on her like a mediaeval hangman's.

I said: "I'd like to take you away from all this. We need to talk. Somewhere private would be best."

She tossed her pen on the table and said: "Anything you have to say to me can be said here."

I shrugged. "Have it your own way. I wanted to describe to you how you killed Danny Bernstein."

She flashed me a look of pure hate. It felt like the heat from a solar flare.

"I don't have to listen to this," she snapped.

She shuffled her papers together untidily and stood up.

I said: "Sit down."

My voice carried around the auditorium, like I was a sergeant major who barked out orders on a parade ground.

The air in the auditorium suddenly felt colder. Everyone stopped talking. All eyes focused on Evelyn.

The silence was so thick you could have bottled it and sold it to insomniacs.

Evelyn glanced around. Saw the others giving her their hard stares. She dumped the papers on the table and sat down.

I said: "When Danny Bernstein realised he'd received what everyone thought was Max Miller's Blue Book – the one with his best jokes – he did something you found unforgivable."

"And what was that supposed to be?"

"He refused to share it with you."

"That was his business," Evelyn said.

"Yes, it was. But you'd worked with Danny since the war. You knew more about his business than he knew himself. And for the first time, he'd cut you out of something. And not just something ordinary. Potentially, the sensational Blue Book. That must have made you very bitter."

Evelyn shrugged. "We had some words about it."

"But you never got to see the Blue Book because Danny locked it in his desk drawer."

"I accepted it was none of my business."

"But you didn't accept it. It fuelled your resentment of Bernstein. That resentment turned to hatred. It led to everything that followed."

Billy Dean and Jessie O'Mara moved closer and sat down. This was going to be better than anything they'd hear on stage.

Evelyn shot them a contemptuous glance. "I might have

known you'd want to stick your noses in."

I said: "You wanted to talk here. But let's get back to the Blue Book. A couple of weeks ago, you did get a glimpse of it."

"I don't know what you're talking about."

"I was told Danny liked a drink at lunchtime. Often, he'd fall asleep in his office for an hour afterwards. One day, I imagine, he failed to replace the Blue Book in the locked drawer before he had his kip. He left it on his desk – long enough for you to see what it really was. Not a book of jokes, but a message and a code. And a code that could lead anyone who solved it to a million dollars."

Evelyn said nothing. She fiddled with the papers on the table.

Teddy Hooper and Plonker joined Dean and O'Mara on the nearby chairs. They leaned forward to catch every word.

Peter Kitchen came into the auditorium from behind the stage. He grabbed a chair, turned it round and sat astride holding on to the back. He stared at Evelyn. She ignored him.

I said: "But that wasn't all. One afternoon Ernie Winkle came calling. Winkle hadn't been on good terms with Danny since the time they'd fallen out over the Blue Book. You realised there was only one reason they were getting together again. They needed to use their joint knowledge of Max Miller to solve the code and pocket the cash."

"That's a crazy flight of fancy."

"Is it? I think that afternoon you decided that if a couple of lame-brains like Bernstein and Winkle couldn't solve the million-dollar code you'd do it yourself. But you needed sight of the Blue Book for long enough to copy the contents. And you had to do it without Bernstein suspecting. I'm not sure how you got a key to Bernstein's desk drawer. I expect when he wasn't around, he'd leave it in the lock. When he wasn't looking, perhaps you slipped into his office and inserted a similar looking key while you borrowed the real one and had it copied. Dockerill's is near your office and they cut keys. I expect when we question them, they'll remember you."

"You wish," Evelyn said. "You can't prove it."

"In fact, I think we can. The cops found a key in the desk drawer's lock. But they also found a key for the desk drawer in Bernstein's key folder. The second key – the one in the lock – must have come from somewhere. And the most likely explanation is that it was copied by someone who could lay their hands – if only briefly – on the original."

"That's terrible," Hooper said.

"Little Miss Thief," Plonker said.

Evelyn turned on them. "And you can shut your mouth. Both of them."

I said: "But getting a key to Bernstein's desk drawer wasn't the most difficult part of your plan. You needed access to the drawer when Bernstein wasn't around – and there was little danger of anyone else interrupting you. That wasn't easy because Bernstein used to arrive late in the morning and work into the early evening. Sally, the receptionist, used to watch people come and go. You decided to make an early morning visit to the office in the hope you'd avoid Bernstein and trick Sally into thinking you weren't there."

"This is rubbish," Evelyn said. She pointed at the comedians. "Each of them had a motive to kill Bernstein. It could have been any one of them."

I said: "It was very convenient for you that there were several suspects – each with a good motive for killing Bernstein. And each of them could have had the opportunity – because none had an alibi for the time of the killing. But none of the comedians killed Bernstein."

Evelyn tossed her head like she thought I was an idiot. "They may not have had an alibi. But I certainly did. I was in my flat in Eastern Road. I didn't reach the office until at least half an hour after Danny was killed. Sally confirmed that."

"But that's not how events panned out," I said. "You'd

managed to get into Bernstein's office without Sally realising you were in the building. You'd used the desk drawer key you'd had made and you'd found the Blue Book in the drawer. You were about to start copying it when something completely unexpected happened."

"And what was that supposed to be?" Evelyn asked. Her voice dripped with contempt.

"Bernstein arrived at the office early," I said. "I don't know why he broke the habit of a lifetime. But I expect it was because he had the code in the Blue Book on his mind. The prospect of pocketing a million dollars encourages people to get out of bed. In any event, he found you in the office and was furious. He'd worked with you for decades. He thought he could trust you. And now you were about to ruin the one hope he had of a comfortable retirement. He seized the Indian club from the wall and advanced on you. But you grabbed the sword and were quicker. You lunged at Bernstein to ward him off, but he came on faster than you'd expected. The sword pierced his heart and he fell dead in his chair."

"I wonder whether they'll ever make a film of this," Plonker crowed.

"Shut up you twisted lump of wood," Jessie said.

I said: "You now had a serious problem. You'd killed Bernstein. The idea of copying the Blue Book and replacing it as if nothing had happened had flown out of the window. Perhaps you thought of that very window image. Perhaps that gave you the idea. You would make it look as though the theft of the Blue Book was the motive for Bernstein's killing. After all, there were plenty with a motive. You opened the window and tossed the cigar box which had contained the book into the yard. Then you grabbed the Blue Book and made your escape."

Evelyn sat up straight and looked at me like she wanted to see me pecked to pieces by ravens.

"None of this makes any sense," she said. "Sally saw me

arrive at the office minutes after Danny had been killed."

I grinned. "Yes, she did. Because she was meant to see you arrive on that occasion – and not before."

"You're crazy."

"So people constantly tell me, but I still seem to land the big stories. And this will be one of the biggest."

"Get on with it," Dean chipped in from the next table. "We want to know what happened."

"Shut your gob," Jessie snapped.

I fixed Evelyn with my evil eye. "Earlier, I mentioned this case was rather like *Alice Through the Looking-Glass*, where time runs backwards. And this is when I realised how clever you'd been. You'd murdered Bernstein in his office shortly after half-past eight. But if you could make time run backwards in your life – if you could make it seem that you'd arrived at the office at nine-thirty when you'd really been there shortly after eight-thirty – it would provide you with the perfect alibi."

"If she could do that on stage, she'd make a fortune," Kitchen said.

I ignored the interruption and said: "An hour before Sally saw you arrive at the office, you slipped in through the front door. Sally was busy signing for a registered letter the postman had delivered so only caught a glimpse of a figure slipping up the stairs. You crossed the corridor on the first floor and came down the backstairs to the ground floor close to Bernstein's office. It was the perfect way for you to get into the office without Sally taking a close look at you."

"Now you really are mad," Evelyn said. "The police and all press reports say it was a man who went upstairs. And he left a few minutes later."

"Yes, but in your Looking-Glass world you are a man, aren't you Evelyn? At least you were in your stage act before the War. You were a male impersonator – not as famous as Vesta Tilly or Hetty King whose playbills hang on your office wall – but you got bookings under your stage name of Valentine Redcar. I noticed the playbill on the wall of your office – next to Tilly's and King's. If you were as good as them, you could pass as a man at a few yards, certainly enough to fool Sally as long as she didn't get a good look at your face."

"And how would I manage that?" Evelyn snapped. "Every time someone walks through the door, Sally looks up to greet them."

"But you arranged it so that she wouldn't be looking up. You sent a registered letter to yourself. Then you hung around outside the office until the postman arrived. You hurried in after him, knowing that Sally's attention would be diverted. But she did see enough to believe it was a man who'd slipped upstairs. And she saw you come back down the stairs wearing a raincoat you didn't have on when you came in."

"Why should I do that?"

"Yeah! What is she – some kind of a magician as well as a male impersonator?" said Jessie.

"She thought she was a mistress of misdirection," I said to Jessie. "But the raincoat wasn't part of her plan. It became necessary when Evelyn slayed Bernstein with the sword. The cops told me the blood splatter was the worst they'd seen. Evelyn would have been covered and she needed something to hide it. So she hurried to retrieve Bernstein's raincoat which he'd left, as always, in the cupboard under the backstairs. Only someone familiar with Bernstein's routine would have known where his coat was."

I turned back to Evelyn. "After you'd donned the raincoat, you went through the door to the backstairs, taking care to bolt it after you. Then you raced along the first-floor corridor and down the front stairs. You crossed the foyer towards the street door. From the angle of her desk, Sally could only see your back as you left. So there was no danger that she would see through your disguise. You hurried back to your flat, changed into your skirt and blouse, and returned to the office – as far as anyone knew, for the first time that day."

Evelyn raised her hands and started to applaud. Slow and rhythmical. A taunting clap. She knew that, as it stood, I didn't have a shred of evidence that would withstand cross-examination in court.

Plonker's eyes popped at the applause. "I didn't think it was that good," he said to Hooper.

"Shut up," Hooper said.

"You can't prove any of that," Evelyn said.

"But I can," said a new voice.

Everyone turned to see who'd spoken.

Ted Wilson stood framed in the doorway. There were two uniformed cops behind him.

He held up a book.

A Blue Book.

He crossed the room to where we were sitting.

He said: "Miss Stamford, can you explain how this book came to be in your flat?"

Evelyn looked from me to the comedians. She glanced at the papers on the table. And at a single spotlight that lit the stage.

She threw back her head and laughed. The laughter built inside her until each convulsion shook her body. Tears ran from her eyes. Her cheeks grew red. And still she laughed.

Her shrieks echoed off the roof and the walls. It was a laugh without humour. Without warmth or compassion. Without humanity.

The laugh of a cold-blooded killer.

The comics sat goggle-eyed. For once, none of them had anything to say.

Evelyn stood up and took a slow bow to all corners of the room.

Ted Wilson and the uniformed cops moved towards her.

She threw back her head and declaimed in her loudest voice.

"La commedia è finita. The comedy is over."

Chapter 24

I handed Shirley a copy of the night final edition of the *Evening Chronicle*.

I said: "That headline will sell another twenty thousand copies of the paper."

The headline read: WOMAN DRESSED AS MAN TO KILL.

It was early evening and we were in Prinny's Pleasure. After a hectic afternoon, it was the one place in Brighton we could guarantee some peace and quiet.

The place was empty. Jeff perched on a stool. He had his elbows on the bar and his head in his hands. We could hear his snores from our table by the door.

Shirley said: "I can see why Figgis wanted you back on the paper. What I can't figure out is why that Evelyn Stamford thought she'd ever get away with stealing the bearer bond."

I said: "Brandenburg J Bekker had sent the Blue Book with the puzzle privately to Max Miller. But then both of them died within a few days of one another. Bekker never foresaw that. I expect Max had hidden the Blue Book in the cigar box while he worked on solving the puzzle. The news of Bekker's death would have come as a shock to him. But before he'd decided what to do about it, he pegged out himself. So then nobody knew about the Blue Book – and the hidden bearer bond – until Bernstein opened the cigar box."

"And I guess those great cobbers at St Dunstan's wouldn't have known that a million smackeroos were heading their way."

"That's right. A bearer bond effectively belongs to anyone who has it. It's not like a cheque made out to a payee."

Shirley hoisted her lager and took a good pull at it. "But Evelyn knew Bernstein and Winkle were working on the code. She must've thought she could crack it before them. What would have happened then?"

I shrugged. "I don't know. I guess with a million dollars in her purse, Evelyn would have taken off into the wide blue yonder, never to be heard of again. Bernstein and Winkle wouldn't have been in a position to complain about that."

"But Winkle could have made trouble after Evelyn killed Bernstein," Shirley said.

"Remember that Winkle wouldn't have known who'd killed his partner in crime. And he certainly couldn't make a fuss. As he stood to gain, he could even be a suspect. The cops might think he'd got greedy and wanted the full million for himself."

"Evelyn seemed to have it all worked out," Shirley said.

"And she'd have got away with it if Bernstein hadn't unexpectedly turned up early at his office. Nobody would have known that she'd copied the Blue Book."

"She nearly got away with it anyway. What with dressing up like a guy. Say, did girls really dress up as men on the stage?"

"Yes, it started in the music halls in Victorian times."

I told Shirl how Vesta Tilly and Hetty King had been stars in their day.

I said: "Evelyn, under the stage name Valentine Redcar, was never in their class. She never achieved their star status, but she was good enough to fool enough people into believing she was a man."

"Evelyn must've been devastated when she read in the *Chronicle* that the bearer bond had been burnt," Shirley said.

"She was already a killer. When I saw her, she looked like a woman beyond devastation."

I told Shirley about her "comedy is over" exit line.

"She's got a 'roo loose in the top paddock," Shirl said.

"Maybe she'll end up in Broadmoor high security mental institution rather than Holloway women's prison," I said.

Shirley lifted her glass and finished the last of her drink.

"I feel sorry for those St Dunstan's guys," she said. "They've missed out on a million dollars."

"Yes. When a bearer bond disappears so does the money that goes with it."

"I suppose it was the bearer bond Mary-Lyn grabbed from the deposit box," Shirley said. "After all, no-one else saw it."

"It must've been. She kept hold of it like her life depended on it. In the end, it did."

"There wasn't anything else?" Shirley asked.

"Of course!" I said. "There was. When the lights went out, I edged myself along the wall to the deposit boxes until I found the opened one. I had a feel around inside. There was another small piece of paper in there. It was pitch black at the time and I couldn't see what it was."

"So that's an end of it," Shirley said.

Somewhere in my tired old brain, a sleeping neuron sprang into life.

"No. I've just remembered. In the confusion, I stuffed the paper into my jacket pocket."

I rummaged in the pocket and pulled out a handful of stuff. A small notebook, three used train tickets, a couple of restaurant bills, a press clipping I'd forgotten to return to the morgue, a receipt for my rent at the Widow's…

And the slip of paper I'd retrieved from the deposit box.

I pushed the other stuff aside.

Shirley leaned forward and looked over my shoulder. Her brow wrinkled.

Together we read a verse four lines long.

"What does it mean?" Shirley said.

"It means we have to pay another visit to Hannington's"

Two hours later, Shirley and I walked into the safety deposit box vault at Hannington's.

Earlier, I'd called Ted Wilson and told him what I suspected.

He sighed wearily. "I hope this isn't another of your newspaper stunts."

"Would I pull a newspaper stunt on you?"

"We all know the answer to that. But I'll do what you ask – if only to tweak Tomkins' nose."

Ted had been as good as his word. He was in the vault with Hannington's manager, a plump man with a beer belly and a permanent frown, called Walter Trant. He came up and shook my hand as Shirley and I walked in.

He said: "I hope this isn't going to mean more bad publicity for the store."

"By the time this is over, you'll want to hire me as your PR man."

His frown deepened at that prospect. "Well, let's get on with it," he said.

I said: "Last night, we thought that deposit box 49 held a bearer bond worth one million dollars. We shall never know what the document that was supposed to be the bond said because it was burnt to cinders. But I do know that it wasn't the real bond. There was also a note in the deposit box. I managed to retrieve it. It's in the form of a poem. I'll read it now."

The poem I read went like this:

You've opened the box with the first barer bond
But remember our friendship crosses the pond
And its true value lies in you dear old Max
Yes, Miller, the man with a million cracks.

"We've got to remember that Brandenburg J Bekker, the donor was playing a game with Max Miller. He was challenging him to solve clues to find the bond. The first line of the poem is a clue that the bond in box 49 was not real. In it, bearer isn't spelt as it should be. It's spelt B A R E R. If something is barer it effectively means there's nothing there. And the fact that Bekker describes the bond as 'the first' provides a clue that there's another one. It's in one of these deposit boxes."

"That's all very well," said Ted. "But we can't bust them all open."

"I absolutely forbid it," said Trant.

"We don't need to open them all. The last two lines of the poem give us the number of the box and the four-digit code we need to open it. Look what the third line says: *And its true value lies in you dear old Max*. The code is based on Roman numerals. There are two in the name Max. the M stands for 1,000 and X stands for 10. But as we realised yesterday, the Romans didn't have a symbol for zero, so we need to knock out the noughts."

"That leaves 11," Shirley said.

"Yes, we should open box 11."

"We need a code number to do that," Ted said.

I was pleased to see he was keeping up.

I said: "The clue to that is in the final line: *Yes, Miller, the man with a million cracks*. In other words, the number is hidden in the name Miller. And, as it happens, there are four Roman numerals in the name – M for 1,000, I for 1, and two Ls each for 50. So, once we've eliminated the zeros, the code we need is 1155."

Trant moved forward and adjusted the rotors on the front of the box. We held our breath as he pulled on the handle.

The box swung open. He reached inside and took out a single sheet of paper.

He looked briefly at it, then handed it to me.

It was a handsome document printed on thick paper designed to imitate vellum, the parchment mediaeval monks made from the skin of calves.

There was some of that curly printing at the top which is meant to look like eighteenth century penmanship. The words Bearer Bond took up the top half of the paper. Then there was some dense type and a larger figure towards the bottom.

"Well," Shirley said. "Don't keep us all in suspenders. Did old Bekker leave St Dunstan's a million smackeroos?"

I finished reading the small print carefully.

I looked at them. Shirley's mouth had dropped open with tension. Ted's eyebrows were drawn together more tightly than usual. Trant's frown had deepened like that crinkly cardboard they wrap round fragile items.

"No," I said. "Bekker hasn't left St Dunstan's a million dollars. It's two million."

"I'm struggling for a headline for this story," Frank Figgis said.

It was the following morning and we were in Figgis' office at the *Chronicle*.

He said: "In a way, it's a pity that Brandenburg J Bekker with his Korn Krunchies wasn't the murderer."

"So you could call him a cereal killer," I said.

Figgis harrumphed. I'd stolen his punchline. But then I'd been writing stories about a bunch of comedians. I thought I deserved one.

He said: "This is the best front-page splash we've had since, er…"

"My story yesterday." I said.

"But if we ignore that, the best since, um…"

"The story I filed the day before that."

He said: "As the money was left to St Dunstan's, I've been trying to think of a clever pun with 'blind' in the headline. How about 'blind date'?"

"Not relevant."

"Blind leading the blind?"

"No."

"Blind drunk."

"Definitely not."

"Blind man's bluff."

"That's a children's game."

Figgis leaned back in his chair and stared at the ceiling.

I had a quick look, but there wasn't anything up there that would help.

I tore a sheet of paper off Figgis' writing pad. Took the pen off his blotter and wrote something in capital letters.

"Try this," I said.

I pushed the paper across the desk. It read:

THE CHRONICLE CRACKS THE CODE

Figgis read the paper and his mouth morphed into a smile. He looked so happy that with a bit of imagination I could have believed his yellow teeth were gold.

I said: "I suppose you'll be writing the other story yourself."

Figgis gave me a sharp look. "What other story?"

"The story about how Sidney Pinker has been released from police custody without a stain on his character."

"Oh, that story. That might be a little difficult…"

"I thought you'd say that. That's why I've written it already. The copy is up with the subs. Cedric will bring it down for you shortly. He's running an errand for me at the moment. I promised Sally Ashworth, the receptionist at Bernstein's office, a new packet of tissues."

"She'll need more than tissues. With Bernstein dead and Evelyn on a murder charge, she'll need a new job."

"She struck me as a resourceful young woman. With a tale to tell, she won't be out of work for long."

Figgis relaxed a little. "I suppose Pinker couldn't thank you enough after you'd sprung him from the cells."

"In Pinker's case, enough means not at all. I think his exact words were, 'Took you long enough to get me out of here.' Incidentally, I mentioned in my copy that the *Chronicle* has reinstated Sidney to his old job with a salary increase."

Figgis twitched irritably. "His Holiness won't like that."

"His Holiness should learn to stick by his staff," I said.

Figgis fumbled through a pile of papers in his in-tray and found a packet of Woodbines. He shook out a fag and lit up.

He said: "It was a bit of an eye-opener for me when I met that landlady of yours."

"She said something similar about you."

"It must be a bit of trial living with someone like that."

"We get by."

"Ever thought of moving?"

"Not at the moment."

Figgis took a long drag on his fag. Blew out a stream of smoke. It formed a mist over his desk.

"Mrs Figgis mentioned to me that we've got a spare room she'd like to let to a lodger. The right kind of person, obviously."

"I hope you find him."

"You could do worse, you know. We have toad-in-the-hole on Friday evenings and play Ludo afterwards."

"It sounds irresistible. But, now, I've got work to do. I want to write a sidebar on how that comedy club helped to unravel the mystery."

"Which of the comedians won that Laugh-a-thon competition?"

"None of them. It was cancelled. So the last laugh was on them."

Figgis nodded. "Of course."

I stood up and headed for the door. I glanced back.

Figgis looked sheepish. He wanted to say something.

He made an elaborate show of stubbing out his dog-end.

He gave his ashtray a hard stare as he said: "It's good to have you back."

"I'm pleased to hear it," I said. "And, by the way, your secret is safe with me."

Figgis' eyes flashed in alarm. "What secret?"

"What you were doing that afternoon you were playing hooky. The afternoon Pinker's copy with the Bernstein libel got into the paper."

Figgis pointed an angry finger at me. "That must never go any further. You understand."

"Completely," I said. "It's good that we both trust one another."

I stepped out of Figgis' office and closed the door behind me.

I hadn't a clue what Figgis had done when he'd played hooky. But the fact he thought I knew would keep him off my back. Well, perhaps for the rest of the day.

Epilogue

The sun came out just as the man and the woman walked into the Pavilion Gardens.

It had been one of those mornings when the sun acts like a fugitive. Sometimes hiding behind clouds, sometimes slipping all too quickly through a patch of blue sky. Now, as the last of the clouds sailed east, it looked as though the afternoon was set fair.

The man glanced at the sky, then at the woman.

The sun suited her. It made her blonde hair glow. She smiled with pleasure as the warmth flooded her body. She was sixty-five, but could have passed for a woman twenty years younger. There were the beginnings of laugh lines around her mouth. But otherwise her skin was as smooth as a baby's.

She wore a sleeveless blue and red paisley print dress. She had a pink chiffon scarf looped loosely around her neck.

She grinned at the man in that way which still made her look like a cheeky schoolgirl. She looped her hand through his arm.

The man was seventy-one and time had etched his face with lines around his eyes and mouth. It was like a sculptor had set out to fashion a face for eternity. He was as slim and erect as he'd always been and walked with a bounce to his step. He wore a white linen jacket over red chinos. He had a blue checked shirt and brown shoes. Nothing matched, but it never had.

He pointed with his right hand and said: "It looks as though a crowd has gathered."

To one side of the gardens around fifty or so people were standing in a group.

In the middle of the group a statue on a plinth had been covered with a large white cloth. A cord was attached so that, at the right moment, the cloth could be pulled from the statue to unveil it.

"Let's join them," the man said.

"No. Let's sit on the bench over there and watch," the woman said.

"Observers rather than participants?" the man asked.

"Makes a change for you," the woman said.

She nudged the man playfully and grinned.

"Yes," he said.

The two sat on the bench and watched as someone important approached the statue. He stood on a small dais and made a speech.

A few words drifted across to the pair on the bench. "One of the greats of comedy… a star like we shall never see again… the pure gold of the music hall."

At last the man on the dais pulled on the cord and the cloth slid silently from the statue.

It showed a man dressed in a jacket that flapped around his body like a tent. He wore plus-four trousers which ended at the knee and stockings on his lower legs. He had a kipper tie and a homburg hat. He was pointing and his animated face looked like he was about to deliver the punchline of a joke.

The man on the bench said: "The sculptor has caught his subject well. Max Miller used to look just like that when he was performing his stage act."

"But he's not holding his Blue Book."

"Max always had a secret about that. The book was only a stage prop. There were never any jokes in it. Just blank pages."

The woman said. "I often wondered whether Max Miller was as great as they said. I mean if all you do with your life is tell jokes, is that really worthwhile?"

The man leaned back and smiled.

He said: "That question reminds me of a similar one in an Arnold Bennett novel called *The Card*."

"Card?" said the woman. "I don't get it."

"It's an old-fashioned slang term for someone who's clever, audacious – a bit of a character."

"In other words, someone like you?"

"You said that, not me. Anyway, in the novel, the Card is a person called Denry Machin. At one point, two characters are talking about him. The first says, 'What's he done? What great cause is he identified with?' And the second says, 'He's identified with the great cause of cheering us all up.' You could've said the same about Max Miller. The point is there's plenty of trouble in the world and we all get our share of it."

"You more than most," the woman said.

"Perhaps. In every life some troubles and tears will come our way. But no matter how many of them we get, we all need someone to cheer us up. That's why laughter is so important. It's the elixir which chases away worry and sadness. It's the magic mushroom which makes us want to live life."

The woman nodded thoughtfully.

"Yes," she said. "Laughter is important. But love is also important."

She leaned over and kissed the man tenderly on his lips. His hand reached out and took hers.

"Yes," the man said. "Love is very important, too."

Crampton of the Chronicle will be back in a new adventure
published in Autumn 2019

Read more Crampton of the Chronicle stories at:

www.colincrampton.com

Author's note and acknowledgements

I'd been thinking for some years about introducing Brighton's comic hero Max Miller into one of my Crampton of the Chronicle books. And this, as you will now know, is the one! Some of what you've read about Max in this book is true and some is fiction. If you want to sort out the one from the other, I can strongly recommend John M East's biography, *Max Miller – The Cheeky Chappie* (Robson Books). I read it from cover to cover and was enthralled.

On one point I can be clear. Max would never have tolerated an agent like the fictional Daniel Bernstein. From 1929 until his death in 1963, Max had an excellent agent in the person of Julius Darewski. He played an important role in guiding Max's successful career. During his life, Max had a reputation for being a bit of a tightwad and there were rumours he had money in safety deposit boxes. But he could also be generous. It is true that Max lent his house Woodland Grange to St Dunstan's during the Second World War.

If this book means you've been bitten by the Max Miller bug, the Max Miller Appreciation Society has a wealth of information and memorabilia on its website at www. maxmiller.org.

Sadly, the idea that St Dunstan's received a big donation from a cereal magnate is a piece of fiction. But the outstanding work that St Dunstan's does lives on at the Brighton Centre of Blind Veterans UK. If you wish to leave a donation to fund the work of this excellent organisation visit www.blindveterans. org.uk.

I've mentioned before that a Crampton of the Chronicle adventure couldn't appear without help from many people. Barney Skinner has designed the cover and typeset and formatted the book for both the e-book and paperback editions. Barney is also the designer behind the Crampton of the Chronicle website. Members of the Crampton Advanced Readers' Team read the manuscript and made many helpful suggestions and corrections. The members of the team who helped are (in alphabetical order) Nancy Ashby, Jaquie Fallon, Andrew Grand, Jenny Jones, Doc Kelly, Amanda Perrott and Christopher Roden. Thanks to you all! Needless to say, any errors that remain are mine and mine alone.

Finally, a big thankyou to you, the reader, for reading this book. If you've enjoyed it, please recommend it your friends! In these days of internet sales, online book reviews are very important for authors. So if you have a few minutes to leave one on Amazon and/or Goodreads, I would be very grateful. Thank you.

Peter Bartram May 2019

About the author

Peter Bartram brings years of experience as a journalist to his Crampton of the Chronicle crime mystery series. His novels are fast-paced and humorous - the action is matched by the laughs. The books feature a host of colourful characters as befits stories set in Brighton, one of Britain's most trend-setting towns.

Peter began his career as a reporter on a local weekly newspaper before working as an editor in London and finally becoming freelance. He has done most things in journalism from door-stepping for quotes to writing serious editorials. He's pursued stories in locations as diverse as 700-feet down a coal mine and Buckingham Palace. Peter wrote 21 non-fiction books, including five ghost-written, before turning to crime – and penning the Crampton of the Chronicle series. There are now 11 books in the series.

Follow Peter Bartram on Facebook at:
www.facebook.com/peterbartramauthor

Follow Peter Bartram on Twitter at:
@PeterFBartram

More great books from Peter Bartram...

HEADLINE MURDER

When the owner of a miniature golf course goes missing, ace crime reporter Colin Crampton uncovers the dark secrets of a 22-year-old murder.

STOP PRESS MURDER

The murder of a night watchman and the theft of a saucy film of a nude woman bathing set Colin off on a madcap investigation with a stunning surprise ending.

FRONT PAGE MURDER

Archie Flowerdew is sentenced to hang for killing rival artist Percy Despart. Archie's niece Tammy believes he's innocent and convinces Colin to take up the case. Trouble is, the more Colin investigates, the more it looks like Archie is guilty.

THE TANGO SCHOOL MYSTERY

Colin Crampton and girlfriend Shirley Goldsmith are tucking into their meal when Shirley discovers more blood on her rare steak than she'd expected. The pair are drawn into investigating a sinister conspiracy which seems to centre on a tango school.

THE MOTHER'S DAY MYSTERY

There are just four days to Mother's Day and crime reporter Colin Crampton is under pressure to find a front-page story to fit the theme. Then Colin and his feisty girlfriend Shirley Goldsmith stumble across a body late at night on a lonely country road…

THE MORNING, NOON & NIGHT TRILOGY

Three books in one

The adventure starts in *Murder in the Morning Edition*… when crime reporter Colin Crampton and feisty girlfriend Shirley Goldsmith witness an audacious train robbery

The mystery deepens in *Murder in the Afternoon Extra*… as the body count climbs and Colin finds himself hunted by a ruthless killer.

The climax explodes in *Murder in the Night Final*… when Colin and Shirley uncover the stunning secret behind the robbery and the murders.

Read all three books in *The Morning, Noon & Night Omnibus Edition* or listen to them on the audiobooks available from Audible, Amazon and iTunes.

Printed in Great Britain
by Amazon